PRAISE FOR EV[E]
TEXAS EMPIRES SERIES!

CROWN OF GLORY

"Ms. Rogers' clever cast of characters will give the readers some chuckles and some moments of clenching tension!"

—*Romantic Times*

"Ms. Rogers brings to life the struggles to create a new life in a new, rugged land, as well as a realistic love story that brings two strong-willed people together. I loved *Crown of Glory*. It's the beginning of an excellent series you won't want to miss."

—*Rendezvous*

"*Crown of Glory* is an exciting adventure with an unusual approach to romance. Rogers' characters make this story unforgettable!"

—*Affaire de Coeur*

"*Crown of Glory* sizzles with history: rowdy Indian fights, anti-slavery issues, the pioneering days of the beef industry, all peppered with the Spanish flavor of Texas."

—*Calico Trails*

LONE STAR

"Ms. Rogers gives us such vivid descriptions that you feel the pulse of the times. She has gifted her readers with a sensitive, refreshing romance spiced with great characters and a powerful love story skillfully plotted."

—*Rendezvous*

"*Lone Star* is a wonderfully woven tale that is sure to captivate your romantic heart."

—*Bookbug on the Web*

"TOO FAR ... OR NOT FAR ENOUGH?"

"It's a strange world we live in," he said. "Men surrounded by women. Women surrounded by men. Yet we're supposed to live celibate lives."

He didn't expect her to play coy.

She didn't.

"Celibacy is not a problem for women," she said. "It is a part of our nature."

"All women? That's not been my experience."

"I speak for myself, then. It is not a problem for me."

"Has no man ever made your heart pound from just the thought of him? Have you never lain awake at night wondering what the touch of a man's hand on your body would be like? Have you never wondered about the taste of a man's lips?"

She swallowed, and he watched the play of muscles in her throat.

"You go too far, sir."

"Too far ... or not far enough?"

TEXAS EMPIRES: Longhorn

EVELYN ROGERS

LEISURE BOOKS   NEW YORK CITY

A LEISURE BOOK®

February 2000

Published by

Dorchester Publishing Co., Inc.
276 Fifth Avenue
New York, NY 10001

Copyright © 2000 by Evelyn Rogers

Cover Art by John Ennis, Ennisart.com

ISBN 0-8439-4679-2

Printed in the United States of America.

*This book is dedicated to my sister Loretta White,
who teaches me what being a heroine is all about,
and to the real life Helen—Helen Owens,
who reminds me how much love and goodness
exist in the world.*

Longhorn

Chapter One

New Orleans
April 1864

When the Yankee soldiers finally got to Madeleine Hardin's house, they came in fast and they came in mean.

Maddie was in the kitchen slicing bread, anticipating the rare taste of wheat on her tongue, letting herself dream of butter and strawberry jam slathered from crust to crust. Then came the pounding at the front door.

By the time she got to the foyer, with Will close beside her, heavy boots were kicking and splintering the wood. Fear pounded in her breast. She must not give in to it. She must not let it show, otherwise she would betray herself.

A gloved hand reached through a jagged hole and twisted the knob. Three Yankee soldiers strode inside. With them came the smell of dirt and sweat, strong enough to cover the scent of the bread.

It all happened fast, too fast, and all she could do was watch. Beside her, Will growled. She grabbed his arm. His powerful muscles bunched beneath the worn cotton of his shirt.

"No," she said, unmindful of the soldiers. "Please, no."

"You don't have to do what she says." It was the nearest soldier who spoke, a sergeant, big and burly and dark as the shadows in the nearby rooms. "Ain't you heard about Lincoln's proclamation?"

Maddie took a deep breath and lowered her eyes, as was her habit over these past two years. Through practice and necessity, she had learned to observe much from such a position.

"He is not a slave, m'sieur," she said as politely as she could, stressing the accents of the French language she had used since birth. She was tall, but she tried to pull herself in, to look small and meek, to sound and look less like an enemy.

Though, in truth, she was their enemy with all her heart and soul. These men, or others like them, had been raiding homes throughout the Vieux Carré over the past few weeks. Today it was her turn, and she hated them for it. They could bring her life to ruin.

A corporal smirked at her over his sergeant's shoulder. Big and dark like his superior, he dwarfed the third soldier, a pale, inconsequential private who lurked behind the burlier men.

"Should'a figured he wasn't no slave," the corporal said. "These women, specially the Frenchies, got to pass the time some ways, what with all the white boys out killing innocent Feds."

So much for subtle impressions. She clenched her fists and concentrated on the scuff marks left by the soldiers' boots. It was her father's toughness she would have to depend on today, not the gentle strength of her French-born mama. Both were dead and buried, her father just months after she was born, but she had been raised on stories about him and she felt her parents' blood pumping in her veins.

Too, she thought of her brothers. Cal and Cord had proven their courage against overwhelming odds in Texas. She would do the same today.

"I work for Miss Maddie," Will said, the words growled out from deep within his broad chest. "I have since she was a little child."

Her longtime friend and servant loomed larger than any of the soldiers, a head taller and twenty pounds heavier, but that didn't keep the foolish sergeant from sneering up at him.

"Call it what you like. But we ain't fools."

Maddie felt the tension ripple through her old

friend. He should not be talking out the way he was, no more than she. She tightened her hold on his sleeve and dared to glance quickly at the sergeant.

"You can have no business here," she said. "This is a private home."

Even so slight a protest could prove a risk. By decree of the occupation government, insolence to Federal soldiers labeled a woman a whore, vulnerable to any kind of treatment. She needed no trouble from them. More than they knew, she needed them gone.

"Ain't no privacy for Rebs," the sergeant said. "Ain't you heard?"

New Orleans had been an occupied city for more than two years, its citizens open to the humiliations that went with their fallen status. She knew very well the loss of her rights. But she held her tongue, letting the resentment burn in her heart.

The ranking soldier, his small eyes blinking, scratched at the stubble on his cheek. His brown hair was shaggy beneath the blue Army cap, and when he stared at her, her stomach clenched into a knot.

Behind him, the corporal loomed equally dark and menacing. Only the third soldier, the spare, pale private, seemed capable of civilized behavior, nodding at her as if he apologized for the rudeness of the other two. But he stared at her in the same way—no, worse, she decided. He studied her as she would a strange animal he had come upon unexpectedly, one he would like to dissect.

The thought was absurd, but it would not go away.

His two companions glanced from the threadbare rug centered on the floor to the small crystal chandelier overhead. The prisms were polished to a shine, ready to catch the flickering light of candles, though they had not done so since shortly after the Yankees sailed up the Mississippi and cut off such luxurious supplies.

Maddie kept the fixture as pristine as the rest of the house, the way her mother had kept it when she was alive. She would scrub the house from wall to wall after the soldiers were gone. And make what repairs she could to the damage they would no doubt inflict.

The sergeant rested his hand on his gun. "Get out of my way," he said, more to Will than to her. "Unless you want to hand over whatever it is you're hiding."

Maddie's heart caught in her throat. They knew. But no, they couldn't. No one did, except Will.

Like her, Will lowered his gaze to the soldier's dusty boots, but she could feel the anger heating inside him. If he had a mind to do so, he could snap the bluecoat in half before the man's gun cleared its holster. And then her world would truly explode.

"What are you going to do, sergeant?" she

asked hastily. "We have nothing of interest here for the brave Army of the North."

Again the pinpoint eyes looked her over. She had bound her golden hair into a tight bun and covered it with a black net morning cap. Her dress was likewise black, ill-fitting and as worn as Will's shirt. Much to her disgust, at age twenty-four, despite a meager diet, she had not totally lost her figure. Though her breasts were tightly bound, she could not completely disguise her woman's body.

The sergeant seemed to know what was beneath the dowdy dress. What he did not realize was that in her left hand, hidden in the folds of her skirt, she gripped the handle of the serrated bread knife. She hadn't purposely brought it with her, but she would purposely use it if she saw the need.

It mattered not that a far more dangerous-looking knife was sheathed at his waist.

"Nothing of interest, eh?" The sergeant grinned. "That's a lie if I ever heard one."

"We have no money," she said.

"You Rebs have a way of hiding what you don't want us to know about, and lying to cover up. Lying's a sin, I was taught by the preacher, and hiding oughta be, too."

"We have nothing to hide." Her voice slipped easily over the lie. "Look for yourself." She stepped aside, and, far more reluctantly, Will did the same.

The intruders started in the drawing room,

the first two with rude energy, the quiet private moving slower, watching as if he needed to know her reaction. They tossed pillows, kicked at the rug, emptied the contents of a small cabinet that held little more than the sheet music she used on the rare occasions when she sat at the piano to play.

Using the butt of his gun, the sergeant pounded against the walls, listening for hollow sounds that would indicate a hiding place. He came to a small tear in the flocked wallpaper.

"What's this?" he growled.

Before she could respond, he ripped the paper and a jagged section came away in shreds, revealing nothing more than the plaster beneath. Grunting, he moved on with his pounding.

Leaving a trail of destruction behind them, they moved to the dining room and into the kitchen.

The sergeant spied the bread and his small eyes narrowed to slits. "Where'd you get this?"

Maddie ignored the question. Will had brought her the wheat last night, already ground into flour. She hadn't asked where he got it. It was the first such flour she had seen in months, full of weevils though it was, and she hadn't wanted to know its origin, or what he had done to get it.

"Looks like contraband to me," the corporal said.

Maddie watched in silence from the doorway

while the bluecoats tossed each other chunks from the loaf until the precious bread was consumed. Even the private joined in. Within the folds of her skirt she gripped the knife handle and waited for them to move on.

After the invaders were done in the kitchen, after they had raided the skimpy larder, cutting open the last sack of cornmeal and kicking its contents across the floor, they moved on to the chamber where Maddie slept. Fear turned to panic, but again she remained in the doorway, staring straight ahead lest she give them a clue where to look.

They tossed the bedcovers, ripped the lace curtains at the window, opened the chest at the foot of the bed and with their dirty hands lifted out her undergarments, the good petticoat she had been saving for Julien's return, and the chemise she had embroidered to go with it.

The sergeant and corporal did most of the searching, the grunting, the threatening, but the private was never far behind, watching her until she wanted to scream.

Through it all, she remained outwardly calm, and so did Will, who kept his post close beside her. Even when they threw open the wardrobe, she did not so much as blink.

The sergeant smirked at her meager supply of clothes, then stopped. "What's this?" He reached on the shelf above her lone spare black dress. She watched in horror as he lifted out the china doll with its faded lavender gown. Her precious gift from her mother. She had forgotten all about it since it could not possibly be of interest to anyone but her.

"That was my mother's, m'sieur," she said, barely able to hide her panic. "It has no value to you."

He took notice of her distress and shook the doll hard. Its cracked, painted face bobbed from side to side.

"Could be something inside," the corporal said.

"Just what I was thinking." The sergeant reached for the knife at his waist. "Let's cut the thing open and find out."

"No," she cried out. "Please, I promise it's a simple stuffed doll, nothing more." She spoke the truth, almost willing to reveal her treasure rather than see her beloved keepsake destroyed.

He tossed the doll high in the air, poised to catch it on the point of his blade. Will sprang into action. He knocked the knife aside and sent it clattering onto the floor, and before the sergeant could react, went for his throat.

But the corporal acted faster than Maddie thought possible, catching Will in the temple with the stock of his gun, slowing him enough to weaken his hold. Will and the sergeant crashed to the floor, and the corporal again delivered a sharp head blow, this time accompanied by a kick to Will's ribs, and another and another. She heard the crack of bones.

Maddie screamed and flew around the bed, the bread knife raised in front of her. The fair-haired private stepped in front of her, more a blue blur than a man, as she slashed out and caught the sleeve of his uniform. Crimson sprouted like a flower on the tip of the knife.

At her feet, Will moaned. Beneath him, the sergeant lay still. It was the corporal who turned to her. In his eyes she saw the hatred of all the world and, worse, anticipation of the pleasure he would get from hurting her.

A hairy hand reached out quick as a snake and ripped open the front of her gown, exposing her white skin and the patched camisole stretched thinly over her bound breasts.

Beside her, the young private whimpered and gripped his arm. She stumbled against him and pressed the blade against his throat, her free hand trying with ill-disguised desperation to pull her torn garment back in place.

"I'll kill him," she whispered, but the words were loud enough to carry from wall to wall. A drop of blood smeared the soldier's skin, but she didn't know whether it was from the residue on the knife or from a fresh wound.

For a moment all was still in the room, and it was as if eternity spun out in that small space of time.

"Killing won't be necessary."

The deep voice came from behind her and she gasped. The private scrambled backwards, away from the serrated blade. Lowering her weapon, she slowly turned and looked into the dark, probing eyes of yet another soldier. An officer, a captain, she noted as rational thought returned. With rationality came a new kind of fear, and a trembling she could not hide.

Here was someone else to threaten her dreams. No matter how hard she tried, how much she fought, fate denied her any victory.

This newest intruder was tall, his skin tanned from the outdoors, his dark hair trimmed evenly above the blue collar of the hated uniform. He filled the doorway as much as Will, with the same strength and quiescent power that in her old friend brought her comfort.

But this man's strength unnerved her. Unlike Will, he carried no kindness in the eyes that stared out at her from beneath the low brim of his uniform hat. His strong presence and softly spoken words sucked the air from the room.

Praying for Hardin courage, she held her head high and ceased the feeble attempts to cover herself. For too long she had been meek; it had done her little good. The shredded front of her gown fell, but she stood with all the quiet dignity she could muster. With Maddie, it was a great deal.

"I want to bring charges against these men."

She spat out the words and saw a hint of admiration flicker across his face. Or maybe it was amusement at her foolish daring.

"They're vandals, not soldiers," she added. "They should be put in jail."

The captain made no response.

In the silence, Will slowly rose from the floor to stand beside her and to stare with equal daring at the officer. He must be in terrible pain from his cracked ribs, but he gave no sign of distress.

Groaning, the sergeant pulled himself to his feet, his hulking figure bent, and managed a shaky salute. "Cap'n Dan—"

"Captain Kent," the officer corrected.

"These are mean 'uns, Captain," the corporal growled.

Kent stopped him with a look. "The sergeant will report."

The sergeant rubbed the back of his head. "He's right, Cap'n. We'd heard there was contraband around. We was only following orders, seeing what we could find. Her man here attacked without warning, and she came at us with a pig sticker."

"A bread knife," Maddie said. She tossed the inadequate weapon on the bed, which stood between her and the captain. "There has not been a pig on the premises in two years. Not until today."

The captain studied her for a moment, then gave the same careful attention to her ruined gown. The camisole, worn from years of washing, provided scant covering for the inadequate binding over her breasts. He saw everything. She read the interest in his eyes.

In all her life she had never been so exposed before a man. And now she was surrounded by gaping men. The private had unnerved her; Captain Kent brought her shame.

The captain looked from her to the rumpled bedcovers, the torn lace curtains at the window, the scattered undergarments his men had pulled from the chest at the foot of the bed. At last, he stared at the twisted doll, lying like a broken child atop the camisole Maddie had embroidered as she waited for her fiancé to return from the war.

"Sergeant, you and your men are to report to headquarters immediately. I'll want to hear your complete story. And I'll want it in writing. If that's possible." Captain Kent looked at the private. "See to your wound. Cuts fester."

The sergeant looked as if he wanted to say more, but a hard stare from his captain silenced him. The soldiers tromped out, but the stench of their insolence lingered. Neither Maddie nor Will moved.

The captain gave his full attention to her.

"Miss—"

"Hardin, m'sieur. Mademoiselle Madeleine Hardin. For the report. Your thugs neglected to inquire who I was."

"You are French?"

"On my mother's side. William Jackson has long worked for the family. He is also my friend. He did nothing that was not provoked, nothing other than try to protect me."

She spoke bravely, but she could not resist covering herself with her arms. And she resorted to her old way of keeping her eyes downcast.

The captain glanced at Will. "Mademoiselle Hardin is safe. Perhaps, however, she could use a bit of spirits."

"We have no liquor in the house," she said. "If we had, your men would have long ago disposed of it. As contraband."

The captain's mouth twitched. "Water, then. Bring her a glass of water."

Will hesitated, but at Maddie's nod, he left the room.

The captain came around the bed to stand in front of her.

Maddie's arms tightened across her breasts, and she concentrated on the fine black boots so close to her worn slippers. "You said I was safe."

"So I did."

She knew long strands of her hair had pulled loose from the black net morning cap. In her torn gown and with her yellow hair in disarray, she must appear dissolute to him, a fig ripe for the plucking. Had she not spoken brazenly to him? Did not that, by government decree, label her a whore?

Her hand itched for the bread knife on the bed.

He read her mind. "I will not so easily be cut, Miss Hardin. I am not a boy."

Slowly she raised her eyes and dared to meet his stare. "Neither are you a gentleman. We are in my private chamber, sir. And we are alone. A gentleman would apologize and leave."

He stood tall before her, brutish in his size and with his strong features, but she saw an intelligence in his eyes that separated him from the departed soldiers. Whoever he was and whatever his character, he would not be easily fooled by subterfuge or lies, no more than he would be intimidated by anything she might do.

"There are no gentlemen in war," he said. "It is something that you as the enemy should remember."

He stepped closer, and the air was filled with the scent of him. She caught no stench of insolence, but something else, the outdoors and horses—he rode often, she was sure—and still something more, a manly scent she could not name.

The smell of horses was perfume to her, sweeter than the aroma of bread that had so recently filled her home. The other scent, the manly one, frightened her. She stepped away and again, with more reluctance than before, lowered her eyes.

He reached out to take her hand, staring at

the long, tapered fingers and the neatly rounded nails resting against his hard palm. Then he dropped it as if it burned.

"This matter is not done," he said. He paused, looking as if he wanted to say more, and then he was gone, as quickly and quietly as he had appeared. In the silence that followed she wondered at the intimacy that had passed between them, though they had touched only briefly and their words had been curt.

Intimacy was too strong a word, she told herself, yet she could think of no other to describe the awareness of him that had momentarily filled her senses.

She was struck with a rare light-headedness. Staring at the floor, she tried to picture Julien's graceful features, the glint in his pale eyes as he talked with her about their future, the kindly smile that was almost as familiar as her own. For some unknown reason, she needed very much to recall everything about him now.

Instead, she saw a lined brown face and deep-set dark and knowing eyes, a hard, square jaw and grim lips that twitched at unexpected times. How much more she preferred Julien's appearance, which comforted far more than it disturbed.

Her fiancé's latest letter, smuggled to her from his parents' ruined plantation outside New Orleans, had disturbed her greatly, declaring as it did plans far different from the ones they had made before the war. The Confederate cause was not hers, though she would burn in hell before admitting such to the enemy. And it must not remain Julien's.

Once she saw him again, she would convince him that their earlier dreams had been right. She had no choice.

Giving in to the dizziness, she collapsed on the bed. Will brought her the water and she drank, but she did not draw pleasure from the cool liquid as it trickled down her throat. Too clearly she remembered her fright as the soldiers tore their way through her home. Worse, she remembered the rescue that in an inexplicable way presented a greater threat.

This matter is not done. The captain's authoritative voice echoed in the room.

With a womanly instinct, she understood that if she were to get through these hard times in any kind of peace, she must do two things: she must hold on to her dreams and she must never see Captain Daniel Kent again.

Chapter Two

Twilight shadowed the front of Madeleine Hardin's home by the time Dan returned to knock at her crudely repaired door.

Like the residences on either side, the house was a simple, low structure made of mixed wood and brick, built on concrete blocks above the wet New Orleans soil. A tiled roof extended over the front stoop and broad sidewalk to provide protection from the elements, which on this quiet day offered no more than the threat of dark clouds.

The sill of the darkened drawing room window held a half dozen pots of aromatic plants. He recognized the scent of rosemary. His mother kept a similar container in the kitchen window of their Kentucky home.

He shook off the memory. In Kentucky he had always been considered an honorable man. Right now, staring at the faint light in the window of her bedchamber, he felt more like a hound dog than an officer and a gentleman.

What the devil he was doing sniffing around Mademoiselle Hardin he had no idea. But he didn't try to lie to himself. It was she who brought him here, not any drummed-up need to report on all he had done since leaving her a few hours earlier.

The servant Will answered his knock. Dan was good at reading men. From the Negro's nod, he got the feeling he had been expected. But that didn't make sense; he hadn't known himself he was coming until halfway through his evening walk.

He had the right to barge inside the house of a southern sympathizer. Instead, he said, "Is Mademoiselle Hardin receiving?"

As if he were a suitor, which he definitely was not.

Will stepped aside and gestured toward the drawing room, a slight wince the only evidence of his beating earlier in the day. Dan walked inside and stood in the dark as Will bolted the front door closed, then disappeared. He felt an urge to take off his hat and smooth his hair and even, foolishly, straighten the cravat at his throat, but he stayed the way he was.

With the front window closed, blocking out fresh air and the scent of rosemary, the room was close and damp. The wool uniform coat lay heavy on his shoulders, as heavy as the questions about what he was doing there.

When Madeleine Hardin entered from the direction of her private chamber, holding aloft a single lighted candle in its pewter holder, he remembered. In her silent approach, she appeared ghostlike, but he knew that if he touched her, she would prove warm and real.

She had discarded the hideous net cap, revealing light golden hair, worn parted in the middle and bound severely in a knot at the back of her neck. A drab black dress lay loose on her tall, thin body. In the dim flickering light her cheeks were gaunt, her features delicate, her skin the color of milk.

She should have looked weak, vulnerable. Somehow she managed to retain a strength and a regal beauty that oppression could not dim. He remembered the way she had pulled out the knife and held it to the soldier's throat. She was not a woman he should ever underestimate.

Should he ever be tempted to do so, there were her eyes to remind him of her spirit. They were wide and deep, thick-lashed, a startling blue: he had never seen eyes like them. Now they were staring coolly at him, and he wondered if they could ever lie.

He looked at the long-fingered hand curved delicately around the candleholder, and again he remembered the knife. He smiled.

"Do I amuse you, Captain?" she asked.

He met her stare, held it, then watched as she looked at the floor, as if she suddenly remembered that she was supposed to look down in the face of the enemy.

"No, Mademoiselle Hardin, you definitely do not amuse me."

She used the candle to light a pair of wall sconces on either side of a small, scarf-covered piano, then set the pewter holder aside. In the increased light, he could see where she had attempted to repair the wallpaper torn during the afternoon search. The pillows were all back in place and the furniture upright.

Like him, she had been busy since last they met.

"I would offer you tea, sir, but I assume this is not a social call."

"I'm sure you agree a social call would be unsuitable."

"As well as unwelcome."

She spoke sharply, as if she addressed herself as much as him. Unwelcome, was he? Maybe, but then, maybe not. Women were harder to read than men, but not impossible, even when they tried to dissemble. Mademoiselle Hardin did not dislike him quite so much as she would have preferred.

Or maybe she was simply lonely. Loneliness he could understand.

"I've not come looking for treasure," he said,

then couldn't refrain from adding, "not of any material kind, if that's what you fear."

She did not pretend to misunderstand. "You'll find nothing to please you here, Captain." She abandoned her study of the floor. "Material or otherwise."

"I came to report about what happened after I left here. Both the sergeant and the corporal have been reprimanded."

"That must have been devastating to them."

Dan recalled the anger of the two when he had threatened them with charges should they ever again ransack a residence with robbery their only motivation. The occupational Army had long since abandoned such practices on the conquered populace, though a few miles away in unconquered territory, Louisianans were still at war.

"They won't bother you," he said. "You have my word on it."

"And the private?"

"He was following orders. Without the influence of the other two, he will not go out on his own."

She stared at him, as if she believed little of what he said.

Dan knew his treatment of the boy was weak. But he was only a boy, probably had lied about his age to join the Army, leaving troubles at home, like so many others seeking glory on the field of battle. And he'd been sent to a southern city that must be as foreign to him as Paris, where he was looked on with scorn by both his fellow soldiers and the people he had come to conquer.

Dan doubted the woman before him would be impressed by his reasoning at letting the boy off.

"Besides," he said, "you frightened him more than I could. Would you have cut his throat if I had not arrived when I did?"

"I would have done what was necessary to protect Will."

"Who, as I recall, was fighting to protect a doll."

"The doll has great sentimental value. But I doubt you're a man to appreciate sentiment."

"You have no idea what I might appreciate."

He almost told her—green fields where frisky horses grazed, a hilltop home filled with love, a smart-mouthed sister, a brash young brother serving his country somewhere in the East. It was his brother Tom who stayed in his mind.

Since leaving home two years ago, he had described such scenes, such people, to no one. Why he thought of them now, he did not know.

Suddenly he grew impatient with the woman's bravery and her strength.

"Your servant's life was not in danger. There are thousands of men being killed on the field of battle. Think of them, too, when you get angry."

"I did not start this war."

"Neither did you swear allegiance to the

United States when you were given the chance."

"Chance? By orders of General Butler, you mean."

"Be glad the general came here after your defeat. Your streets stank with refuse. He cleaned them up. Since he arrived, the epidemics of yellow fever have ceased."

He did not expect an apology or thanks, and he did not get them.

"All out of the kindness of his heart. The same kindness that brought you here, no doubt, Captain."

She gave a French pronunciation to his name, somehow softening the sarcasm, reminding him what a complex creature she was.

He took a long time to study her, all of her, from the tightly bound hair to the breasts he knew too well were purposely flattened, to the black slippers visible beneath a frayed hem. Despite the signs of hardship, her air was that of a fine filly, her spirit flaring within the confines of her life. Mademoiselle Hardin would give a man a splendid ride.

"Whatever brought me here, it wasn't kindness," he said.

"Robbery, then. Sacking and pillaging. You have taken up the failed mission of your men."

She gave every sign of looking coolly at him, but she couldn't hold the look for long. Something had her agitated, something beyond his taunts and certainly beyond his manly presence. Her servant Will had expected him, but she had not. The longer he remained, the greater her agitation. He doubted she was physically afraid of him. The threat he represented went beyond mere harm to her body.

Robbery, she threw at him. *Sacking and pillaging.* In her distress, she revealed her greatest fear.

"As you pointed out," he said, picking up the candleholder, "this is not a social call."

He walked past her, coming close, so that her skirt brushed against his trousers, and strode across the foyer into her bedchamber. She hurried after him.

Like the drawing room, the chamber had been straightened, giving no sign of the earlier invasion. Before he arrived, the soldiers had searched the room with ruthless thoroughness. Except for the wardrobe. The doll had delayed the inspection. That much he had been able to observe before she began nicking the throat of the outmatched private.

Setting aside the light, he threw open the doors of the wardrobe. One black dress hung inside, as drab as the one she wore. The doll rested on a high shelf, alongside a plain black bonnet. He knocked against the back wall and was rewarded with a hollow sound. He regarded the woman, who stood unmoving inside the chamber doorway.

"Whatever it is you're hiding, you need to

choose a better place. The three men who came today will not return, but I can't promise there will not be others."

"I'm not—"

"Don't tempt me to look further. I don't want to know what's there, and, believe me, you don't want me to know."

For a change she showed the good sense not to snap out a reply. Instead, she stared at him. Neither looked away. His stomach knotted, as it had not done since he was seventeen.

At last, she said softly, "I don't understand you, Captain Kent."

"Sometimes I don't understand myself."

He closed the distance between them. She was taller than most women, but still, the top of her head scarcely came past his shoulder. She had to tilt her head to look at him with those remarkable eyes.

For all her appearance of frailty, he once again felt the strength that flowed through her body. He saw it in the way she held herself, and he saw it in her eyes. Her parted lips were full and moist. The urge to kiss her was almost too powerful to resist. He hadn't kissed a woman in a long while. He doubted he had ever kissed anyone like her.

"It's a strange world we live in," he said. "Men surrounded by women. Women surrounded by men. Yet we're supposed to live celibate lives."

He didn't expect her to play coy.

She didn't.

"Celibacy is not a problem for women," she said. "It is a part of our nature."

"All women? That's not been my experience."

"I speak for myself, then. It is not a problem for me."

"Has no man ever made your heart pound from just the thought of him? Have you never lain awake at night wondering what the touch of a man's hand on your body would be like? Have you never wondered about the taste of a man's lips?"

She swallowed, and he watched the play of muscles in her throat.

"You go too far, sir."

"Too far . . . or not far enough?"

She closed her eyes. "You insult me."

"That is not my intent."

"I have neither wanted nor invited such talk. Please go."

He hesitated, then backed away. He was forgetting himself, who he was, and who she was, and why he was in the city where she lived.

He gave a slight bow. "Forgive me, mademoiselle. But do not forget my warning. The soldiers were stupid today. As I have promised, they will give you no more trouble. But others may come to search. Blind luck brought me by your house today. The next time you may not be so fortunate."

* * *

Maddie listened as the front door closed behind the Yankee captain. She wrapped her arms around her waist and suppressed a shiver. He frightened her, just as he had done this afternoon, far more than the three soldiers, even the private with his strange, obsessed stare.

Instead of fear, she should be filled with indignation over all that he had said to her, the talk of touching and kissing, of celibacy, the way he had dared stand close and study her until she couldn't breathe. But the indignation would not come, not right away. It was overpowered by a far darker emotion that shook her soul.

She couldn't lie to herself as to its cause. He asked if her heart ever pounded from thoughts about a man. She could answer yes. Her heart was pounding now.

She should have told him that she didn't have to wonder about the taste of a man's lips brushing against hers. Julien had kissed her. More than once. Before leaving for the army, he had gone so far as to abandon his courtly butterfly touch and to kiss her long and hard.

But even that last kiss hadn't shaken her the way the mere talk of kissing had tonight. Because she did, indeed, wonder how Daniel Kent's kiss would be different, and how she would react to the touch of his hand.

She was a foolish woman. She had been alone too long.

Will came into the foyer outside the chamber door.

"You left me alone with him," she said.

Will nodded.

"He could have attacked me."

Her old friend's dark eyes watched her, but he made no attempt to defend himself.

She sighed. "I know I'm being silly. You were nearby. You are always nearby."

She dropped her head into her hands, but she could not give in to thoughts of all that had taken place between her and the Yankee captain. She certainly couldn't dwell on the way he looked with his tall, strong body and his dark hair and eyes and the way he held his mouth in a mocking, almost smile. No, she must not recall any of these details.

The memories, the personal recriminations would come later, when she was lying in bed unable to sleep. As he had predicted, in his devious, roundabout way.

Julien, please come home.

She sent the cry eastward more fervently than ever, hoping he would sense her need and return. It was a foolish thought. She was being selfish. Others had sacrificed more than she. Others had lost their loved ones, their homes, their fortunes.

The plantation of the Delarondes was in ruins because there were no slaves to work the fields. Julien had never thought to inherit from his parents; that bequest was destined for his older brother. But he loved the land on which he was raised. It would break his heart to see his family living close to poverty in a once grandiose home they could no longer maintain.

Julien was more fortunate than any in his family. He had her. She wasn't being vainglorious, simply honest. She was rich.

Moving to the open wardrobe, she turned to Will. "We've got to find another hiding place."

He could have said *I already told you so,* for he had, more than once. But she had been so sure her cache of jewels and gold coins was safe in the secret compartment behind the wardrobe's back wall. She hadn't taken into consideration Captain Kent.

"The floor of my room," Will said with a nod.

His room was attached to the main house behind the kitchen. It was a perfect hiding place. The Yankees would never suspect that she trusted her servant so much; but then, they didn't understand the close relationship that could exist between a southern white woman and her male Negro friend.

The soldiers had tried to make the relationship sound obscene. Will was her friend, her best friend; he had been such since shortly after she was born, when her mother bought and freed him and his sister Cinda, then put her only child into their care.

40

Later, with rumors of war beginning, Cinda had fled to Illinois. Will had remained in the South. Maddie would trust him with her life. Why not the treasure she had been left by the frugal and wise woman who had given her birth?

The false wardrobe panels slipped out easily. When Will was gone with the small wooden cask that held her future, she sat on the side of the bed and pulled out the latest letter from her fiancé. Julien's father had received it last week and brought it into town. A once proud man, he still managed despite his troubles to view her as unworthy of his son. But he honored that son's request to deliver the letter to the future Mrs. Julien Delaronde.

Gabriel Delaronde did not know Maddie was wealthy. It was something only Julien knew, and even he did not understand the value of her jewels and coins.

But he knew it was enough to satisfy their dreams—at least the dreams they had shared before this cursed war.

Texas. Land. A ranch. That was the plan. And eventually a family to build an empire, much in the way of her brothers, Cal and Cord. They were, in truth, her half brothers, but she scarcely bothered with that detail. The three Hardin offspring had shared a father, though each was born to a different wife. Fifteen years separated them, but Maddie felt an overpowering desire to live the kind of life they had carved for themselves in the rugged land west of their native Louisiana.

Each of her brothers had come to his land by accident, thinking his stay temporary. Fate had deemed otherwise, sending them strong, loving women who had helped them settle their respective ranches and, in the doing, changed their lives.

In that, Maddie was different. She already had her land picked out, offered by a friend of the Hardin brothers who had been trapped in New Orleans at the outbreak of the war. Her brothers did not know of her plans. She wanted to surprise them after she was settled in her new home.

She even had a name for the place she and Julien would found: Longhorn Ranch. Years ago, while visiting Texas on the occasion of Cord's marriage, she had seen herds of the wild cattle roaming the countryside. They had looked beautiful to her, with their curious pointed horns and the feral light in their eyes. They were still there, waiting for anyone determined enough to tame them.

Maddie knew she could be that person, with Julien's help, and the help of the brave and loyal men they would hire. Working together, they would capture the wild beasts, they would breed them to more domestic stock, and they would prosper.

But now she had his letter to consider.

The cause of the Confederacy is just, Maddie. And just causes must prevail. When this terrible but necessary conflict is done, our fledgling country will need stout hearts and true believers willing to sacrifice all to see that she will survive and flourish. We cannot allow despots to determine our destiny. I know that in this resolve, you will remain at my side.

Poor, deluded Julien. The Confederacy's cause was no more just than it was destined to succeed. This was a belief she had not revealed to anyone, not even Will.

Neither did she embrace the principles of the United States, where self-serving men preached the preservation of the Union over all else, no matter how many of its people had to be slaughtered to keep it whole.

Texas was a part of the Confederacy, but she knew there were many Texans who did not want any part of the war. Slave owners were present, but they lived in the eastern and southern portions of the state. Maddie was looking farther west.

Folding the letter, she tried to picture Julien, tried to feel the love that had led her to accept his hand in marriage. With him far away, risking his life before enemy fire, it was dishonorable of her to doubt her devotion.

It seemed especially wrong now that a Yankee captain had made his appearance in her home. Had she met Daniel Kent only this afternoon? It seemed she had known him all her life.

A ridiculous thought. She didn't know him. She only endured his taunts.

With a sigh, she got up to prepare for bed, as she did every evening about this time. Some citizens of New Orleans attended balls, went to the opera, gave parties, much as they had done before the Yankee invasion. Not Maddie. She hadn't been much for such entertainments—except the opera—before Julien left, and she hardly felt it right to participate in them now.

The one activity she missed was horseback riding. Her mother had taught her to cook and sew, to weave, to garden, to keep books, to maintain a home. She had also made sure her only child knew how to ride. Nothing gave Maddie more pleasure than galloping on the long, flat road beside the levees, the wind catching in her hair. Riding, she felt alive.

But the horses and the carriage had been confiscated long ago by General Butler's troops when she refused to swear her allegiance to the United States. Riding became another of her dreams.

Dan Kent would have said she should be grateful that her home had not been taken from her. Gratitude was not something she could allow in her heart. It would be an act of disloyalty to Julien.

Later, when she was lying beneath the light

coverlet, unable to sleep in the mugginess that warned of an approaching storm, she tried to concentrate on memories of her rides. Instead, she thought of Daniel Kent. Even dreams of Texas would not supplant him in her mind. She doubted she would see him again. He had teased her and, yes, he had flirted, but there had always been about him the air of the conqueror taunting the conquered.

He sensed her loneliness. If he thought that would make her more susceptible to his all-too-evident charms, he was very much mistaken. No matter what the future held, she would be true to Julien.

And, no matter the arguments Julien presented when he returned, she would see that her dreams came true.

Chapter Three

Two days after the invasion of Maddie's home by Yankee soldiers, one of them returned.

She was in the kitchen dredging fish fillets in corn meal when she heard the sound of footsteps in the dining room. They were moving her way. She turned to see Daniel Kent standing in the doorway. She jumped and gasped.

"I didn't mean to startle you," he said.

The crown of his captain's hat came close to the top of the door, and his shoulders blocked any view she might have of the room at his back. Anyone would have been startled, she told herself. It wasn't *who* the man was but *what* he was that disturbed her.

With the back of her hand, she brushed a strand of hair from her eyes. Her morning net wasn't doing a very good job at suppression, and neither was her sense of composure.

"I didn't mean to cause alarm," he said.

She wondered if he spoke the truth. His deep voice in her quiet home was almost as unsettling as his presence, and he had to know it. He wasn't menacing, but he was so very *there*. Everything about him was foreign to her, and to the subdued, get-through-these-years-as-best-you-can manner in which she was living her life.

She cleared her throat. "I'm used to visitors being announced, that's all."

"Your servant suggested that I come on back." He watched her for a moment. "Do you have many visitors, Miss Hardin?"

None, she could have replied.

"I volunteer at the charity hospital three days a week," she said, "and I care for my home. I have no time for visitors."

His thick, dark brows furrowed. He read the *none* in her response.

"Besides," she added, "who do you think would call? My friends have left the city."

Most of them, anyway, and those who remained numbered among those who had taken up once again the parties and balls of the antebellum days. They danced with boys and old men and with former soldiers whose injuries did not totally impair their social life. Maddie preferred to stay home and think of Julien and their future together.

But this was none of the captain's business. She had already said more than she should.

He stepped deeper into the kitchen, and she saw Will standing in the dining room at his back. If Will caught her glare of admonition, he gave no sign. Instead, he nodded and disappeared. He certainly seemed unconcerned that an enemy officer might bring her harm.

Maddie was not so sure.

She returned to her preparation of the two o'clock meal, feeling the enemy's watchful stare on everything she did.

"Fish," the captain said. "I never cared for it."

"Your wife must not know how to prepare it."

"I have no wife."

She saw her comment from his point of view, and her face warmed. "I wasn't trying to find out," she said, wondering if she spoke the complete truth.

"But still, you did."

She wiped her hands on her apron and looked at him. "Did you call to learn what we're having for dinner? Little else besides the fish. Put that in your report."

His lips twitched, as if he would smile, and her heart took a quick little turn. She had definitely been alone too long.

"I came to let you know that the two soldiers who invaded your home have left the city. They were sent to another command."

"You sent them?"

"It was on my recommendation. They instigated a fight in the barracks. I decided all that energy could be put to better use elsewhere."

"Shooting and killing."

She snapped out the words without thinking, and the atmosphere changed in the room, from one of awkward wariness to confrontation.

He took a moment to respond. "It's what soldiers do, Miss Hardin. On both sides of the battle."

"I am well aware of the pattern and consequence of war, Captain."

"I doubt that. Most southerners aren't. At least, I'm certain they—you—weren't when you began this hell."

He spoke with a vehemence that surprised her, and she understood what a passionate man this coolly composed officer could be. The floor seemed to be moving under her. She could not allow herself to get into an argument with him over the reasons for the war, or her part in its inception. She would leave such matters to zealots like her fiancé.

"You said two soldiers."

"Yes, the sergeant and the corporal. There is no chance they will bother you again."

Maddie thought of the pale young soldier's eyes. Over the past two days, they had haunted her more than she would have thought.

"You forget the third man," she said. "The private."

"He has caused no trouble."

"He wants to. But he lacks the nerve."

"It's as good a reason as any for causing no trouble."

"I would prefer a code of ethics, Captain Kent, one that would govern misbehavior. But then, that would be the difference between you and me."

"One of them." His voice softened. "But not the only one."

His insinuating tone stirred her as no confrontation could. He came up beside her. She dared to look into his eyes.

"Why I came puzzles me as much as you. But you can be grateful for one thing: I would consider it highly unethical to take advantage of you. To kiss you, as I want."

"Captain—" she began, but she didn't know what else to say, and she found herself unable to move. The most she could manage was to stare into his eyes.

He brushed a finger against her cheek. She remained calm, but her heart was beating fast.

"Cornmeal," he said. "You wear it very well."

His behavior was unconscionable, but so were her thoughts. She wondered how his kiss would compare to Julien's.

She closed her eyes. A woman could look at Daniel Kent only so long without making a complete fool of herself.

"If circumstances were different," he said softly, so close she could feel his breath on her cheek, "I would request that you give me a sample of what you can do."

"Captain—"

"I refer to the fish, of course. I love my mother dearly, but she is a terrible cook."

Her eyes flew open. "You're laughing at me."

"Would that I were, Miss Hardin." His expression darkened, and she could see a solemnity in the depths of his eyes that she had not seen before. "Would that I were."

With a bow, he took his leave, so quickly she grew dizzy. But she could feel him in the room. The strength of him, the force, even when he spoke softly, could not easily be ignored. It did not help her composure that in a grim, taunting kind of way he was one of the most handsome men she had ever seen.

Maddie had never given much importance to appearance. She could not begin to do so now with Daniel Kent.

Twice over the next two weeks she caught glimpses of the captain, once in front of the hospital when she was arriving for her volunteer work and again when she was at the waterfront market near Jackson Square picking over the poor selection of vegetables. Neither time did he seem to notice her, much less approach.

Coincidence, she told herself, and she also told herself that she was relieved his presence was nothing more.

The Texan who was offering her the dream

land for sale came by one evening to say he had several other potential buyers interested in what he had to offer, but he was holding it for her because of his friendship with Cal and Cord. Was she truly serious about wanting to make the purchase?

"I'm offering four thousand acres of rich grassland and water, and the finest stone house in the county. There's not much civilization around—that's why I'm giving it up, as I told you earlier, being a city man myself and not in the best of health. But location is all that's wrong. Location and the hard work that's needed to make it pay."

Maddie realized he exaggerated. Amid all that grass were probably enough rocks to build a dozen houses. And the house itself was probably plain and small. But houses could be added to and rocks could be cleared.

"I'm not afraid of hard work. I definitely want it, but not until my fiancé returns."

"You wait too long, little lady, the land'll be taken up by someone else."

Maddie blinked innocently. The Texan wanted money. For all his friendship with her brothers, he was a man of commerce and he did not want anything so bothersome as a war to impede a sale.

She didn't like his pushiness when he knew it might be years before she could travel west. She also knew that as wonderful as his proffered ranch sounded, there would be other places she could buy after the war.

"We shall both have to wait, m'sieur," she told him. "As we both are well aware, these are hard times."

He protested, but at last he left, and she went back to her daily, wary existence.

On the evening of the last Sunday in April, while she was hurrying home after a walk down to the river, debating whether she had done the right thing in putting the Texan off, she saw another man she recognized—the pale-haired, pale-eyed soldier who had invaded her home. He was coming from the opposite direction on the same walkway. His path would bring him directly in front of her.

When his eyes locked with hers, she shivered, as before unnerved by the intensity of his stare.

The street on which she walked was for the moment deserted. Her uneasiness grew to an irrational panic. He halted twenty feet away and waited for her to close the distance. Drawing a deep breath, she kept walking. When she came abreast of him, she tried to give him a wide berth.

"Ma'am," he said, "I've been wanting to see you again."

She ignored his words, kept her eyes downcast, hidden in the protection of her bonnet. But in the surreptitious glance she dared give him she noticed that his hair was long and scraggly and his uniform unkempt, far more so than when she'd first seen him at the beginning of the month.

Before she could get past him, he grabbed her wrist. His grip was strong. She could not break away.

"Let go of me," she snapped, more angry than afraid. He was a boy. She could handle him.

"We gotta talk. I keep thinking about you all the time."

His voice was wheedling, but there was threat in it, too.

"Let go of me or I'll scream."

He smiled, as if he liked the idea, and an icy fist took hold of her heart. Will had wanted to accompany her, but she had assured him that she needed only a breath of fresh air and would not be gone long. She wished he had not listened to her.

"There ain't nobody to hear," the private said. "Go on and scream."

Looking around, she realized that there were no lights in the windows of the surrounding buildings, most of them being business establishments that had closed or been ordered closed since the occupation began. Even the streetlights along the block had not been lit. They were alone in the growing dark.

She must not panic. It would be an admission of weakness. Instinct told her that this soldier, surely no more than eighteen, would enjoy finding someone weaker than he.

"Say what you have to say and be gone."

"I'm real sorry about the other day."

He didn't sound sorry. He sounded whining. And he did not let go of her wrist.

"Your apology is accepted. I know the other men talked you into doing what you did."

"You think I'm nothing but a kid."

"I think you were following the orders of men with higher rank."

His fingers tightened, bruising her skin. "I never seen nobody pretty as you."

She used great force of will not to twist and try to get away. Instead, she looked at his sidearm. She had never fired a gun, but she was willing to give it a try.

"You're lonely," she said, "that's all. I understand. Let me go and we can talk about it."

"I ain't letting you go. You'll run, and I'd have to catch you, and that wouldn't be good."

"I won't run, I promise."

"Women don't tell the truth. My mama lied all the time."

Maddie dared to look at him straight on. He had an innocent face, but it was without character, his features not yet those of a man, and she wondered if he even had to shave. The one feature that got her were his eyes, turned blank this evening in their expression, as if they stared inward instead of out at the world. Where once he had stared at her, he now stared at himself.

"I'm not lying," she said. "I'll listen. But I need to be on my way. People are waiting for me. They know I'm here. They'll be looking for me any time now."

"That ain't good."

Without warning, he jerked her into a nearby recessed portal, throwing himself against the door. The two of them crashed into the dark interior, and he slammed the door closed.

Maddie choked on dust and fright. Her breath was ragged, shallow, but the soldier did not seem to breathe at all.

"Maybe if you was to give me a little kiss, I'd know everything was all right. I got into some trouble with the captain and I'd like to tell him there ain't no bad feelings between you and me."

She thought hard about what to say. She must get out of this without further harm. Nothing else was a possibility.

"You don't want to do anything that will get you in more trouble, do you?" She spoke softly, an older sister giving advice.

"I ain't never had no pretty girl kiss me."

He spoke as if he heard nothing she said. She glanced around, and in the remaining light of day that seeped in through the dirty windows, she saw a counter running the length of the room. Otherwise, all was empty in the once-bustling establishment.

"I guess one little kiss wouldn't hurt," she said, willing her arm to give no resistance under his hold, thinking of the gun, feeling the itch in her free hand to grab it when she had the chance.

But first, she had to get closer and in the right position to reach out for the weapon.

"You're trying to trick me," he said.

"No, I promise, I'm not."

She managed a smile, but in the dimness he didn't seem to see it. She turned her body to face him and made her move, her fingers grabbing for the handle of the gun.

But he was quicker and stronger than she had realized, far more so than he had been when she fought him in her bedchamber. With a curse, he let go of her arm and slapped her across the face. Her head snapped and she stumbled backward, trying to catch herself but still falling, it seemed forever, until pain fierce as lightning exploded in her head.

The last thing she realized was an enveloping darkness as she fell into a deep, impenetrable void.

Chapter Four

Maddie drifted along the edge of pain and light, falling effortlessly back into the release of darkness before emerging once again to a wall of blinding pain.

The pattern repeated itself again and again, but she was beyond counting the number of times, beyond understanding, beyond reckoning of any kind.

For a while she seemed to be floating, then fighting a foe she could neither see nor identify, his voice deep and low, the words he spoke indistinguishable. But her efforts to defend herself had no force, and she soon ceased her struggles.

When she awoke to full consciousness, she was aware of a dim light and blurred surroundings and, most of all, a throbbing in her head that drove her to the brink of madness.

Considering the force of the pain, she could have been burning in hell. Instead, she was lying on a soft mattress, a pillow supporting her head and shoulders. They brought her no comfort. She lay still as stone, terrified without knowing the cause.

A shadow loomed over her. She gasped, then saw that it was Will. She clutched the covers. The mattress was her own, she realized, and the pillow, too; the dim light was from a single candle on the bedside table. All should be well. She told her heart to cease its pounding, but her heart would not listen.

Something was wrong, terribly wrong. As familiar as everything was around her, she should not be here. She tried to sit up, but the throbbing drove her back against the pillow.

"What happened?" she whispered. "What's going on?"

Will knelt beside the bed. "You're safe, Miss Maddie. You're fine, jes fine."

She tried to smile, but the simple movement involved worsened the pain. "Why wouldn't I be fine? Why do I hurt? Why—"

She rubbed at her temples, then pressed the heels of her hands against her head. She had too many whys to put to him, and she did not know where to begin.

She dropped a hand to her throat. "I'm in my nightgown," she said, as if that fact was the most curious of all. "Why am I in my night-gown?" She forced herself to think, to try to remember. "I was out walking. I was on my way home, and then . . ." She blinked up at Will. "And then nothing."

"You don't remember who did this to you?"

"Who did what? What happened?"

Will took a long time to respond. "No point in not telling. Someone hurt you. You was late getting home, Miss Maddie. I found you in an old building nobody uses no more. The door was crashed in. You was lying on the floor—"

He broke off, as if he was embarrassed to say more. But she heard more than simple embarrassment in his voice. He spoke with a fury she had never heard in her old friend, even in the days before the war, when as a freedman he had endured insults no man should have to endure.

Will had a great tolerance for insults, but only to himself. The closest he had come to this kind of anger was the day the soldiers came into her home.

The soldiers . . .

Something stirred in the back of her mind, and the terror returned. She held herself very still, willing it to go away.

"You say I've been hurt."

Nodding, he stood and backed away.

"You needs a woman now, Miss Maddie. But we ain't got one. I undressed you, but I ain't sorry and I ain't apologizing. You're like my child. I got some water in the basin, and some soap in case you want 'em. I'm leaving, got some chicken stewing on the stove. I don't know how much you been hurt. You tell me what you want old Will to know. You tell me who did this to you. I'll take care of the rest."

It was a long speech for him. It frightened her as much as her aches, as much as the blanked-out period of time. Hours must have gone by since she had gone out walking. She felt as if she had lost a piece of her life.

When he was gone, she slowly pulled herself up and sat at the edge of the bed. Her head continued to hurt and she felt a general achiness throughout her body, and she felt dirty, very, very dirty, soiled in a way she had never been.

Stripping off her gown, she made her way to the basin on the far side of the bed. Wringing out the cloth, she dabbed it against the lump at the back of her head, winced, but went on, wiping at her arms and stomach, feeling a knot of discomfort low on her abdomen.

Fetching the candle, she studied herself. Her body seemed the same as ever, thin and pale, except for a bruise at the top of her thigh. And the smear of blood, of course, that trailed along the inside of her leg into the thatch of dark private hair.

She could not draw her eyes away from the blood.

A shaky hand set the candle on the table. She moistened the rag and rubbed at the smear, and on beyond it, between her legs, in intimate places that hurt where she had never hurt before. She wiped herself a hundred times and still felt soiled. The filth was inside her.

At last she understood what Will had tried to tell her, what he had most feared. She had indeed been hurt. She could never wash the filth away.

When she had bathed herself as best she could, she glanced around the room and spied her walking clothes lying beside the wardrobe. Quickly she went to them. The dress was soiled with dirt from the floor of the abandoned building where Will had found her. So, too, was the petticoat.

She stared most at the underdrawers she had worn next to her body. The torn underdrawers were stained with another smear of blood.

Something else dirtied the garment, yellowed and stiffened it. She was not completely ignorant about the workings of the body, both of a woman and a man, and she suspected what had caused the stain.

In his haste to do his will, her assailant had not bothered to undress her. She gagged and threw up onto the pile of clothes.

For what seemed hours, she crouched on the floor, naked, unable to move. She tried to draw solace from thoughts of her mother and of her brothers, but she did not feel clean enough to bring them into her mind.

In disgust of herself, she stood, pulled out clean undergarments, brushed her hair until it crackled with electricity, put on a clean black dress. Gathering up the clothes, along with the nightgown, she set them in the basin of water and went out to find Will.

She found him in the kitchen beside the stove.

"These need to be burned," she said.

He took the basin from her.

"You remember," he said.

"I remember. It was the quiet one, the private who broke into the house. He saw me on the street and he—"

She could not bring herself to say *raped me*. No genteel southern woman ever said the word *rape*, much less endured it. The fact that she had no memory of the violation did not lessen the brutality of the act.

When Will was gone with the basin and the clothes, she wandered without purpose into the parlor and sat at the piano, removed the covering scarf, and mindlessly fingered the keys. She was not an accomplished pianist, but the sound of the music partly dissipated the cruel silence of the house.

Without willing them to do so, her fingers picked out a melody written in a minor key.

She told herself that she ought to cry, to rant and wail about her fate. What would other women of her class and upbringing do? Should she end her life and in the doing end her misery and shame?

It was a stupid thought, a weak thought. Maddie was not a weak woman. She did not react to troubles in the usual womanly way. Her anguish had been spent in the cleansing of her body, and in its place a cold resignation and abiding hate set in.

One other thought lingered, almost inconsequential as it flitted through her mind, yet basic to how the rest of her life would go. It was the conviction that her fiancé Julien would not easily forgive what had happened to her nor forget she was no longer pure.

How curious it was that only now was she considering the effect it would have on the man who should be the most concerned about her welfare. Would he look upon her as soiled beyond forgiveness? Would he somehow lay the blame of the violation at her feet?

She did not know. She wondered at how little she truly knew the man with whom she planned to spend the rest of her life.

If they heard the news, Cal and Cord would ride to her defense, doing whatever was necessary to avenge the terrible wrong that had been done her. This she understood, and it was the reason she could never tell them. That, and the fact that they might look upon her with pity.

Pity was the one reaction she could never tolerate.

For some reason, she considered how Captain Daniel Kent would react. He was the one person who could most easily avenge her. After the invasion of her home, he had taken action, albeit inadequate to her way of thinking, with the reprimands and transfer of the two ranking soldiers. Surely he would do something of far worse consequence to the private.

Hanging came to mind. Or skewering on the point of his saber.

But it was not vengeance she wanted; she wanted and needed release from her sense of shame. Surely nothing would come of this night except the shame. Fate could not be so cruel as to leave her with child.

The conclusion came after much thought: No one must know what had happened on this day. It would be her great secret, one she shared only with Will, one she would take with her to her grave.

When Captain Kent came calling two days later, Maddie had the opportunity to report the assault. But the disgrace of what had happened must be her secret; she could no more reveal to him her terrible secret than she could swim to France.

She also could not look him in the eye.

"Tell the captain I'm not receiving today," she instructed Will when he knocked at her chamber door. Returning to take her place in the chair by the front window, she watched as the captain mounted his horse.

The animal was beautiful, a chestnut gelding broad in the shoulder like the man who rode him. Kent knew horses; she could tell by the way he held the reins, at once casual and masterful, and the way he sat in the saddle, more at home than he would be in any parlor.

Fine horsemanship was a trait she appreciated more than any other. She looked away, unwilling to think favorably of him, of any Yankee soldier, of any man.

Another day, when Will was gone from the house—he had taken to absenting himself for long periods of time—the captain again came calling, but she refused to answer his knock. And she did not look at him through the window as he rode away.

Much to her regret, she had learned he was not a man to look at and forget. After the last time, when she'd studied him on the horse, he had lingered in her thoughts far longer than was right or wise.

Over the remaining week of April and into early May she occupied her time sewing new gowns for herself, pretty gowns, nothing black. The pieces of cloth, enough for several dresses, she had found on an early morning visit to the market the day after the assault. Will, of course, was close beside her, and although she was apprehensive, she made herself look at people, talk to the salesclerks, discuss fabrics and appropriate trim.

There wasn't much to discuss: The goods offered for sale were sparse and of a quality she would never have considered before the war. But times were different now. Different in every way.

Will thought her actions wrong, but she had to get out into the world right away, otherwise she might never leave the house again.

Her bruises and her physical discomforts passed quickly. Finding the need to keep herself busy, she sewed by candlelight late into each night.

But she could not bring herself to wear the pretty new clothes. Not just yet. She was dressed in black, hair net in place, when the captain again came, on a Sunday afternoon, exactly two weeks after the attack. She saw no way more effective to get rid of him than to tell him in person to go away.

She joined him in the parlor, where Will had directed him. He stood with his back to her. She would have expected to feel fear at the sight of his broad shoulders and imposing size. Instead, she felt a small, inexplicable tingle that came close to pleasure. It was the same tingle she had felt when she watched him mount his horse.

"What is it you want, Captain?" she asked, determined to send him on his way.

He turned, they looked at one another, and

she found herself unable to look away. He had been much in the springtime sun, and his skin was brown as toast, drawn tight over sharp features, his brows thick and dark as his hair, his brown eyes lit with an unexpected spark.

Why she should find comfort in the company of an enemy captain, she had no idea. But it was definitely a comforting warmth that stole from her heart to her throat and face, a warmth so strong she thought surely she must look flushed.

The war, the opposing sides on which they found themselves, held little importance at the moment. Daniel Kent wouldn't hurt her. Tall, muscled, darkly intriguing, he would not use his strength against her. She knew it in her heart.

The hate she carried with her she directed solely at a small, pale, weasely creature who wanted to think himself a man.

The realization brought her unexpected relief, but she could not let the captain know the thoughts that raced through her mind. She resorted to as stern an aspect as she could muster.

He doffed his hat and made a slight bow. "Miss Hardin, it is good to see you again."

"Surely this is not a social call."

"Of course not. That would be unthinkable."

"Most certainly."

They both spoke too quickly, too sharply, for either to believe the other.

"I have news that you may find of interest. The young private who came to your home—"

Maddie's heart leapt to her throat and she looked away, her hands clasped at her waist. "I have no interest in him."

"I'm certain that you don't. Still, I wanted you to know. He disappeared from the barracks sometime during the late hours night before last. Early this morning his body washed onto the riverbank south of the city. I've only just this past hour received word."

She glanced beyond him to see Will standing in the doorway to the dining room, watching, listening. An icy chill washed over her. She forced herself to regard the captain with what she hoped appeared no more than the slightest interest.

"Do you have any idea what happened to him?" Her voice sounded thin, reedy, far too concerned.

The captain gave no sign that he noticed.

"None. Several soldiers reported that he had not been himself the past week or two, moody, withdrawn more than usual. He acted like someone who had received bad news from home, but he never received letters. I don't believe he knew how to read or write."

"It sounds as if he was despondent. Perhaps he brought about his own death."

"Suicide, you mean? It is a possibility. But I'm told he had a fear of water. I do not believe he would have chosen drowning. A gunshot to the head would have been more in character."

Maddie shuddered and hugged herself.

"Please forgive me, Miss Hardin, for speaking so bluntly. I am too long removed from the company of women. I forget your sensibilities."

"You speak of sensibilities, yet I think you would rather say weakness. I am not a weak woman, Captain. With me you may say what you wish."

He smiled. "If only that was true."

There was much more than polite concern in his eyes and in the way he held the smile. Maddie had lied when she protested his thinking her weak. At the moment her knees could barely support her.

"Do you ride?" he asked.

The question was unexpected; it took a moment for her to understand what he meant.

"I used to. But the mare I had owned since she was a filly was taken from me two years ago by orders of General Butler."

If he caught the criticism in her voice, he gave no sign.

"I can make a horse available to you, if you would like to ride again. Not the mare, I fear, nothing so fine as you knew. But an animal of sufficient spirit, if that is what you choose."

"Why would you do this?"

"Because I want to. If you ask why I want it, I say it's a question best not asked."

She closed her eyes for a moment. Much

innuendo lay in his words, hints at something that ought to repel her. He had no idea what he offered her. With all her heart and mind, she wanted to cry out, "Yes."

But the word caught in her throat. Riding with the captain, accepting his bounty, would be a betrayal of herself. Any pleasure she derived from the outing would be bought at a terrible price, the remains of her self-esteem.

She had no chance to put her thoughts into words. In the pit of her stomach she felt an all-too-familiar discomfort that had assailed her over the past few days, a discomfort that demanded her complete attention.

She swallowed a bitter taste. "Thank you for the offer, but I really can't discuss anything further at the moment. You'll have to pardon me for asking you to leave, but I'm suddenly feeling ill."

"I'm sorry. If I've disturbed you in any way—"

"Oh, no. I'm certain whatever is wrong with me will pass. But I would very much appreciate your showing yourself out."

She didn't wait for a reply, but instead hurried past him through the dining room, past Will, and into the kitchen, where she sought a pail hanging from a hook by the back door.

Leaning low over the pail, she promptly emptied her stomach of all that she had eaten since early morning. As he had done yesterday and the day before, Will brought her a glass of water so that she could rinse the taste from her mouth.

With the moment of release, the nausea passed and she stood to face her old friend.

"Is he gone?"

Will nodded.

"You heard, of course," she said.

Again, Will nodded.

She tried to think of the dead boy, to summon feelings of hate, of relief, even of sorrow for a wrongly spent life. But all she could think of was Will.

"Do you need to leave? I know you receive letters from your sister in Illinois. You could join her and her family there."

"I laid no hand on the boy."

"I'm not saying you did. I'm not asking. What I'm telling you is that I'll get by. You need to think of yourself."

"No need to leave. I didn't touch him, jes' followed and watched. No crime in that."

"He saw you."

"No point in following if he didn't know it."

"And so—"

"He ran. I ain't never seen a more running boy than that one."

"And you followed."

"Down to the river. I don't think he knew where he was. The bank was slippery with mud. The tide was coming in fast and jes' swept him away. Wasn't anything I could do."

With a shrug, he fell silent.

Wasn't anything I could do.

The words echoed in Maddie's overburdened heart. She felt the same, but in a way far more desolate than her friend could ever know. There was, truly, nothing she could do about all that had gone before.

At last tears came to her eyes, tears that had not fallen in as long as she could remember. This day should mark the ending of what had happened to her. She should be able to get on with her life.

But there was the nausea that she could not ignore. She had not grown strong enough to consider exactly what it meant.

And yet, she knew. She knew.

Chapter Five

When Maddie missed her monthly flux, she admitted the truth to herself. Fate had dealt her its cruelest blow. She was with child.

The admission came in the middle of a stormy night as she lay sleepless in her bed. She couldn't move, couldn't even cry, not with a heavy heart anchoring her in place. Instead, she listened to the thunder and thought of the life growing inside her.

Barely growing. The assault had been little more than three weeks ago. She had been prepared to deal with her violation. Now another human was involved.

It's too soon to know for sure she told herself. But the attempt at rationalization was in vain.

She knew the truth. She understood the disgrace.

There were women not far away, practitioners of the dark art of Voodoo who offered potions that could end the condition. She knew of them; everyone who lived in the Vieux Carré did. She had friends who had purchased other vials to solve their problems, love powders to capture the heart of a wanted suitor.

For a price, the Queen of Voodoo herself, Marie Laveau, would provide what she needed.

Maddie considered the idea for no more than an instant. By the time dawn brought in a clear sky, she was fiercely determined to protect the new life that grew inside her. Already the infant was a part of her. Acceptance was the only way she had of defeating Fate.

With artfully designed dresses and, later, seclusion, she could keep the condition secret. The worst would come after the birth. She cared little for herself, but she could not visit her disgrace on an innocent child. She had a practical mind and a heart that yearned for love. Surely she could discover what path she must follow.

More than anything, the child needed a father. But Julien was far away, had been for two years, and she knew in her heart he would not accept another man's leavings. Especially under the circumstance by which the child came to be.

No, her betrothal to him was definitely at an end. The news would please the Delarondes, but it saddened her. She had loved their son, and she knew he loved her. And they had made such plans for their Texas ranch.

But his letters proved he had changed too much for those plans to reach fruition. And now, so had she.

But if Julien could not step in as the father, then who? There was no one else who cared for her, no one to whom she could turn. She must think, she told herself as she arose to begin her day. Something would occur.

Within an hour of her arising, Daniel Kent came to call.

Captain Kent? In desperation she considered the possibility. He was interested in her—she knew it—but only as a way to pass the days that grew lonely for everyone. Perhaps one of the Voodoo love potions could be put to work. She appreciated the irony in considering a Yankee as the replacement father.

But when she thought about this particular Yankee, the size and power of him, the self-assurance, the trembling way he made her feel, she knew he was a man she could not allow in her bed.

There were also other reasons, of course. He would never agree to marriage under these circumstances, no matter the strength of the potion; also, he was the enemy.

"Inform him that I am not receiving," she told Will, and the captain went away.

Over the next few days life went on as if all was well. She spoke to the few neighborhood friends who still remained in the city, did the shopping with Will close by, cooked, cleaned, and pretended she was content. The nausea passed, leaving her thinner than ever, though her appetite gradually returned.

One small problem remained: she found herself given to tears over the smallest of matters. The sight of a broken-winged bird lying in the street outside her door brought sobs that ended an intended walk before it began. Later, passing a park, listening to the laughter of children at play, she brushed from her cheeks tears that had absolutely no justifiable cause.

She did not know if all *enceinte* women reacted in such an emotional way to events around them, but she had turned into a watering pot.

Will watched as she entered the front door following her embarrassment at the park. He must have seen her red-rimmed eyes, looking her over carefully the way he always did lately.

"I caught some catfish down at the river," he said. "I got 'em cleaned and gutted for dinner."

She nodded and went toward the kitchen. What she wanted to do was thank him for not mentioning her condition, although he had to realize why she had changed. Mostly she wanted to thank him for not offering sympathy. For that she would always love him.

The captain came to call two more times before Maddie consented to see him. This time she was wearing one of the new dresses, a soft blue with a narrow waist, lace-trimmed rounded neckline, and fitted sleeves. She did not bother to bind her breasts. She found the constriction more painful than ever. She wouldn't be wearing this dress long, not even after she let out the seams as far as they would go.

Why she chose the best of her three new dresses she did not know, but she did not want to wear black. Not ever again. It seemed very important for her to look pretty all the time.

He joined her in the drawing room. She had forgotten the impact of him, the power, the dark suggestion of forbidden secrets he could show to her if she gave him the chance. For just a moment, studying him, she forgot her situation and thought only of him.

In turn, he looked her over with equal care. She felt the need to hug herself. All her worries returned. Could he not see her loss of virginity? Did her pregnancy show in a way an experienced man like Kent could see?

"Your hair is uncovered," he said.

She brushed at a tendril that curled in front of her ear. He sounded as uncomfortable as she felt.

"You look nice," he added.

It was not a rapturous compliment, but she doubted he was a man given to rapture. And it was a compliment, which she discovered she had wanted very much.

So do you, she almost said. Instead, she murmured, "Thank you," then regarded him with a steady eye.

"Why are you here, Captain?"

"I don't know."

That stopped her for a moment.

"Could you venture a guess?"

"I like looking at you. That's the best explanation I can come up with for why I've been making a fool of myself the past couple of weeks."

"Captain Kent, you've done no such thing."

"Of course I have and you know it. You seem a blunt-spoken woman. I assumed you would prefer to speak with a blunt-spoken man."

She studied his uniform for a moment, the dark blue jacket with its captain's insignia, the white collar at his throat, the dark cravat.

"But you're not just a man."

"Oh, I can assure you, Miss Hardin, that right now, a man is all I am."

She looked away, blushing, the way an innocent young woman would do. But she was no longer innocent, and she no longer felt young. It seemed wrong to be talking to him in this flirting way, as if every word, every glance was a lie. Surely he could see through her mask of insouciance to the pounding heart that lay beneath her gown. Surely he could see that she had been altered in a way even he could never forgive or forget.

She ought to ask him to leave, but she could not say the words. This was her first real conversation with a man since the assault, discounting Will. She took great relief in the fact that though she felt guilty and unsure of herself, she was not afraid.

"I suppose we could sit down," she said, gesturing to one of the chairs in front of the fireplace.

She felt his eyes on her. "Is that what you want?"

"What I want—"

She broke off. She had so many wants, most of them conflicting, she could not begin to answer him.

"Yes," she said, "it is very much what I want."

She sat in a facing chair and watched as he stretched out his long blue-clad legs. The pistol secured to the right side of his leather belt required a moment's maneuvering so that it could fit in the narrow seat. The chair appeared dwarfed by him. He made the entire room seem small.

He took off his hat and gloves, laying them across his lap. She followed the movements of his hands; she studied them as they rested against his thighs. Could those hands be cruel? Could they grab a woman and drag her—

She stopped herself. Danger lay in that way of thinking. Thus far she was managing the visit without major distress. She must not allow what had happened with one weak creature to sour her on the rest of the world. She had already decided Dan Kent was not a mean man.

She gave attention to the thighs beneath the hands. He was, however, very much a man.

"Would you like some tea, Captain?" she asked, too loudly in the small, quiet room.

He shook his head, then watched her until she shifted uncomfortably in her chair, wanting to brush from her face the strands of hair she had left loose.

"Why the change?" he asked.

"I don't know what you're talking about."

"The dress, the chair, the tea. Have I so charmed you that you've forgotten who and what I am?"

For the first time in her life, Maddie wished she were a simpering miss, one given to equivocation. She had never been much good at lying; she had not tried it often.

"I have not forgotten. And it is not so much your charm as your persistence that has worn me down."

She wasn't lying completely, except for the part about the charm, although she wouldn't have called what he had charm. That was far too mild a word for what caused the stirrings he aroused simply by being near.

"Besides, I have reconsidered your offer to provide a horse so that I might ride."

81

The declaration surprised her as much as it did him. She hadn't realized the thought of riding lurked anywhere in her mind.

"Of course," she added, "there are those who will curse me for accepting, but there are also others who attend dinner parties with our conquerors. A simple ride in the country does not seem nearly so wrong."

"You southern women could turn a man's head with such flattery."

"You're making fun of me, m'sieur."

"At us both. I'll be riding with you. Do you understand this?"

"I understand."

"Will you need a chaperon?"

She hid a bitter smile. "No, I will not need a chaperon."

"This is Thursday. Are you free to ride Saturday?"

She nodded, and the time was set at midmorning, before the heat of the day set in. He left quickly, and she went to her room to pull her riding costume from the chest at the foot of her bed. It needed mending, probably taking up in the waist, too, since she was so very thin, and it certainly needed a thorough cleaning. She hadn't worn it in two years.

She worked quickly and with great industry, willing herself not to question what she was about. Already she had dismissed the captain as a possible solution to her problem. He would be sympathetic to her situation, but he would also declare that the culprit had come to an end that should satisfy anyone's sense of justice.

If he did anything further, it would probably be to offer her some kind of financial help for the child, perhaps through the United States Army, and to offer his sympathy. Then he would leave and she would never see him again.

It was while she sat on the floor holding her riding habit that a different idea occurred, a possible solution to her problem that was as evil as it was reprehensible. But it would not go away.

What if she seduced him—soon—and convinced him the baby was his?

She buried her head in her hands. What had she come to? She was a good person. She was against slavery, against the war. Never in her life had she wished harm on anyone.

Except one villain, who had already gone to a watery grave.

She had only one excuse for considering the idea: the welfare of her unborn child. For that child, she had already given up her dreams of moving west, of founding the Longhorn Ranch. She did not mind the sacrifice of her chance at happiness. She would sacrifice her soul.

But would she seduce Daniel Kent? The idea refused to leave her mind. Could she do it? That was a more reasonable question. Doubt assailed her: He was too smart to fall for any ruse she might use to trap him. No, marriage to the captain was out of the question. To consider it for even a moment, she must be out of her mind.

And if she managed for a short while to fool him? As evil as the idea would always be, worse were the consequences if he ever realized what she had done.

"What the hell am I doing?"

Over the next two days, Dan asked himself the question regularly. He was making a fool of himself; he had already done so with what Madeleine Hardin called his persistence, and he was not yet done.

His quest for her company was caused by more than just loneliness. With her innocence, her strength, her honesty, she had him bewitched.

And of course there was the way she looked. Thin, too thin, but that was temporary, brought on by the hardship of war. He liked her spun-gold hair and he liked the tilt of her chin. She also had the finest eyes he had ever seen.

Men were fools. They fought wars and they sniffed after women who were as wrong for them as they could possibly be. There were hundreds of young Kentucky women waiting for their men to return home. He had no particular woman waiting for him, but he knew that he would eventually settle on one as his wife.

He was twenty-nine years of age. His life would be assuming control of the horse farm when his father could no longer remain in charge, taking residence in the family home with his sister and her family nearby, taming his young brother Tom to the daily chores, once Tom decided to settle down.

But that did not mean he should cut himself off from all female companionship. Madeleine Hardin wanted nothing permanent from him, just as he wanted nothing from her.

This was what he told himself as he went through the routines of the next two days. When he rode up to her front door on his chestnut gelding, holding the reins of a second gelding, this one white, he watched her walk out the front door.

For the moment he could not remember his name.

Her riding habit was deep green, a soft material that clung to her body and outlined a pair of breasts that were definitely not bound. The open throat revealed a teasing expanse of white skin and a long, graceful neck leading to the tilted chin, the full lips that almost smiled, the straight nose, the blue eyes.

She had bound her hair underneath a matching green bonnet, but fine curls lay against her face and neck. She was artfully dressed. Clearly she had taken much care to look pretty today.

He was glad. He let his reaction show in his expression. If anything was to happen between them, and he suspected that perhaps it might, it ought to be soon. He was, after all, part of an army of war. He could be called away at any time.

He dismounted and offered her a helping hand. She accepted it, allowing him to encircle her waist and lift her into the saddle. She moved so lightly, so effortlessly, he got the feeling she could have mounted the gelding all by herself. The fact that she had not done so he found encouraging.

With great care she distributed her costume over the sidesaddle as was required, and her well-worn gloves gripped the reins with practiced ease.

"Shall we go?" she said. With little urging on her part, her horse started off at a trot down the street.

Dan had to hurry to catch up.

She chose a route that took them quickly to the edge of the French Quarter and along a road at the base of the Mississippi River levees. Occasionally she would ride to the top of a levee and watch the slow-moving river flow past.

They encountered few people, and these mostly soldiers who saluted their captain at the same time they gave him knowing looks. He could not tell whether she noticed.

After a half hour at a leisurely pace, suddenly she dug her heels into the gelding and took off cross-country, winding through a stand of moss-draped oaks, the horses' hooves crunching the leaves that lay on the damp, flat ground. She did not stop until she came to the edge of a bayou that wound through the countryside far off the main road.

"We can water the horses here," she said when he reined to a halt beside her.

"You've ridden this way often."

"I used to. A lifetime ago."

She dismounted without help, and Dan did the same.

Her bonnet was slightly askew, and her hair was not so neatly bound as it had been at first. He found the flaws endearing. It was a word he had never used before.

On their own, the horses went for the water, leaving their riders to stand on the bank and to stare at one another, as a breeze ruffled the branches around them.

She licked her parted lips. It was more than Dan could take.

In two strides he was in front of her. Taking her in his arms, he kissed her. For a moment she fought him, shoving her hands against his chest, twisting her head, but when he eased his hold on her and moved his mouth from hers, he heard a sob catch in her throat. When they again kissed, this time it was she who held him and took his lips.

She tasted sweet, her lips soft and yielding, and he felt himself falling into a void. His desire was not subtle. His erection was immediate. If she felt it as she pressed her body against his, she gave no sign.

Though she was tall, she felt doll-like as he held her in his arms. He was on fire. He touched his tongue to her lips. For him the feeling was electric. But she had a far different reaction. Crying out, she jerked her head away. Her gloved hand flew to her mouth as she stared up at him. He had no choice but to let her go.

"What were you doing?" she asked.

"A man's tongue has never touched yours? Clearly not. For a moment there I wanted you so much, I forgot everything else."

She turned away and stared at the water. He could see that the breaths she drew were as ragged as his.

"Forgive me," he said. "I took you to be more experienced."

She turned to face him. Her eyes looked as if he had wounded her in some way.

"Of course you did. It was what I led you to believe."

"You have me confused. Why would you do that?"

She looked away. "Because I am attracted to you, when I know it is wrong. I wanted this ride more than I have wanted anything in a long while." She shifted her gaze to him once again. "And I wanted to be kissed. I did not think of it as being complicated."

He fought a smile. At the same time he recognized the urge to pounce on her again.

"The use of a tongue is complicated?"

"It made me feel strange."

"I felt more than a little strange myself. But I know the cause. I want you. It isn't gallant of me, and it isn't gentlemanly. But when we first met in your bedchamber, you knew I was no gentleman. And you told me so."

"So I get what I deserve?"

Her sharpness caught him by surprise.

"That's not what I meant," he said.

"So tell me what you think of me." She gestured to the horses and to the secluded setting. "Tell me what you think of all this."

Her forthrightness took him aback. He wasn't used to such honesty from women. He knew they liked to play games.

But Madeleine Hardin did not seem to be playing. He had never seen a woman look more serious. Or more beautiful.

He took a moment to look around him at the thick trees, the oak and the cypress along the bank, at the sunlight filtering through the branches to the leaf-covered ground, at the dark bayou moving past toward the river. Across the water, he heard the rustle of a wild animal. Alligators abounded in the swampy land around the city, but so did deer and muskrats, and even black bears and wild cats.

He felt no danger from any of them. They

were not so threatening as Madeleine Hardin's eyes.

"I think I can't breathe in this setting. I don't know if it's the closeness of the air or the way you look at me."

"Have I completely taken away your good sense? I don't think so. What I have done by my boldness in accepting your invitation is heighten other senses. I'm a conquered woman. Easy prey."

Dan smiled. "You're about as conquered, Maddie, as the wild animals in the woods. You don't mind if I call you Maddie, do you? When we're alone. Should we ever be alone again."

"Haven't you got things out of sequence, Captain? Shouldn't you have called me Maddie before you kissed me?"

"And shouldn't you be calling me Dan?"

She pulled off her gloves and thrust them into a pocket of her riding habit, then picked up a twig and began striking at a leaf on a long-hanging branch beside her.

"Will you be leaving soon?"

Her question took him by surprise. "Will you care?"

"I don't know." She abandoned her attack on the leaf to stare at him. "I rather think so, but your leaving has nothing to do with us right now. I simply want to know."

"Probably not. The Western campaign goes well for us. My unit should remain in New

Orleans for a while." He rubbed his chin. "Surely you don't want the details."

Her gaze followed his hands. He found her watchfulness as erotic as anything about her.

"If you gave it a few days, you could grow a thick beard, could you not?" she said. "It's not yet noon and already you could use a shave."

"And I believe, Maddie, it is time you had another kiss. This time I'll be gentlemanly enough to warn you what I'm about."

He pulled off his gloves and tucked them under his belt, then tossed his hat aside. He did the same with her bonnet, and for a moment watched the breeze catch in the loose strands of her golden hair.

"Without the tongue," he said, "if that is what you prefer. Ever the gentleman I am, where you are concerned."

She stared up at him with great solemnity.

"Let's try it both ways, Dan, and I'll let you know which I prefer."

Chapter Six

Tongue. Definitely with the tongue.

As soon as he invaded her mouth, she knew the truth. The trouble was that with the way he was holding her and touching her, she couldn't think beyond the one question. She had to remain in control. She had to reason through everything she did.

She must not like this too much. She must not like Dan.

So why was she standing on tiptoe, her arms wrapped around his neck, her body pressed to his, her mouth opening wide to anything he might want to do? She should be repulsed by him, by any man, but *should be* was not a consideration she could take seriously. She had no memory of any ugliness. And there was nothing ugly about what was happening now.

Dan's tongue felt thick and warm and sweet inside her mouth, and a little rough as he deepened his exploration. She responded in kind, thinking tongues had far more pleasurable uses than for the simple tasting of food.

Tasting a man . . . tasting Dan . . . satisfied her in a way no food had done, satisfied at the same time it made her hungry for more.

His hands were strong on her back. They stroked and massaged, then eased lower to grip her waist, and lower, to the roundness of her hips as he pressed her against him. At first she thought the hard object pressing against her belly was his gun, and then she realized her error. For a woman with child, she was incredibly ignorant.

She was on fire. She wanted him to touch her, to stroke her, to lay her on the ground and do whatever he wanted to her. She had no motivation other than her need for him to put out the flames.

And she would think of things to do to him. There was so much of him to touch, to stroke, that the completion of her journey might take a very long while.

He was the one to break the kiss, to ease his hands back to her waist, to lift his head and stare down at her. All the heat she felt in her body she saw reflected in his eyes.

"Maddie—"

"I'm doing something wrong."

"Good God, no. That's the trouble."

She stared at his parted lips and thought about his tongue. "I'm trouble."

"Yes. Or I am. I'm not sure right now."

"Then let me go."

She tried to look stern, to look proud, to act offended. The effort proved difficult.

"We can ride back into town," she said, "and forget any of this happened."

"You're doing things to me," he said, as if he heard not a word she said.

"You're doing things to me."

"I knew you would be sweet, but I didn't expect—"

He was clearly having trouble with words. She tried to help him out.

"You didn't expect me to be so willing. You think I'm terrible."

"I think you're as lonely as I am. What I didn't expect was this need I feel to protect you. I've never wanted any woman the way I do you, but I've never wanted to hurt anyone less."

"Would you hurt me?"

"Not in any way you're thinking. I would like to believe what might pass between us would be the height of pleasure. But there might be consequences neither of us could face."

He would never understand how cruel his words were.

"Do I need to explain?" he asked.

94

The injury deepened until she thought she might cry from the injustice of the world.

She slipped from his arms. "The horses are rested, I believe." Scooping her bonnet from the ground, she shook off the clinging bits of leaves and thrust it in place. "We ought to return now. I very much appreciate the ride."

"You're upset. Don't I get some appreciation for having a conscience?"

"You make me feel that I don't."

She spoke the truth, but in a way he could not begin to understand.

"That's not what I meant at all. I don't want to take advantage of your innocence."

"What changed your mind? When we rode out here, I had the feeling that was exactly what you wanted."

Suddenly she was weary of all the word play, the subterfuge. This moment held many levels of meaning only she understood. The most surprising realization was that she truly cared for this man. He was honorable. And he made her feel loved, if only for the afternoon.

She rubbed the side of her head. "Please don't answer. It was a bold question that should not have been asked. We were unsure about each other. And now we know the possibilities. They must concern you as surely as they worry me. The worst thing is, I want you to kiss me again, and for that I cannot forgive myself."

Before he could respond, she walked to the

bank where the horses were cropping grass. This time she did not play coy and let him help her mount. Tugging on her gloves, she positioned herself in the saddle and watched as he did the same.

On the ride back to her home, she made no stops by the river. What she wanted to do was keep riding, far, far to the west, to get away from the war, away from her circumstance. But she would carry her condition with her. She would ride with her troubled mind.

On this day her problems had multiplied. Against all common sense and expectation, she found herself caring for Captain Daniel Kent of the U.S. Army. She could almost call it the first stirring of love.

Dan came to call the next day, a Sunday. She hadn't expected him, yet she was not surprised. She wasn't pleased, yet she was happier than she could have believed to see him standing at her door.

She welcomed him in. "This time you'll have tea."

"This time, yes."

They sat in the drawing room and she apologized for being unable to offer him cakes and sandwiches.

"My mother would have served a three-course meal, all on a dainty plate you balanced on your knee. But the supplies are limited, you understand."

"Tell me about your mother," he said, and she did, recalling the gentleness edged with strength that had helped Adrienne Hardin through the years of motherhood. She mentioned that her mother had been married twice, the first time to a Frenchman who died young of yellow fever.

She did not mention that the Frenchman had been wealthy. It was a fact few people knew or had known at the time.

"I don't remember my father. He was much older than she and died of a heart attack when I was only six months old. But I have two brothers—half brothers from different wives. My father was thrice married, you see."

"Do the half brothers serve in the war?"

"The oldest, Cal, no, but he has a son who has joined the Confederate forces. Cord is a cavalry officer. They live in Texas, so I don't get to see them often, but they are dearer to me than anyone in the world. Except Will, of course. Do not mock me, Yankee, when I say he is like an uncle to me."

"I would not mock you, Miss Hardin."

"Miss Hardin? What happened to Maddie?"

"We are not alone. I assume your uncle is close by."

"So he is, Captain Kent, and don't you forget it."

She listened while he described his home in Kentucky, his beloved parents, the feisty sister

97

and her growing family, and mostly his brother Tom.

It soon became clear that Tom was the one he felt closest to, the one he loved the most.

"So you raise horses," she said.

"It's what you do in Kentucky if you're lucky. It has the finest grassland in the world."

"My brothers say the same of Texas."

"For cattle, maybe. Not fine horseflesh."

Pride shone in his eyes, and she did not argue. She liked a man who took pride in his home.

She more than liked him. And that was why she accepted another invitation for a horseback ride.

"The same place?" she asked. "Is that all right?"

"Yes," he said, and she had to look away lest he see the same heat in her eyes that she saw in his.

When they were once again in the woods, by the bayou, feeling the warm breeze and hearing the cry of unseen birds, he kissed her in the manner he had used before. It was a kiss filled with complications, all of them designed to drive her wild.

This time she was the one to pull away. Her hands were shaking. She clasped them at her waist, unwilling to let him see how much he affected her.

"You're right," she said. "We shouldn't be doing this."

"I'm right that we're wrong? You have me confused, Maddie."

"I have me confused."

"I've thought about nothing but you since we first met."

"When you leave, you'll be thinking of someone else."

"You keep mentioning my leaving."

"Because it is inevitable. Will I know where you go? Can you write? Already I sound clinging and foolish, but I want to know."

He told her the possibilities of his assignment, the probable troop movements that could involve him, then assured her that he would let her know where he was.

She listened to only the last; it was all he said that mattered.

As they stood beside the water, she touched his cheek.

"When we do this again, and I guess we will—"

"We will."

"Let's not talk of anything while we're together. Let's not talk at all."

He took her hand and held it against his face for a moment, then kissed her palm. She felt the touch of his lips all the way to her toes. There was no way she could hide her shaking.

"Do you know what you're saying?" he asked.

"I know." She pulled free and studied the moving water. "It is not something I have considered lightly. Our . . . being together is something I want very much."

"I won't be able to see you for a week," he said. "Maneuvers."

"I don't want to know what you're doing."

"There are rumors of an enemy ship off shore. We need to make certain our defenses are ready."

She covered her ears. "I don't want to know," she repeated.

"All right," he said with a smile. "I won't burden you with war talk."

Maddie could not return the smile. Instead, she kissed him and held on to him, and at last she let him go. When next they met, she would let him make love to her. And then she would have a decision to make, the hardest any woman could face. She loved him. Could she deceive him into letting him believe the child she carried was his? To do so would ensure marriage to the man she cared for in a way she had not known existed. To do so would give her child a name and a chance for a life without shame.

Everything in her cried out that she must attempt the deception. He didn't love her, not yet, but perhaps one day he might. She would make him the best of wives. She would forsake her plans, she would wait for her Yankee captain, and she would follow him wherever he wanted to go.

But she remained troubled, so much so that

the lie was all she could think about. Her decision came three days later when Will, summoned by one of the Delaronde slaves— former slaves—returned to town with a message.

The note was terse and carried all the more impact for it: Julien had been killed in battle, felled by a Yankee bullet.

Blindly, she stumbled into the drawing room and fell in a fireside chair. She read the note again and again, but tragically the words remained the same.

Julien was dead. Dear, sweet Julien, who, despite his wild enthusiasm for the southern cause, had never been equipped to go to war. He would not have known how to protect himself.

He had loved her; he had expected her to wait for him. The fact that he had wanted to change all their plans mattered not.

She wept for him, her first love and almost husband, a gentleman in the best sense of the word. Her grief was genuine. For the rest of her days, he would dwell in a corner of her heart, along with her grief.

As she sat, another emotion struck: contempt for herself. Julien was an honorable man. In her mind she had denied him the chance to prove that honor and to accept her child. She had betrayed him in spirit the same way she had planned to betray him with her body in only a few days.

And she had been prepared to betray Dan, too.

She could not do it, not now. Not even for an unborn innocent. There was another way out of the desperation that fell upon her, a way she had not considered until now. The solution was not perfect—it wasn't even a true solution—but it would have to suffice.

Brushing tears from her eyes, she went to the back of the house to find Will and to tell him exactly what they must do.

When Dan rode up to Maddie's house, it was with the realization that today would probably change the rest of his life.

He was falling in love with her. It made no sense, but there it was. He could not deny the way he felt when he thought about her, and he could not deny the soaring pleasure when he held her in his arms.

One thing he had to do: make certain she felt the same. Then whatever happened today by the bayou would be glorious.

As he dismounted and secured the two horses to iron plugs by the street, he noticed the lace curtains were no longer fluttering by the open window of her bedchamber. They had probably been taken down to be cleaned. Maddie was a woman devoted to cleanliness.

It was a fine trait in a wife.

If that was the way things worked out.

He had chosen to wear trousers and a shirt

other than his uniform. He was off-duty. He thought she would be pleased. Today they were a man and a woman intent on exploring the possibilities of what they meant to each other. He would not ask her to gaze upon the differences that could keep them apart.

And when she undressed him—he had the particulars worked out in his mind—he did not want her touching Union blue. The most he had allowed himself to wear was his gun.

A man answered his knock, a stranger to him.

"If you're selling something, I ain't buying."

The man was tall, scrawny, with narrow eyes and an unshaven face. Dan took an immediate dislike to him.

"I've come to see Miss Hardin."

"She's gone," he said and started to close the door.

Dan's booted foot kept him from succeeding.

"What do you mean, she's gone? Where?"

"I ain't supposed to tell."

Dan shoved him into the foyer and grabbed him by the shirtfront.

"Where?" he repeated.

"I don't know for sure. She moved, that's all. You let go of me and I'll tell you what I know."

Reluctantly, Dan did what the man asked.

The stranger dragged his fingers through his long, scraggly hair, then rubbed the back of his hand across his nose.

"She said she needed to get out of town. I

sold her some land she's been wanting. Over in Texas. She gave me the house as partial payment. Then she and that nigger she keeps with her skedaddled. Middle of the night, it was. I figured she was heading for Rebel territory. I got the feeling she was sick of being around the Yankees, what with her fiancé being dead and all."

"Her fiancé?" Dan felt like a fool.

"Julien, or some fool name like that. A Frenchie, like her. They'd been planning to buy the land and move west, but the war slowed 'em up. I figure what with him getting shot down in battle, she decided to go on her own."

Dan rested a hand on his gun. "I'll kill you if you're lying."

Sweat beaded on the man's brow. "I ain't lying. I swear."

Dan wanted to smash the man's face, like the ancient Greeks taking his pain out on the bearer of bad news.

Instead, he took a quick look around him, then left fast, slamming the door behind him. Without looking back, he rode down the street, the white gelding meant for Maddie in tow. Leaving the horses at the stable, he went to the small private room that was provided an officer of his rank, sat at the edge of the hard bed, and poured himself a stiff whiskey.

He drank it down fast and thought about all he had been told.

They'd been planning to buy the land. In talking about herself, she hadn't mentioned any such plans.

She decided to go on her own.

Dan could not have been so wrong about her. But the evidence was there. She had kept secret her engagement to a Rebel soldier and she'd questioned him about Union matters, all in the guise of worrying about whether he might leave.

She had gone so far as to cover her ears, pretending she did not want to hear what he said. Madeleine Hardin was a very clever spy. A hell of a lot more clever than he.

Would she have let him make love to her? It was something he would never know.

He was progressing fast toward drunkenness when a letter was delivered to his door. He had to read it three times before the terrible message registered. His brother Thomas had died in a Confederate prison, the hellhole known as Andersonville.

Dan's world shattered around him. He hadn't known Tom was taken prisoner. He should have, he should have felt it in his bones, close as they were. He should have sensed his baby brother was dead.

But he had been concentrating on someone else. In that moment he admitted to a feeling he had never felt before with such purity: hate.

He hated the war, he hated the Rebs and

their shoddy cause. Most of all he hated Madeleine Hardin. She was a southern spy, as much a cause for Tom's death as anyone.

In a sudden rage, he threw the whiskey glass against the wall. It fell in a thousand pieces on the floor. The destruction brought no relief.

He dropped his head in his hands. He needed to write to his parents. He needed to think about Tom. He needed to mourn.

For all of this, he needed a sober mind that would keep him from thinking about Maddie and of the tremendous mistake he had almost made, the confession to her of how he had begun to care.

How he used to care. The admission of his love would have no doubt caused her much amusement. The one thing he could hope for in this world was that some day he would see her again. On that day he would make her pay for all she had done.

Chapter Seven

Maddie got her first look at her future home on a hot, cloudless summer afternoon. It was not the best time for viewing any portion of South Texas. From what she had already seen, there probably was not a good time.

She sat unmoving on the narrow wagon seat that had been her perch since leaving San Antonio six days earlier. Her head and hair were soaked with sweat beneath a sun bonnet, her calico dress clung to her back, and she ached from eyes to toes after endless hours of bouncing on the buckboard and staring into the sun. Now that her journey was done, all she could do was stare straight ahead.

Mon Dieu, she thought, and burst into tears.

She had been assured the stone house of Longhorn Ranch was the biggest such structure in the county. Of course it was; it was the only one. She hadn't seen a building of any kind—stone, brick, or adobe—since crossing the county line two days ago. This one would have fit inside her New Orleans drawing room, with maybe a little intrusion into the foyer on one side and the dining room on the other.

The scout who had accompanied her during the last part of the journey—for an exorbitant fee—had given her warning.

"You might be a hair disappointed," he said as they rode onto what her deed showed was now Hardin land. "There's not much anybody'd want here in the Strip."

It was the last thing she got out of him before he sneaked off. He chose a moment when she was concentrating on guiding the wagon along a patch of nonexistent road and making certain none of her belongings pitched out of the back.

Bâtard.

A wind hot enough to bake biscuits ruffled her bonnet. She wiped away the tears. All they did was sting her eyes.

Securing the reins and throwing her gloves onto the seat, she dropped to the ground and went closer to the house. The ground lay hard and cracked beneath her heavy shoes. The wind stirred dust and whipped her skirt between her legs. A few brave weeds and low clumps of grass grew between the wagon and the front door; except for the three-foot cactus by the house, the only other vegetation close by was a copse of oaks and another of mesquite trees throwing pitiful patches of shade a dozen yards away.

The lone front window, small and square, was boarded up. The gray, splintered door squeaked back and forth on its rusted hinges. She looked up at the chimney and saw a narrow ribbon of smoke diffusing into the outside heat.

Her heart started to pound. Once again she cursed the runaway scout.

Stepping backwards, stumbling over a rock, she returned to the wagon and grabbed the shotgun that lay under the seat. She knew how to fire it, having done so once as practice when she bought it in San Antonio, but she wasn't sure about her aim.

Whoever was squatting on her land would not know that. Brushing a strand of hair from her eyes, she headed for the house. If she had any sense, she would be terrified. But a long time ago Maddie had lost her ability to react like a normal woman.

She had been heartsick for so very long, she welcomed another kind of feeling, even if it was alarm. But terror, no. She hadn't the strength.

She started for the front door, then thought better of it. Planting her feet firmly on the ground, she thumbed back her bonnet to get a better view and raised the shotgun.

"Come on out. All of you. I've got six men backing me up. Every one of them is a sharpshooter. When you clear the door, I want to see your hands raised."

There, that sounded Texan enough. She had been picking up the lingo since she first crossed into the state from Louisiana two months ago. French, she long ago decided, would do her little good.

The door creaked open a couple of inches, and a grizzled gray head peered around the edge.

"Where're the men?"

The squatter's voice was hoarse, as if he carried a week's worth of phlegm in his throat.

She took heart. He didn't sound so tough.

"They're where I can call them if I need them."

He spat tobacco in her direction.

"You put that gun down, little lady, and I'll come out."

"You raise your hands and I won't shoot."

"You might's well pull the trigger. I'm out'a whiskey, anyways."

He staggered out the door, tripped, and

barely righted himself. Well, sort of righted himself. He swayed, tilted westward for a couple of seconds, then circled his body around in a clockwise direction, all the while managing to keep his feet in place. His arms hung loose, but she decided insisting he raise them would be his undoing.

His shirt and trousers were caked with dirt and sweat; his boots were cracked, the heels worn almost completely to oblivion. He was scrawny, not much taller than she, his gray hair long and scraggly, and his rheumy eyes blinked repeatedly in the bright sunlight.

The wind shifted and she got a whiff of him.

"You've been drinking," she said unnecessarily.

"I'm a drunk."

"A drunk who is out of whiskey. Are you alone?"

He nodded toward the house. The motion almost sent him falling backwards. " 'Cept for the harem inside. And Brutus, of course."

He whistled, and the ugliest cur Maddie had ever seen lumbered out the door. With yellow mangy fur, short bowed legs, and a big head on a squat, thick body, Brutus was missing an ear, and his left eye had a milky cast to it. The flaws should have made him look mean; instead he looked pitiful. He leaned against his master's leg, man and beast propping each other up.

The squatter eyed her carefully and scratched

at the side of his red-veined nose, then reached down to scratch his dog's head. "There ain't no six men."

She gripped the shotgun. "I'm a liar."

She was also very much alone, thanks to the cowardly scout, who had proven himself no better than the rascal who sold her the ranch. Even a Brutus of her own would have given her comfort right now.

She shivered, cold despite the heat. Where were the settlements, the ranches, the neighbors she had been assured were nearby? Over the past two days she had not seen even a single wild cow, which made the name Longhorn Ranch more than absurd. And its owner more than a fool.

It was all too much. Her heart was already broken. Over the past year and a half she had been through troubles no woman should have to endure. A few weeks ago she had said goodbye to Will, and to her only chance at happiness. And now this.

Suddenly, the gun seemed to weigh as much as the wagon; she lowered the barrel, collapsed to the ground, and came up with a fresh supply of tears. This time they did not stop.

The squatter sat, too, watching her from a dozen feet away. Sobs racked her. He didn't say a word, just watched, blinking from time to time. So did the dog.

When she had finally emptied herself, she

rubbed at her face and wiped her hand on her skirt. It was not a time for linen handkerchiefs. There probably was not one within a hundred miles.

"My nose must be as red as yours."

"Yep."

She sniffed. "You're squatting on my ranch."

"You own this place?"

"More than four thousand acres. It came from an old Spanish land grant. A lawyer in San Antonio said the deed was valid. It's mine, all right."

"No wonder you're bawling. You have my sympathies."

There was something in his voice this time that gave hints of a better time, even a smattering of education.

"Who are you?" she asked.

"Owen. Don't ask for no other name. I'm too poor to have more'n one."

"What are you doing here? Besides sheltering your harem, that is."

"Passing time. What I am, y'see, is what's called a drifter. I got hold of some whiskey over in Illusion, at a place called the Grog Shop. I decided to rest up here for a while. Seeing the grandeur that was available and all."

"Illusion's a town?"

"Calling Illusion a town is like calling this place a ranch. No more'n a couple dozen people, most of 'em living in tents or dugouts. They thought they was moving to Paradise. Sort of like you, I'm guessing. But there ain't no Paradise nowhere near this part of Texas."

"I covered a good part of the county to get here. I didn't see a soul."

"Illusion's easy to miss. Most everyone there wisht they had done just that."

He staggered to his feet, frowned in the direction of the afternoon sun, and hitched his pants. "Brutus and me best be moving on."

Maddie panicked and hurriedly stood. "No," she cried, and then, embarrassed, added, "What's the rush?"

"Illusion's a half day's hard ride, and I'm on foot. Caesar—that's my horse, or at least he was—stepped in a hole a week or so back and I had to shoot him. Had to leave him to the buzzards, too. Neither Brutus nor me could bring ourselves to eat him. We're sentimental that way."

She knew he was trying to look and sound pitiful. If she hadn't been hardened to the plights of men, he would have succeeded.

She took a deep breath. "Would you like to work?"

"If you're gonna cuss, little lady, I'll have to leave. Anyways, I was thinking more of being a guest."

"Quit calling me 'little lady.' I'm offering you a job. I'll pay you to stay until I get settled and can hire some real men."

"Can't say as I care for the way you put that, little not-a-lady."

"Real ranch hands, that's what I meant."

He blinked, looked around, stared at the wagon, then back at her.

"You don't seem all the way demented. What possessed you to come out here alone? El Desierto Muerto ain't exactly friendly to women."

"Doesn't *muerto* have to do with death?"

"Yep. The Dead Desert. That's what this part of the country used to be called, when it was part of Mexico. It's known now as the Nueces Strip."

"I've heard it called the Strip."

"The Nueces River ain't far away. The Strip lies between it and the Rio Grande. El Desierto Muerto still fits better. Only creatures that thrive are snakes and desperadoes."

It was another fact her Texas land dealer had neglected to mention. Along with Lipan Apaches that frequently raided across the border, or so she had been warned in San Antonio. And the true state of the house.

"I hired a scout. He was supposed to stay until I got set up. He said he knew some vaqueros who could work for me cheap."

"Don't tell me. You already paid him."

She shrugged. "I don't have much good luck when it comes to men." The admission was as close as she could come to thinking about the past, at least in the bright light of day. "I've got a lot of supplies that need unloading. There's a bottle of whiskey in there somewhere. For medicinal purposes, in case I got bit by one of those snakes you mentioned."

She held out her hand. "My name's Madeleine Hardin. Maddie."

He wiped his hands on his pants, which was not an encouraging sight when she considered the state of the pants. Brutus wagged his tail, then collapsed, exhausted.

"Whiskey, you say?" Owen asked.

"A whole quart. I heard there were lots of snakes."

They shook. His hand was rough; it was like grabbing onto cactus.

"Is there water?" she asked.

"There's a pump out back and an old cistern full of holes. But don't be looking for no other refinements. You want a privy, you'll have to go behind a tree."

"I would have been surprised at any other arrangement. Give me a minute to look around. It won't take much more than that. Then we can start unloading the wagon."

His look of interest lasted only until she started listing what she had brought.

"I've got crates of tinned food, flour, things like that. And dishes. Be careful of the dishes. They belonged to my mother."

Owen ran a tongue over his teeth. "You want to tell me where the whiskey is? That way, I can be extra careful with it, too, when I'm moving it."

"Be extra careful with everything. I'll get the whiskey when we're done."

"How do I know you've really got it? You already said you lied."

"You don't know. You'll find out when the wagon's empty."

Squaring her shoulders, she went inside to inspect the place from which she would direct the founding of a third Hardin Texas empire.

The dark single room reeked of whiskey and sweat. A low glow from the fireplace provided enough light for her to make out a rumpled bedroll on the wooden floor, a beat-up tin coffeepot on the hearth, one table, one bench, and nothing else. In a couple of places someone had hung cowhide over the stone walls, she supposed as insulation. The hide could never be mistaken for decoration.

She took a deep breath, then let it out slowly. Here was the home in which she had expected to spend the rest of her life. She prayed for the strength to make it through one night.

Maddie woke sometime in early morning and sat up with a jolt. It took a minute to realize where she was: lying atop a thin pallet on a hard, splintered floor, in a ten-by-twelve-foot cabin in the middle of hell.

She had loosened some boards at the window to let in air, but no light made its way inside along with the breeze. With the fire out, she was sitting in ink. Sleep wouldn't come again. It never did when she woke up like this in the night. She couldn't remember a night when she hadn't awakened. It must have been before the war.

Feeling around in the dark, she located the shawl that served as a wrapper, shook out her shoes in case spiders or snakes had crawled inside—the precaution had been Owen's suggestion, and she took it for a good one—and made her way cautiously to the front door. Supplies were scattered everywhere around her. If she tripped, she would probably break a leg.

Outside, the unloaded wagon loomed twenty feet away from the house. Nearby, embers from a fire glowed in the dark. Owen was sleeping under the wagon. The wagon horse was standing still, head lowered, in the stand of oaks beyond Owen's makeshift bed.

A quarter moon hung low on the horizon, but it was the million stars that got her attention. She hadn't known a night sky could look like this one, like diamonds thrown against black velvet. And the breeze—the blessed breeze—had cooled the air so that she had to pull the shawl tight around her shoulders.

Lifting the hem of her nightgown, she dared go around to the back of the house where she could study the trees shifting in the starlight and where the breeze could catch in her hair. She ought to be crying again, the way she had this afternoon, but her tears were spent. Giving in to despair was not only tiring, it was wasteful. She needed her energies to survive.

Besides, not everything was terrible. Seen like this in the cool of the night, her land was beautiful. On the journey she had observed vast stretches of grassland, some of which had to be on her property, and there had been trees; nothing like Louisiana trees, of course, just scraggly live oaks and ash and mesquite, but still, they were there. Despite Owen's talk about snakes and desperadoes being the only creatures to survive, she knew wildlife abounded. She had learned that from the scout.

Of course, nothing made up for what she had lost. Nothing ever could. Closing her eyes, she gave in to weakness: she thought of Grace, beautiful Grace, with the tiny hands and the upturned nose and the perfectly formed lips. Darling Grace, born on the first day of this year, born so small, so weak.

She had not been able to care for her beloved daughter as she should, and now her little girl was gone. She welcomed the pain that came with remembering; it was payment for her inadequacies. She had awaited Grace's birth with a desperate eagerness, as something beautiful that could come out of the worst time of her life. Grace was the only child that she wanted and now, according to the doctor who had attended her, most likely the only child she would ever bear.

But Grace was gone.

The knowledge, the memory, struck too hard to consider them for more than a few minutes at a time.

And so she thought of Will, who had been treated badly ever since they'd left New Orleans, worse even than before the war. They had fled to Shreveport, the Confederate state capital after the fall of Baton Rouge. There, he had been a freed Negro in a land of slaves and then, after the war, he was an enemy in a country where all Negroes were viewed as part of the hated Reconstruction.

Will had got her to San Antonio. She had been right to insist he join his sister and her family in Illinois. If she needed help, she had two brothers she could call on. In the meantime, she was traveling with others. She would be all right. He had promised to join her at the ranch, but she knew he wouldn't. He did not belong here.

Did she?

It was a question she had been asking herself since she'd left San Antonio, moving slowly down the Presidio Road that eventually led to Laredo, down on the Rio Grande. Her company, her protection, had been a dozen settlers moving west, fleeing the devastation of their southern homes. With their plans undetermined, they had talked about joining her, but as they left the lush hill country near San Antonio and the land grew more harsh, they had decided, family after family, to keep moving on.

She should have let Cal and Cord know what she was about. They were prominent ranchers in the state, and they were her only family. It would have been easy. Cord had friends in San Antonio. All she had to do was reach out to one of them.

But she was stubborn, like them, and had kept her presence secret. Having failed so cruelly, so completely at so many things, she had wanted to prove herself worthy of the Hardin name.

All she had done was prove herself a fool.

What would Daniel Kent say if he could see her now? A thousand times she had wondered what he must have thought when he went to her house for their ride—and more, for the promised yielding to his lovemaking—and found her gone. What did he think of her now, more than a year later? Did he think of her at all? She doubted he remembered her name.

She had known him such a few short weeks, yet he had remained with her in ways that would make him laugh. Hearing him, seeing him in her mind was not the worst of it. When she closed her eyes and tilted her head, she could feel his lips on hers. And she could feel him in her heart.

He could not have felt the same, the handsome Yankee captain lonely for companionship in his temporary home. She had been a dalliance, a woman willing to sacrifice her virtue for a few rides in the country. It was the only view of her that made sense. He did not know she had lost that virtue in an abandoned building in the center of the Vieux Carré. Or that the rides she so readily accepted had little to do with why she had been desperate to make love to him.

She truly was crazy. She ought to be remembering the way another soldier had dragged her into that building. She ought to remember the horror of when she awoke and discovered what he had done.

Instead, she thought of Will and Grace and Dan, of what they had brought to her life, of whether she could survive now that they were, each in a different way, gone.

She stood for what must have been hours, until the first faint glow of the day edged the eastern horizon. The house had been built on a rise, the highest point in the county for miles around. In the dim light she could barely make out the rolling landscape, covered with stunted trees and scrub brush, that stretched in every direction. But she remembered how it looked under a blazing sun: endless, forbidding, untamed.

She stirred herself to move. The desert was still cool at this time of morning, but it would not remain that way for long. She needed to get as much work done as she could within the next few hours.

She would need more furniture than the slanted table and wobbly chair. She had an ax to cut down trees, and the tools for planing and hammering together a simple bed. Too, the cistern would need repairing, right after a privy was built.

So many things awaited. She had never cooked on an open fire, but she could learn, a stove being as inaccessible to her as the stars. Surely her new employee could teach her a few of the thousand skills she needed to know. If she could wake him up.

Crouching by the wagon, she gave his boots a shake. He did not stir. Neither did his dog.

She should not have given him all the whiskey. On the other hand, she did not have any more to give. If he wanted to buy some in Illusion, at the Grog Shop, he could not do so until he actually performed some work and earned his pay.

In dealing with a man, she was learning, a woman had to hold back something of herself, something that she possessed, whether it was her heart or her purse.

It was a lesson for which she had dearly paid.

Chapter Eight

August burned its way into September and then October. Maddie managed not only to survive but to allow a ray of optimism into her life. She was not a woman given to inactivity. Through all her hard work, she found an easing of her heart's burdens that bordered on hope.

Probably it came from the hint of fall in the air, the rains that sometimes fell in the night, the green sprouts that were beginning to peek through the garden she had planted at the side of the house.

She had hired a vaquero to begin the construction of a corral, in preparation for the wild mustangs she planned to capture. Carlos spoke little English and, naturally, absolutely no French, but Owen knew enough Spanish to communicate with him. He was teaching Maddie what little he knew.

The fact that Owen was still there, sleeping under the wagon beside Brutus, even in the rain, grousing but doing his share of the tasks, amazed her. He had his own horse, a sway-backed nag he called Caesar II that he kept staked out in the woods away from the house. He had come back from a trip into town with the animal tied to the back of the buckboard.

Caesar II—he spelled the name out for her in case she did not catch what "the Second" would look like—was the equine equivalent of the dog, but he could support his owner for long periods of time as he rode about the ranch with Maddie.

Still, when she paid Owen his wages, he would usually forget Caesar and take the horse and wagon with Brutus slumped in the back, disappearing for a few days. Always he returned. And he hadn't begun the disappearing until Carlos moved into a dugout a half mile from the house.

As for the house, it was clean, which was the most she could say for it. With more than a little arguing, she and Owen had constructed a small bed, and she had sewn a sheet into a mattress stuffed with grass, leaves, and feathers from the wild game he sometimes shot for their meals.

As a gesture of farewell to the past, she had

added to the stuffing the undergarments embroidered for her marriage to Julien.

Gone were the cowhides from the walls, along with the cobwebs and mold. The table and chair were still the only other furniture, but she had put up some rough shelves for her precious dishes and pots, using the crates she had brought with her.

The best shelf she had saved for hanging over the bed, a place of honor for her mother's china doll.

Around the ranch—Maddie was determined to call it a ranch—she had taken to wearing trousers. She and Owen wore the same size; at her instruction, he bought them each two pairs and a couple of shirts in a general store that had opened in Illusion. He had surprised her by adding a fringed buckskin vest. She topped her ensemble with a floppy straw hat as protection from the sun, and a red bandanna she wore around her neck.

Her proudest possession was the horse Carlos had got for her from a rancher he once worked for down near the Rio Grande.

"You ain't never gonna see that vaquero again," Owen had warned her when she gave Carlos money for several purchases.

But Carlos returned with not only a high-stepping blood bay mustang, but also a tooled saddle and matching bridle, so fancy with their silver trim, they were totally incongruous with everything else at the ranch, including their new owner.

Being less inclined than Owen toward classical nomenclature, she named the mustang Sunset, in recognition of the sun that colored the western horizon a fiery red each twilight.

Carlos had also bought a mule, *"para Señor Owen,"* he said with a grin. What with his own horse and hers added to Caesar II, the dray horse she was now calling Dependable, and the mule, the newly finished corral looked downright crowded.

What little shopping was done, Owen took care of in Illusion. Not once had Maddie gone into town. She did not want to see people. Her obsession was her land. At least once a day, she saddled the mustang and went riding, usually with one of the men unless she could get away alone.

She found a dry creek bed not far from the house; she explored the grasslands as possible pasture, and she eventually caught sight of the Longhorns that had been so much a part of her dream.

On horseback, she stared at the beasts from a distance of a hundred yards, watching as they moved through the brush, tearing at the grass with their stubby teeth. The longer she looked, the more depressed she became, and eventually resigned. These were far from glorious wild creatures roaming the countryside. Her

Longhorns had dangerously pointed horns and mean little eyes, and they spent their time pawing in the dirt.

When Christmas came, Owen killed an especially fat wild turkey, and they dined on greens from the garden. She gave the two men shirts she had made from her now useless riding habit. Much to her surprise, Carlos gave her a basket he had woven from straw. With much flare and noise, Owen brought in a rooster and two hens he had purchased in town.

"Carlos here's been keeping them in the dugout for the past week," he explained.

Carlos said something in Spanish that she loosely translated to express pleasure the fowl were now hers to contend with. She promised the men a breakfast of the first eggs.

Resting by the fire, Brutus ignored the whole scene and gnawed on a turkey leg.

The next day the men began work on the henhouse and yard for the chickens, putting them beside the house, close to the garden. And Maddie began to think about Grace, more than just in the night, but while she worked during the day. Every day.

The first of January was approaching, the anniversary of her lost baby's birth. She knew she could not bear to be alone. And so she found Owen down by the creek, which had begun to run with clear water after a series of winter rains.

"I want to go into town," she said, then added, "To welcome in the new year," as if the explanation would take the surprise from his face.

"Don't know as how there'll be much celebrating. Illusion ain't exactly given to good times."

"That's all right. I don't expect much. Is there a place I can stay?"

"I always sleep under the wagon."

"Then I'll sleep in it. We'll take all the blankets we've got. And we can do some shopping. I've been wanting a milk cow. Now that we've got the chickens, we need butter and cream to go with the eggs."

"Next thing you know, you'll be wanting a barn. Women. Ain't none of you people ever satisfied."

Carlos remained at the ranch, to care for the growing stock and to watch over the house. Thus far the Longhorn had been spared the attention of Indians and outlaws, but all of them knew it was only a matter of time before such trouble came.

For Maddie, trouble always came.

In Illusion, it showed up in the form of a man. She met him in the hastily built wooden shack that bore the sign GENERAL STORE. Tall and thin, with gray streaks in his brown hair, his features narrow and not entirely displeasing, he watched with pale blue eyes as she entered.

129

She had seen that look before when men stared at her. Why this man was attracted to her, she couldn't figure. She wore a plain cotton gown over which she had thrown a plain brown cloak, and her floppy straw hat was pulled low over her bound hair. Her only decoration, and it wasn't much of one, was the red bandanna at her throat.

Under the Texas sun, her skin had toughened and browned, and there were freckles across her nose and on the backs of her hands. Her palms were callused, her nails cut to the quick, and her boots thudded heavily as she walked inside.

Despite her change in appearance, she remained obviously female. With men, that was enough.

He smiled, doffed his hat, and walked toward her. Immediately she got nervous. He wore a suit and vest and string tie, and he was clean-shaven, all of which should have been in his favor. But he was smiling at her. She did not want to be smiled at by anyone other than Owen and Carlos.

She felt like one of her chickens when the rooster strutted too close. Her feathers were ruffled. She preferred to be left alone.

He gave her no choice. "You must be Miss Madeleine Hardin. Allow me to introduce myself. I'm Edwin Worster."

"How did you know my name?" she asked, none too graciously, wondering where Owen had got to.

Oh, yes, the Grog Shop. She probably wouldn't see him until the next day.

"You're our local mystery woman. Our recluse, as it were. There has been much speculation about why you have kept to yourself. Some thought you had been terribly burned in a fire and had moved to the country to get away from prying eyes. Others decided you were peculiar in the head."

"How do you know I'm not?"

"I don't. But I suspect that for reasons you choose to keep to yourself you simply want to avoid the company of others. I hope your visit keeps you in Illusion long enough so that I may find out."

"Don't the people around here have anything better to do than gossip?"

"Sadly, no. There is, however, what will pass as a celebration at the Grog Shop this evening, in welcome of 1866. I hope you can attend and show them that you are not scarred."

She wanted to tell him to go away and forget she was there, but that would leave her alone again. Tonight and tomorrow, she wanted to be with other people, especially women. It was why she had come to town.

And he was not entirely unpleasant. He wasn't a woman, but he would have to do.

He smiled and backed away. "I will leave you to your shopping," he said.

He really wasn't unpleasant at all.

She caught herself. What was she doing? Except for Will, and now Owen and Carlos, she had terrible luck with men. But it was nice to be smiled at, and he really wasn't being pushy. Besides, he was not wearing the uniform of an Army officer. She had seen so many blue coats in San Antonio, she had fallen ill from worry that one would be worn by a man she recognized.

And so that was why, after she had completed her shopping, making arrangements to pick up the supplies the next day, she decided to attend the New Year's celebration.

Anyway, she was curious to see inside the tent that was called the Grog Shop.

Back at the wagon, which was under a tree at the edge of town, she used part of their water supply to wash her face and hands. Tossing the hat and bandanna aside, she brushed her hair and wore it loose, but there was nothing she could do about the boots. They would have to be her party slippers, probably the only kind she would own for the rest of her life.

Her curiosity about the Grog Shop was soon satisfied. It was indeed a tent, with a wooden extension at the back that doubled its meager size. A few barrels and unpainted boards at one side served as a bar, and a half dozen tables and chairs were scattered around a straw-covered dirt floor. But the lanterns sparkled in the evening light and she could smell good cooking, and there were a dozen people present, men and woman and a couple of children, all of them dressed about the same as she.

Except for Edwin Worster, who was the neatest person in the room. He looked ready to come over and greet her, but Owen got there first.

"I didn't think you'd make it. Thought you'd turn yellow and change your mind."

"And a happy New Year's Eve to you, too," she said.

He was wearing his Christmas shirt, and at some time since she last saw him he had actually poured water over himself, although it was too much to expect that he had added soap. Nor had he trimmed his hair or shaved.

She had not expected to see him here. He looked beautiful to her. She needed a familiar face, even if it came with a nagging mouth.

She felt Worster's eyes on her. She turned her back. "Do you know anything about him?" she asked, rolling her eyes so he would know whom she meant.

Naturally enough, Owen looked right at the man. There was nothing subtle about her hired hand.

"He's new to the county." His voice crackled loudly over the talking in the saloon. "Heard he bought some land just north of yours, but he stays in town mostly. Says he's trying to decide how to use it. There's talk he wants to build himself a grand house. For a man living in a two-room shack in Illusion, he talks big. 'Course, it's the best shack in town, but that ain't saying much."

She turned to watch as Worster approached.

"I couldn't keep from overhearing," he said.

"Did you hear any lies?" Maddie asked. "Anything you would like to correct?"

He shook his head solemnly. "No. I do talk big. But I plan big. As, I think, you do, too. I might, however, add a few details to my biography. I come from Virginia but have no intention of returning, having lost a wife and child there before the war."

Despite her ingrained reticence, Maddie warmed a little to him.

He was not done. "I served with the Confederate forces, I am proud to say. I have now settled in this godforsaken land hoping for a better life."

"You'll never make it as a Texan," she said. "The ones I've met don't have much to say for themselves. And they never talk about the past."

She glanced sideways at Owen. After five months of living close to him, she knew he was a drunk and a drifter, but that was all she knew. Except that he had not abandoned her to her isolation. And he liked to nag.

"As I said, I am from Virginia and am naturally gregarious."

134

Owen snorted.

Worster smiled. "I will be quiet and assume a Texas pose, if that is what you prefer. Although I would like to introduce you around, especially to the women. And there is the food they have brought. They will want you to share, I promise."

Against her will, against her better judgment, Maddie allowed herself to be charmed, and she made no objection when he offered to introduce her to the good people of Illusion, as he called them. He even helped her with the purchase of a milk cow, from a young couple who had decided to leave Illusion and return to their Alabama home.

A week later, when he rode out to the Longhorn to deliver the cow, she went with him for a stroll, then offered him a cup of tea. She served it in the shade of the oaks, unwilling to let anyone other than Carlos and Owen into the small stone edifice that had become her refuge from the world.

As they drank and talked, Owen stood in the background, rolling his eyes, but Carlos kept on clearing out land by the corral for a barn.

And so January passed, bitterly cold some days and almost springlike on others, predictable only in its unpredictability. February was colder still, and March was dry. The ground hardened, and the creek went dry. She had to use precious water from the pump when she planted her spring garden. When the cistern went dry, Carlos hauled water from a spring he found on the south edge of the ranch, and they all talked about beginning a roundup of the cattle that were the source of the ranch's name.

She and Carlos talked, that is, with Owen translating, although she was getting pretty good with her Spanish. She had even taught the two men a smattering of French. Carlos took to the language. Owen hadn't gotten much beyond *mon Dieux*.

In the middle of March, Edwin Worster rode out to warn her about the Lipan Apaches.

"They're raiding again," he said. "You need to stay in town."

"I'll be all right. Owen has been teaching me to shoot. I'm pretty good. And I bought a second shotgun and a rifle. Don't worry about me. Think about yourself and your land."

"I have been. That's also why I'm here."

They were standing by the fence of the corral, where Maddie's gelding Sunset was prancing about in an extra frisky fashion, acting as if he still had all his parts.

"Cut proud," Owen had called the behavior, giving her another phrase to add to her Texas talk.

Sidling close, Worster looked as if he had something he very much wanted to say, something she probably did not want to hear, and the uneasiness she had felt when she first saw him returned.

She kicked at the dirt. "Look at this. It's gray. How can you grow anything in gray?"

"You were used to a different soil."

"Stick your finger in Louisiana dirt and it comes up muddy. I wonder how far I would have to dig to get water here. China, probably."

He eyed her for a minute, in a different kind of way, assessing her on terms she didn't understand. Her uneasiness grew.

"Will you do me the great honor of becoming my wife?"

Maddie was not certain she heard right.

"I'm sorry. What did you say?"

"Marry me. I want you to be my wife."

"You don't know anything about me."

"I know you are lovely and good. These are traits I very much admire in a woman. And in a wife."

He started to take her hand, but she thrust it into a pocket of her trousers.

"I have never married. I do not intend to."

"I will not ask why you feel this way. I honor your privacy. But this is a hard land for someone trying to live alone. Surely there are times in the middle of the night when you grow lonely."

She turned away from him. She had not thought him so wise as to see into her heart.

"Please," she said. "I did not expect your proposal, nor did I encourage it."

"All I ask is that you think over my offer. I am not a poor man, nor am I unpleasant company."

"No, you are not unpleasant. I did not say you were. But there is between us a lack of—"

"Of passion? Of love?"

"Of both."

"I knew love once. And passion. If you are unable to give them, I will expect neither from you. At this time of my life I want the companionship of a good woman. I do not want to live alone."

He sounded sincere, and when she looked into his eyes she could see an earnestness that made her almost believe she could accept such an arrangement.

Love was highly overrated. Twice she had been its victim; she would not be so again.

But no, this was impossible, and she told him so.

"My land is not as vast as yours," he said, "but neither is it a small spread. And I am not without other resources."

"You embarrass me, sir, and insult me."

"Neither was intended. I ask that you not deny my plea outright but give yourself time to think it over."

In all the time he talked, he did not once touch her. How different he was from the men she had loved.

"I'll consider what you have asked," she said.

It was more of an admission than she would have imagined she could make, and he seemed to see it as such. Reminding her of the Apaches and warning her to take care, he left.

Life with Edwin Worster would not be joyous, but she knew that for her such a life could never be. Not without her precious Grace. Not without love. In her heart she had betrayed Julien with her love and lust for an enemy captain. If she married Edwin, she would do the same to him. She would always love and want only one man. She felt truly cursed.

And yet she could not fully dismiss the offer that had been made. Sometimes she grew weary bearing all the responsibility of the ranch. She had help—this she did not deny—but the men ultimately depended upon her.

Troubled more than encouraged by Worster's proposal, Maddie threw herself into work, clearing land for a larger garden, helping with the ground work on the barn, learning from Carlos the art of adobe construction, nagging Owen as much as he nagged her so that he would do his share of the chores and earn his keep.

She also practiced roping and, even more, shooting. She was good with a lariat, but even better with a gun, taking to shooting the way she had taken to riding a horse when she was a child. From a hundred paces, she could snap the leaf off a tree. It was a skill she might need.

The Apaches were indeed raiding—Owen brought back from town stories about their looting and rustling—but thus far she had been spared, and she told herself that perhaps this was one trouble she might avoid.

By early April she was ready to go after the cattle. But for that, she needed men. Carlos left to find what vaqueros he could.

Before he returned, she got all the men she could ever want. But these were not the workers she sought. These wore the blue coats of the United States Army. She was standing in the middle of the half-tilled field where she was planning to grow corn—or at least try to. She saw them riding toward her, kicking up dirt, blocking out the world.

Sunset was tethered fifty yards away, at the edge of the field, too far for her to get to him in time and gallop away.

She was wearing her trousers and a buckskin vest over a plain brown shirt, the red bandanna at her throat. Her hair was braided under her floppy hat. Pulling off her gloves, she reached for the shotgun by her side.

She expected them to overtake her en masse, in the way of Yankee soldiers, little caring for the dust or the alarm they might arouse. These held back. Only one emerged from the troop of twenty-odd soldiers, a tall man, broad in the shoulders, his legs strong as they gripped the flanks of his mount.

He rode right up to her, the flaring nostrils of his horse a scant two feet from her face. His uniform and boots were covered in trail dust, but the pistol and saber he wore seemed clean and lethal, available for use in a trice if he was given any trouble.

Instead of a regulation Army cap, he wore the wide-brimmed hat of a cowboy. It went with the sword and gun, all of them suited for riding the Nueces Strip. As she looked up, she shielded her eyes with her free hand. She saw no recognition in the dark eyes that stared back from under the brim of the hat.

Maddie trembled inside. Two opposing urges tore at her: one, to run for her life, and the other, equally powerful, to throw her arms around his nearest leg.

She took her cue from him and chose neither. Instead, she stood her ground and tried for nonchalance.

"I believe we've met," she said coolly, as if she had winter creek water in her veins instead of liquid fire. "Captain Kent, isn't it? I must admit this is a surprise."

Chapter Nine

She should have shot him when she'd had the chance.

Bivouac! On her land. She would not have it. And she told him so.

They were standing in front of her less-than-grand home, and he was explaining why he was there. The cactus plant was directly behind him. One push and she could make up for not using the gun. It was a contemptible but tempting thought.

Maddie held back a sigh. How quickly all her warm feelings and old desires for him had died. Or, if not died, had banished themselves temporarily from her heart. Later there would be hurt, of course, and crushing pain, but at the moment anger held them at bay.

"You're irritated because I did not recognize you right away," he said, his voice smooth as black silk. "You've changed, you know. I can hardly be faulted for not knowing who you were."

Dan had placed himself, probably by calculation, just far enough from her so that she could get a full view of him without putting herself out, all six-feet-something of blue-swathed muscle and dark confidence. But he was close enough for her to see the new lines around his eyes and the tightness of his mouth.

Too, his face, shadowed by bristles, was leaner than she remembered it, his cheekbones sharper, more pronounced. He could not tug the felt hat low enough to hide the change.

Altogether, he looked harder, sinew and muscle and bone with no room left over for gentleness or consideration. He was not now a man who would make social calls on a woman considered his enemy, not one who would care if she liked to ride or give her the chance to decide how much of his lovemaking she could accept.

Whatever he had been doing the past two years had not brought him much peace. For a moment she weakened, and her heart went out to him. But there was danger in softening and, worse, letting him know it. If he had ever cared for her as more than a dalliance, he did not care anymore.

Neither must she.

"I'm a great deal more than irritated," she said, keeping her eyes locked with his. He could not begin to understand the effort that took. "And your poor memory is most certainly not the reason why I'm so upset. I lived two years under Yankee occupation. I won't do it again. Not for two minutes. You and your men will have to settle somewhere else."

"Nothing you say surprises me. Southerners have never been the most sensible of people. Unfortunately, my conscience will not allow me to do what you ask."

"Your conscience?"

"The word obviously bothers you. It's that sense some people have that tells them right from wrong."

He spoke sharply. It was the first time he had allowed anything other than cool assurance in his voice. But she saw nothing in his dark eyes that would indicate what had brought on the alteration.

It did not last long. When he spoke again, the sharpness was gone.

"Aren't you curious as to what brought me to your ranch?"

"I no longer question misfortune, Captain Kent, no matter what form it comes in." She stood as regally as she could manage in her fringed vest and worn trousers. "As a southerner, I'm quite sensible in that regard."

"Your fiancé guided me here."

"I don't have—"

Maddie stopped herself. He must mean Edwin Worster. Her exasperation mounted. If Dan wanted to believe she was engaged to the man, she would let him. What business was it of his? The next time she saw Worster, she would set him straight about how he spoke of her.

Her tormentor was not done with his lecture. "You should not look at me and my men as misfortune. We could very well be your salvation."

Daniel Kent her salvation? Maddie muttered an obscenity in French.

He looked at her, really looked at her in a way he had not done before, from the top of her floppy hat to the open throat of her shirt with its red bandanna loosely tied, to the vest that barely disguised the shape of her breasts, to the shabby fitted trousers that did not disguise any shape at all.

He made the trip back to her eyes even more slowly.

"In New Orleans, you acted very much the lady. You truly have changed."

"You have no idea how much."

She could not keep the bitterness from her voice. But she could hide the hurt over the *acted*. She had not been acting; she had considered herself a lady, even after the assault, probably more so then than ever. He was the one who began the real changes in her, with his visits, his touch, and finally his kiss.

What would he do, what would he say if he knew all that had happened to her? Would he view her with scorn, as easy prey?

The answer squeezed her heart. This would not do. She had to get control. Stepping away from him, she looked around for Owen, but he had disappeared soon after she and Dan and his men rode in from the field.

Even Brutus had summoned the energy to slink away.

"You'll have to explain things to me," she said, "although the definition of conscience was unnecessary. What exactly did Edwin Worster say to you? Why do you feel obligated to stay here?"

"He said you were a strong-willed yet vulnerable woman who refused to live in town. I assume from the little he told me that your servant Will is no longer with you."

How easily he could strike her with remembrances of what had been. She took a deep breath to draw her strength.

"No, Will is not here. But I have other help. I am far from vulnerable."

"Do not be overconfident. I've seen your help. I agree with Worster. He seemed genuinely concerned when he spoke of his beloved's dangerous situation."

"His beloved?"

"You seem a little slow to understand what I'm telling you. It must be the heat. And the

146

solitude. As I recall, you were not a woman who liked to be alone all the time."

Maddie looked at the saber at his side, long and lethal in its scabbard. How easy was it to run a man through? She shuddered, surprised at the potential for violence in her. It equalled her susceptibility to hurt.

"I quote him," Dan continued. "He seemed quite concerned about you. When he described how your ranch sits on high ground, providing an unobstructed view of the surrounding countryside, I knew this was where we must stay."

His words had a finality to them that would be hard to shake. He demanded to be near her, not because of old longings or even a lingering animosity, but because she lived on a hill. She could hardly believe she had loved him for the past two years.

"What are you doing here?" she asked.

"I've told you," he said as if he was talking to a child.

"I don't mean specifically here, on this spot. I mean in Texas."

"I would have informed you of the reason right away if you had allowed me. Most of the forts that protected settlers from the Indians have been closed during the war."

"Everyone knows about the forts, Captain."

"Then why are you living out here in the Nueces Strip like this?"

"Because I'm a southerner and I'm not sensible. Why else?"

"Why else, indeed. General Sheridan in New Orleans sent me with a band of Indian fighters to scout out the area, to observe the seriousness of the situation. I am here to protect you."

"I don't need protecting."

"So you have already indicated. If you truly believe that, then Maddie, you are a fool."

She ignored the criticism, too caught up in the sound of her name on his tongue.

"Excuse me," he added quickly, "Miss Hardin. We are not familiar enough with one another for me to use your given name."

There went her heart again, squeezed and hurting a little more.

"I agree," she said stiffly. "It would never occur to me to call you Dan."

He could not know how severely she lied. She had been whispering *Dan* in her mind again and again since first he rode up, interspersing it with curses because he had appeared. He was right. She was a fool.

"You misunderstand my question about why you're here in Texas," she said. "I thought, that is, as best I can remember, you were planning on going back to Kentucky. That is your home, is it not?"

She could have told him every word he had used in its description. But it was easier, and safer, to play stupid instead of smart.

"Circumstances changed. When the war was

over, I decided to sign up for another tour of duty."

She longed to ask the particulars, about the mother and father he had talked about, the sister and her family, and, most of all, the younger brother. What had been his name? Tom, that was it. She had thought he cared very much for him.

There was something in the way he had said *circumstances changed*, an underlying emotion that she recognized—pain. Was Tom killed in the war, like Julien? The more she thought about it, the more certain she became that Dan's much loved brother was gone.

In another time and place, she would have reached out to him, touched his hand, stroked his face, and told him how very sorry she was, how she understood the anguish of loss.

She did not dare. With the hardness in his eyes and his chiseled countenance, she suspected that reaching out might cost her a finger or two. He was feeling a sadness she shared, but he was in no mood to accept or pass on sympathy.

So be it. Her heart hardened in a way she would not have thought possible an hour ago.

"Please listen to me, Captain Kent. There is no room for you here. My home is small, as you can see."

"Yes, I did take notice."

"It barely provides enough space for me."

"I do not plan to remove you from your bed."

His eyes glinted. "Nor do I plan to join you there. In case such a sharing was in your mind."

Tears blurred her eyes, and her cheeks burned. "Why are you talking to me like this? When I left the way I did—when I found myself forced to leave—I did not hurt you. I couldn't have. You did not care enough for me."

If she had expected him to question the leaving, to let her know he had been upset, she was disappointed. His only reaction was to stiffen and rest a hand on the high, rounded handle of the saber.

"Do not turn this situation into a personal one."

"It is impossible to do otherwise."

He looked at her for a long moment. Too long. She brushed nervously at her trousers.

"I have been assigned to this part of Texas with the express purpose of looking for Lipan Apaches. Despite our awkward association in the past, an association you insist on bringing up, I will expect your cooperation."

"Our awkward association?"

"What would you call it?"

She had no answer she could put into words.

"My men and I will set up our tents around the highest point of land. Unfortunately for you, or perhaps fortunately if you care about surviving, that point is close to your house. Except for the use of your pump, we will take care of ourselves. Your eggs and milk and privy are yours alone. Ignore us and go about your life as you did before we arrived."

He gave her a mock salute, turned sharply, and disappeared around the corner of the house, returning to his men, who were resting in the shade of the oaks in the back.

Maddie stared at the spot where he had stood. Some things the human mind could not comprehend, nor the human heart bear. Daniel Kent's abrupt return to her life was one of those things. The sun was cruelly bright. She wished to be in darkness to recall all that he'd said.

You've changed, you know.

He was more right than he could ever realize, more than she would ever let him know. And she was still changing. She had always thought of him with love, even when she told herself he'd thought of her as a dalliance. He had never lied to her about his affections. But he had been kind. In her despair over her condition, she had hoped the kindness would grow into love.

He was not kind anymore, not when he could speak so dismissively of a time that had been the most meaningful of her life. The losses, the sufferings he had endured, had wrought an alteration in him equal to any in her. She would forever mourn for the loss of Grace and the absence of Will, but she would never, ever again long to be within a thousand miles of Captain Daniel Kent.

She started for the house.

"You got yerself a situation, damned if you don't."

She turned to stare at Owen, who was stumbling out of the woods.

"I thought you went running," she said, "when you saw the bluecoats."

"The cap'n there would call it a strategic withdrawal. I didn't go far."

"You were listening in on a private conversation."

"Didn't have to listen hard. You and the cap'n had something going back in New Orleans, didn't you?" He clucked his tongue. "You being on one side and him being on the other, it must've caused quite a to-do."

"We didn't have anything going, and there was no to-do. Besides, it's none of your concern. What you'd better be thinking about is twenty bluecoats camping out behind the house. With Carlos bringing another half dozen vaqueros, we'll be crowded with more people than Illusion and half the settlements between here and San Antonio combined."

"Throw in the Apaches and you got something there. Drifting ain't what it used to be. Not by a mile."

"Nothing is what it used to be, Owen. Nothing can ever be the same again."

This time she made it into the house without interruption. She could not hear the sounds of the Army unit setting up their tents, but she could sense them even through the thick stone walls.

She sat on the bench and spread her brown callused hands on the table in front of her. She was cursed. There was no other explanation for all that had happened. After she'd disappeared, Dan must have bought a Voodoo hex doll fashioned in her image and stuck it full of pins.

But that didn't make sense. Her life had begun to go wrong from the start of the war, long before she had ever met the Yankee captain. Besides, arranging for the doll would have required passion. For him, passion involved lust and only lust.

He had not cared what else developed between them, beyond a few stolen kisses, and never had. Through the past months she had tried to tell herself that was the way it had been. Now she knew it for the truth.

Dan thrashed about in the woods, with no purpose in mind except to get away from human company. And to keep to himself the reaction of his body, a reaction that came from doing nothing but seeing and talking to Madeleine Hardin again.

She had glanced more than once at his sword. A slight shift of focus and she would have detected another kind of weapon he had been ready, damn him, to unsheathe.

Why did he want her like this? His reaction did not make sense.

She looked terrible. Her once milk-white skin had turned brown and freckled, her hands were callused, her nails cut to the quick. She had taken to wearing trousers, and the hat she thrust on her head was the ugliest piece of clothing he had ever seen. There wasn't a single characteristic that was soft or feminine about her, not anymore.

Yet she had never looked more beautiful or more enticing. Living like this the way she had chosen, out in a harsh land as different from New Orleans as granite from swamp mud, she must be going through difficult times. But she hadn't broken. If anything, she had grown more spirited, and it was her spirit that had drawn him to her in the first place.

He would not be drawn again. He could not allow himself the luxury or the torture. Still, she looked better in the trousers than any man he had ever seen, better than other women did in a fancy dress. And he was hiding out in the trees waiting for his body to cool down.

Most everything he'd told her had been the truth. He was here on orders from General Sheridan. What he hadn't mentioned was that it was he who had suggested the assignment. He had known she'd bought land in South Texas. He figured that was where she had gone when she fled.

What had really happened to Will? She had said he was like an uncle to her. Maybe she'd fled from him, too. With Maddie, a southern charmer, a former southern spy, actions could have devious motives.

He had known the identity of Edwin Worster's beloved. Worster had called her by name. It was the main reason he was where he was right now. When he rode up to her in the field, he had, of course, recognized her immediately, and it mattered not that he was already looking for her. Neither did it matter what she was wearing or how her hands and complexion had coarsened. She was Maddie, and he wanted her.

It was a hell of a situation. He had Lipan Apaches to deal with, skilled warriors who fought with savage intensity for a land that once had been theirs to roam. For the safety of them all, he needed to concentrate on the Lipans. Not Maddie. Not again.

Despite himself, he remembered her in the lush shadows by a Louisiana bayou, her body clad in a green riding habit, warm, yielding, gentle. And he thought of her the way she was now, standing in men's clothes in front of a shabby stone cabin under a glaring sun.

The thing to do was get from her what she had so tauntingly offered two years ago, and what she shamelessly displayed for him now. If she made so much as a half offer, he would take it and get about the important task at hand.

He no more believed she was an innocent maiden than he believed the world was good and pure.

Her most recent fiancé came to mind, a self-possessed, sharp-eyed man who had spoken of his *beloved* as he might a piece of property recently acquired. Despite his expressed worry over Maddie, he had not seemed particularly enamored of her, no more than she did of him. When she was speaking of Worster, her strongest emotion was annoyance over his concern.

Thoughts of a fiancé had not bothered her when she was seducing him in New Orleans. Another would not deter him here in Texas when the tables were turned.

For Maddie could definitely be seduced. Too well he remembered the way she had kissed him two years ago. She would kiss him that way again. And soon.

"Cap'n Dan."

Dan whirled, pistol drawn. He heaved a sigh of relief. "Damn it, Wilcox, you could have got yourself shot."

Sergeant Mead Wilcox was big and tough, hairy as a bear, strong as an ox, and utterly fearless. He was Dan's best trooper, an old Indian fighter from the frontier fort days. He was better by far at scouting and shooting than the fresh-faced second lieutenant Sheridan had insisted he bring along, and he was smarter, too. Dan could ill afford to lose him before the Indian fighting had begun.

"Something's wrong," Wilcox said.

"Where?" Dan looked past him in the direction of the house. "Is she—" He broke off and started over. "Is the woman all right?"

"Ain't seen her since you left. I was talking about you."

He could always depend on the sergeant for honesty, even when he didn't want it.

"Nothing's wrong. We've been riding for a long while. I needed to walk out some kinks."

Wilcox's grunt was noncommittal. He scratched at his thick brown beard. "We put the horses to pasture and got 'em watered down, but I sure don't want 'em loose at night."

"There's a corral, isn't there?"

"Not much of one."

"Put them in there anyway. If it's too crowded, remove Miss Hardin's animals and stake them elsewhere."

"She won't like it."

"She won't like anything we do. Gratitude, I have learned, is not something to expect from a woman."

"You got that right."

The sergeant's harshness surprised him, but he could read nothing in his countenance that revealed the source of his bitterness.

"We've been riding for a couple of months now, and I don't know much about you."

"Not much to tell. I'm reg'lar army. That's about it."

"Have you ever been married?"

"Nope."

"Neither have I."

"Don't intend to change that, neither," Wilcox said.

"In that we think alike."

It was the most personal exchange in which the two had engaged. Dan couldn't tell which of them was the more embarrassed.

"Go on and take care of the horses. I'll be back shortly. Have the men been fed? Good. As soon as it's dark, we'll get some sleep. Tomorrow we need to be up early and draw plans for sending out scouting parties. The Nueces Strip is a big area to cover. We'd better get started right away."

"We won't have to look far. There's Apache around. I can feel it. I can taste 'em."

"Close by?"

"Could be. Can't say for sure. All I know is we won't have to cross the Rio Grande to run 'em down. You can be sure of that."

"It's not much consolation. We're facing a thousand square miles where they might be riding. There must be hundreds of them. And there's only twenty-two of us."

Wilcox grinned. "That puts the odds right about where I like 'em. We don't have to catch 'em all. Just convince 'em it ain't safe to raid these parts."

158

Dan nodded. "Nothing to it, is that what you're saying? It's a matter of breaking our assignment down to its parts. And setting priorities, of course. We must concentrate on what is important."

"You got that right, Cap'n Dan."

Wilcox left to get ready for the night, and Dan was left to think over his own words. Setting priorities. He had things to do, all right. One of those involved Maddie. Where did she fit in his list?

He honestly could not say. What happened between them tomorrow and over the next few days while they got ready to ride would tell him all he needed to know.

Chapter Ten

When Maddie went out early the next morning to saddle Sunset, she had to walk around and past a dozen small tents, bedrolls, campfires, and a horde of half-dressed men who had set up their miniature fort behind her house.

She could take the tents, but the men were not a pretty sight in their undershirts, suspenders hanging loose around their hips. Nor did they offer a pleasant sound, spitting, scratching, belching, and coming up with other coarse sounds she did not try to identify, all before they realized her presence and did their best to silence themselves.

Her only relief came from the fact that she was upwind of them, and also from the way in which they avoided looking at her as much as she avoided looking at them. Or so it seemed from the glance she could not avoid giving them from the corner of her eye.

Without staring into their faces, she knew one thing: Captain Daniel Kent was not around. These men wore the light blue trousers that were an enlisted man's issue. As an officer, Dan would have been dressed in the dark shade that matched his jacket. Feeling superior, he had probably camped alone in the woods, spitting, scratching, and belching like the rest of them, except in higher-rank solitude.

Maddie did not care to know what men of any rank did in the morning. But she was being forced to learn.

She walked past them as quickly as she could.

"Morning, miss," someone said, but another of the soldiers warned him to shut up. She wondered what kind of warning Dan had given them about her.

She did not know what the proper etiquette was for such a situation. These troopers had more than likely fought for the United States against the Confederacy. But the war was ended—if the hated Reconstruction could be called a time of peace. Army service had become once again a profession freely chosen.

Though she could never call them her friends, neither was she their enemy; that mantle fell to the Lipan Apaches. The soldiers were in Texas risking their lives for the frontier settlers, including her, whether she wanted them here or not.

Southerners have never been the most sensible of people.

Dan's attitude was probably one they shared. Ignoring them seemed the best course, halfway between greeting them warmly with a plate of hot biscuits and ordering them at gunpoint to ride away.

If only she could ignore their captain. He was right—she wasn't sensible. Around him, she had better remain armed. That was why she was carrying the rifle in her hand.

Halfway down the hill behind the house, she came to a halt. The corral spread out in front of her, alongside the land that had been cleared and leveled for a barn. The corral got her full attention. It was filled with Army mounts and pack horses. Sunset, Caesar II, Dependable, Owen's mule—none of them were in sight.

There was no possibility that Owen had them out to pasture already. At the moment he was snug in his bedroll snoring loud enough to rattle the underside of the wagon bed that served as his roof, Brutus lying belly-up at his side. She figured he had wheedled whiskey out of one of the soldiers. It was his way, and he had not been to town for two weeks.

Footsteps sounded behind her. Tightening her hold on the gun, she whirled and saw a pair of dark blue trousers striding toward her. Instinctively, she raised the gun.

"Miss Hardin."

She looked higher than the bullseye of her target—the buttoned placket on the pants—and slowly lowered the rifle. It wasn't Dan. The speaker was a young lieutenant, not much older than her own twenty-six years.

"Sorry I wasn't able to greet you when you came out," he said. "I was . . . unavailable."

Unlike his captain, the lieutenant wore the regulation cap with his blue uniform. Except for a small, light brown mustache that resembled a patch of dust, his square-jawed face was clean-shaven. His hair, two shades lighter than the mustache, was neatly trimmed.

He looked so fair, so young, so out of place in his uniform. The light of morning faded, and her anger turned to a wave of dizziness. Once again she was on a New Orleans street; striding toward her was the private who continued to visit her on the worst of her sleepless nights. She could feel his hand gripping her sleeve and pulling at her.

She covered her lips to stifle a scream.

"I mean you no harm," the lieutenant said hastily. "Nor did I mean to startle you."

The voice soothed at the same time it jolted her back to reality. She caught her breath, and the city of her birth disappeared. Once again she stood on a Texas slope, with the eastern sun casting shadows across the hard-packed dirt. She felt foolish. Except for the similarity in coloring, the officer was nothing like the private. He was taller, his bearing more erect and dignified, and she could detect no desperation in his pale blue eyes.

"I didn't hear you, that's all," she said, sounding more friendly than she would have preferred. He was, she must remember, an ally of his captain.

She sharpened. "What do you want?"

He tipped his hat. "I'm Lieutenant Jason Leigh, ma'am. I have been waiting for you. I knew you would be wanting your horse."

Her sense of foolishness doubled. She had completely forgotten about the missing Sunset.

"What have you done with him and the other Longhorn animals?"

"I did not see any cows, Miss Hardin, just some horses and a mule."

Maddie slowly shook her head. How had an innocent, inexperienced boy like this one found himself in a company led by Dan Kent?

"You're camping on the Longhorn Ranch. My ranch. I meant, what have you done with the horses and mule."

"They were staked out for the night. I can get them for you. Just give me the word."

"By whose orders were they removed from the corral? No, don't tell me. Captain Kent's." She looked past him up to the top of the hill. "I would like to discuss the matter with him. Where is he hiding?"

Leigh's lips twitched into a short-lived smile. "He warned me you would be angry."

"That's all he told you?"

"Actually, he said something about a swarm of hornets." He glanced at her rifle. "I get the feeling I know what he meant."

"Can you tell me where he is, or are you under orders to protect him?"

"He rode out before dawn with the first scouting party. Another will be leaving shortly. We're fanning out, using your place as the center of the tracking. But don't fret, Miss Hardin. A couple of the men will be staying here under my command. Captain Kent was most eager for me to make certain you are safe."

What Captain Kent wanted was to get the fresh-faced lieutenant out of his hair. Maddie could read his purpose loud and clear.

"I understand completely the captain's concern. How long do you think he will be gone?"

"That's difficult to say. The captain is not given to explaining his plans. It could be a week or a month."

Maddie hoped for the month.

"If you'll point me in the right direction," she said, "I will get my own horse, thank you. I am used to taking care of myself."

As she had expected, Leigh proceeded to present arguments against her riding out far. She half listened to him, thinking about how her life had changed once again because of one unexpected event. Like all the other events, at the center of this one was a man. There were times when she grew weary of being a victim, never more so than right now.

She interrupted the lieutenant's warnings. "How do you plan to pass the time? Exactly what does keeping me safe entail?"

"Staying close beside you, ma'am. The captain thought that would particularly please you. I knew he didn't exactly believe what he was saying, but I told him you would not get out of my sight. Not for long, you understand. I know there are times when you'll need, that is, when you will have to—"

"You don't have to explain." She regarded him with great care, glanced back over her shoulder to the corral and the cleared land, then smiled at him. The smile was sincere, but it was not a gesture of welcome. Suddenly she had a plan.

"The captain was wrong," she added. "I will very much appreciate your staying close by the house. About fifty yards away, as a matter of fact."

She started back up the hill, and the lieutenant fell in beside her, moderating his stride to match hers.

"Tell me," she said sweetly, "what do you and the other soldiers know about making adobe brick? Nothing? But you're a smart man. You will learn, and so will your men. I have a project that needs working on. With your strength and your obvious intelligence put to good use, the days will pass quickly and, of course, safely. And all the while you will be earning my undying gratitude."

She stopped short of batting her eyes. In trousers and floppy hat, she felt foolish enough flirting as much as she was. She also felt a little proud of her southern sensibility. If the army insisted on invading her land and destroying her solitude, the least she could get out of their stay was a barn.

Wouldn't Carlos be surprised if she had it half finished by the time he returned with the vaqueros he was hiring for her? Wouldn't Dan be irritated that the work had even begun?

Dan had intended to stay away for at least a week, but a hard rain washed away the tracks he and his men had been following, and there were no other signs the Lipans were anywhere around. Before starting out on a new trail, he needed to go back to the Longhorn and get a report from the second patrol party, or so he told himself.

The rain had skipped over Maddie's land, leaving the ground dry and hard-packed. As he rode in, he took time to really consider it. He knew what had sent her running from New Orleans—the death of her fiancé and the end of her life as a spy. But what had brought her to this isolation? In some ways she was as much an enigma as ever to him.

He approached the front of the pitifully

small house she called home. He had not gotten a look at the inside, but he doubted it was any grander than the front, with its lone cactus offering a prickly welcome to visitors, and its lone resident doing pretty much the same.

His men rode around to the back to find the soldiers he'd left behind. Settling his hat low on his forehead, he dismounted and knocked at the front door. No one responded.

The derelict Maddie had taken on as a hired hand shuffled toward him from the chicken coop, an open tin of dried corn in his hand. Behind him the chickens were squawking and scratching in the hard dirt. What was the man's name? Owen, that was it. Owen, nothing more. Owen took a long look at him, then shuffled away toward a stand of trees behind the coop, where the milk cow was grazing.

The man was almost as irritating as Maddie. Dan started after him.

"I found 'em, Cap'n Dan," one of the men called out from the rear of the house. "Goldurned if I didn't," he added with a laugh.

With a curse, he went to find out what was going on. Given the situation and the owner of the so-called ranch, it could be almost anything.

He spied her at the bottom of the slope, dressed, as always, in the tight pants. She was talking to Lieutenant Leigh, gesturing toward a stretch of wooden forms that were laid out on the ground between the corral and a nearby clearing. The two soldiers he had left to guard the house along with Leigh were standing by the forms. In the center of the clearing lay several dozen logs of varying lengths and widths.

He had been in Texas long enough to know what the scene signified: his men were making adobe bricks for the woman and cutting wood for a frame. His seasoned Indian fighters, carefully chosen because of their skill and experience, had been turned into farm laborers, helping her civilize her land.

He set off down the hill. She caught sight of him when he was halfway to her. Leigh watched him with uncertainty in his eyes. The lieutenant was usually uncertain, wanting to do the right thing, never quite sure what it was.

He had every right to be uneasy. If he had the sense of a lizard, he would turn tail and run.

Dan did not bother returning Leigh's salute.

"What the hell's going on?" he barked, waving toward the cleared land.

Leigh snapped to attention. "The men and I, that is, we were—"

"Acting as guards, right? The way I ordered."

"Yes, sir, I believe that we were. If you look around, you will see that all is safe here."

"That's because there aren't Apaches within a hundred miles."

Maddie slapped a hand against her trousers. "Captain Kent, you have no right to ride in here like this and start behaving in your usually boorish manner. Lieutenant Leigh has done nothing wrong. On the contrary; he's been most helpful."

His eyes cut to her. "I'm sure that he has. But this is a military matter, Miss Hardin. Stay out of it."

Leigh nodded to her as if he was telling her to back off. As if he had influence over her Dan did not. He wanted to smash his lieutenant's handsome face.

With an exaggerated sigh, she backed away.

Dan nodded toward the house. "Get the men and meet me back up there. Has Sergeant Wilcox returned? No, don't bother to answer. I can tell he's still out."

Again Leigh saluted, gestured toward the two soldiers who had been left under his command, and started up the hill.

Maddie wasted no time in starting in again. "Captain Kent—"

"Not yet, Miss Hardin. You do not want the men to hear what I have to say."

"I've done nothing to be ashamed of."

"By your standards, maybe not."

That stopped her, but only until Leigh and the others were well past the top of the rise.

"What do you mean, my standards?" she asked.

"Don't play coy. It worked in New Orleans. It won't work here. At least not with me."

"Coy is the one thing I am not."

He looked her over. Beneath the fringed vest, her dark brown shirt lay open at the throat, exposing a smooth expanse of tanned skin. He counted three buttons that should have been fastened. He thought about doing it for her. She had no shame.

"Considering the way you parade yourself around, I would have to agree. Coy, you are not. But Jason Leigh is a gentleman. He probably never looks below your neck."

She reddened. He was glad she wasn't carrying a gun.

"I do not parade myself around. I dress like this because it's easier to ride and work. Wearing trousers is one way men are smarter than women. It's also the only way I've found."

"You're smarter than Leigh, that's damned certain."

For a moment, her eyes softened. "Why have you taken to cursing around me? You never did before."

"Why do you think?"

"I think that before, you wanted something from me. And now you don't."

If she really thought he wanted nothing from her, she was too innocent to live. He knew she was not innocent, not after the way she had used him in New Orleans. She had to be using him again. Or trying to.

He quit looking in her eyes. Around her, it was getting difficult to find a place where it was safe to look.

He directed his attention to the adobe brick.

"You may have gotten your way with men in

New Orleans, Maddie, but I won't have you pulling the same tricks here."

She did not answer, and he was forced to look at her. She was pale, despite the kiss of the sun on her cheeks, and her remarkable blue eyes appeared sunken, haunted. Otherwise, she showed no expression. She stood as still as the stones of her house.

"My tricks," she said flatly. "I had forgotten all about them. New Orleans was so long ago."

"A lifetime."

"We were both very different," she said. "Softer, kinder."

"At least we appeared to be so."

"Whatever I was then, Dan, I am not soft now, nor am I kind. Take fair warning: I do not want you here, but I will take from this forced occupation all that I can."

"Why is it I get the feeling you mean more than just some adobe bricks?"

"Because you have an evil turn of mind."

"If I do, it's because I was trained to it. The war was not kind to either side."

"No. It was not kind."

They stood looking at one another for a long while. At last she turned from him and walked away, stopping by the logs that lay in the clearing, staring at them as if she could will them into place.

Her thick braid of yellow hair lay against the back of her vest, making her look far younger than her years. Her boots were worn and covered with dust, and her trousers were stained. He remembered the callused hands beneath her leather gloves, and the nails that were cut to the quick.

She was a rare seductress. He almost believed her truly innocent. He had to fight the urge to go to her, to take her in his arms, and to hold her.

Maddie could very well know the fragile, provocative picture she presented, just as she understood how lovely she had appeared in the green riding habit she wore beside a Louisiana bayou, on a day when they had both been softer if not kinder, on a day when she had offered her lips to him.

Too, she had promised more. Much more.

But that was before she received word that her fiancé was dead. That was before she ran.

It was also before he received news that his brother had died in a southern prison, a place where he should have been safe until the fighting was done. She was right. No longer did he have softness in him. He was no longer kind.

Turning his back to her and all she represented, he went back up the hill. He needed to discipline Leigh, to lay down specific orders about what he could do and could not do when he was in charge, to cast off whatever spell Madeleine Hardin had cast over his men.

Chapter Eleven

Maddie got up the next morning to find that the second patrol had returned during the night. Behind her house was the full contingent of soldiers with their tents, their fires, and their noisy, earthy presence.

Bleary-eyed and heavy-hearted, she nevertheless managed to focus on her primary task: to get Dan Kent out of her mind. She could not believe she was letting him hurt her this way, again and again.

Once she had been distraught over hurting him, over trying to trick him into marriage, over running away.

But that had been in another life. She had done what she had to in order to protect him.

In the doing, even though she did not lay the blame on him, she had lost her child.

She was smarter now, if not wiser. In her new existence, she would take care of herself.

She began by dragging Owen out from under the wagon. She even managed to get Brutus to stand.

The dog blinked at her with his good eye and twitched his only ear. Owen scratched his baggy-trousered behind.

"We've got hours of work ahead of us," she told the pair of them, one listening about as well as the other. "I've already gathered the eggs. I'll get breakfast while you feed the chickens and milk the cow."

"I got a feeling that ain't all we're gonna do."

"You told me once you knew how to build a barn."

"I never said no such thing."

"A barn's easy, that's what you said. Nothing fancy to a barn. We're going to find out if you were right. Beginning today."

She had no choice. As an option, asking for Jason Leigh's assistance was impossible. Dan did not want him helping her, the implication being that if he did so, he would be tainted in some way.

By noon, she and Owen had laid out the logs. With Brutus lying beside a corral post, his mangy body positioned carefully in a narrow strip of shade, they were discussing exactly how many more logs would be needed to frame the structure when Dan walked down the hill. She had not seen him all morning. She was not pleased to see him now.

Neither did she welcome the news he brought.

"Your beloved's here," he said. His eyes and his voice were both flat.

She stared stupidly at him. "Who?"

"Edwin Worster. The man you plan to marry. You must have forgotten him over the past week."

She muttered a few French phrases under her breath. Somehow obscenities in that language seemed more acceptable, almost genteel. It was an added advantage that only she knew what she said.

"He's waiting inside your house," Dan added.

"You let him in?"

"Doesn't he have the right?"

"He most certainly does not."

Maddie wanted to say more, but what good would it do? Dan did not listen to much of what she said, or if he did, he did not believe her.

She sighed. Getting angry at him took too much of her energy. He thought she was betrothed to Worster. It was time she set the matter straight. But she wanted to start with her ersatz fiancé. Then Dan could believe whatever he chose.

A Special Offer For Leisure Historical Romance Readers Only!

Get Four FREE* Romance Novels

A $21.96 Value!

Thrill to the most sensual, adventure-filled Historical Romances on the market today...

FROM  LEISURE BOOKS

As a home subscriber to the Leisure Historical Romance Book Club, you'll enjoy the best in today's BRAND-NEW Historical Romance fiction. For over twenty-five years, Leisure Books has brought you the award-winning, high-quality authors you know and love to read. Each Leisure Historical Romance will sweep you away to a world of high adventure...and intimate romance. Discover for yourself all the passion and excitement millions of readers thrill to each and every month.

SAVE AT LEAST *$5.00* EACH TIME YOU BUY!

Each month, the Leisure Historical Romance Book Club brings you four brand-new titles from Leisure Books, America's foremost publisher of Historical Romances. EACH PACKAGE WILL SAVE YOU AT LEAST $5.00 FROM THE BOOKSTORE PRICE! And you'll never miss a new title with our convenient home delivery service.

Here's how we do it. Each package will carry a 10-DAY EXAMINATION privilege. At the end of that time, if you decide to keep your books, simply pay the low invoice price of $16.96 ($17.75 US in Canada), no shipping or handling charges added*. HOME DELIVERY IS ALWAYS FREE*. With today's top Historical Romance novels selling for $5.99 and higher, our price SAVES YOU AT LEAST $5.00 with each shipment.

AND YOUR FIRST FOUR-BOOK SHIPMENT IS TOTALLY FREE!

IT'S A BARGAIN YOU CAN'T BEAT! A Super $21.96 Value!

LEISURE BOOKS A Division of Dorchester Publishing Co., Inc.

"Would you send him down?"

Dan tipped his hat. "Whatever you say, Miss Hardin. Anything else?"

"Yes, one thing. Tell him to bring his horse."

She watched her one-time and never-again love stride back up the hill. Once again she was struck by how gracefully he moved, his legs swinging powerfully one after the other from a pair of taut, lean hips.

She wondered what he would look like in civilian clothes. She considered how he would look without them.

Blushing, she looked away and caught Owen's eye.

"Best take care," Owen warned.

"What are you talking about?"

"You and the cap'n. Ain't none of my concern, I already know, so don't bother to tell me. All I'm saying is, take care."

You're too late.

"I'm always careful," she said instead.

"Nope, that ain't so. You warn't careful when you took me on, not knowing if I'd slit your throat in the night, and you warn't careful with that Worster feller, getting him all excited about taking you as a wife, when you and I know you wouldn't have him if you won him in a poker game. Sure as the devil, you ain't careful with the cap'n, neither. He ain't like me and he ain't like Worster. He's a mite harder to handle. You fool around with him,

177

it'll be like getting hold of a bull's tail."

He wasn't telling her anything she did not already know.

"I like you better when you don't talk," she said.

"You just don't like what I'm saying. I'll hush up now. Here comes your beloved."

Maddie rubbed at her temple. "Please don't call him that."

"Just copying the cap'n, that's all."

Owen went back to studying the logs, and Edwin Worster rode down the hill. He was dressed in his usual suit and vest, his gray-streaked brown hair slicked back beneath a narrow-brimmed hat. He stared at her the entire time, his pale blue eyes holding a hard glint she did not like.

He smiled as he reined in beside her, but the glint remained. When he started to dismount, she raised a hand.

"Don't," she said. "I'll get Sunset out of the corral. He's already saddled. We can ride some-where. I need to talk to you in private."

Her words softened the glint into an interest that was far more disturbing than the harshness. As always, he was misinterpreting what she said.

Mounting the blood bay mustang, she led Worster across the open space, into the trees, and on through low-lying brush to the creek that cut across her land. A foot of water trickled down the bed of rocks, and the trees and shrubs along the banks provided a bower that made this part of the creek like a private room.

It was her favorite place on her land. She did not come here often, preferring to save it for special moments when she needed to think. She did not like bringing Worster here, not because she felt any animosity toward him, but simply because he was not special to her.

But for today's confrontation—for that was what it would turn out to be—she needed privacy. Since the invasion of her land, privacy was difficult to find.

As soon as her boots hit the ground, he was moving in on her. Brutus never looked so eager, even when she threw him a meaty bone. For some reason she thought of the rooster, his eyes beady, ready to peck at some corn.

"Let's take care of the horses," she said.

In silence, they tethered them close to both grass and water. She backed away. Again, he moved close.

"I brought you here, Mr. Worster, so that we could talk."

"Talk? We could have done that out in the field, Madeleine."

"Too many people could listen in. When you hear what I have to say, you will appreciate the privacy."

"I already do. You are a lovely woman,

despite your rough appearance. I am a very lucky man."

"Luckier than you think. I can't be your wife."

"You have accepted my offer of marriage." He said it without so much as a blink. She gave him credit for persistence and confidence, if not a surfeit of sensitivity.

"I told you I would consider it. Nothing more."

"We both know the way a woman likes to play coy."

"What is it with men thinking women are coy? I have never been coy in my life. I meant what I said. I considered your proposal. I have to tell you no."

"Let me guess why. Because you do not love me."

"Yes."

"Nor feel passion for me."

Maddie grew uneasy. Something in the way he said *passion* did not sit well. Besides, it was not a word a gentleman used with a lady. Unlike Dan, that was what Worster considered her to be.

Or so she had thought.

She tried again. "I feel nothing except respect and gratitude because you thought enough of me to make the offer."

She said it in as firm yet polite a voice as she could manage, attempting to be considerate and convincing at the same time.

"What do you know of passion?" Worster asked.

There he went again. It was not an easy question to answer. She decided to take offense.

"Are you insinuating that my virtue is blemished?"

"On the contrary," he said quickly. "I fear you do not know whereof you speak."

Maddie did not know which was worse, being thought of as wanton or viewed as dumb.

"I know that I should feel something for you besides friendship."

In truth, she did not feel even that, but now was not the moment to tell him so. She should not have brought him to the isolation of the creek.

He smiled. "Perhaps the heat in you has never been aroused."

"You are too forward, sir. I have no heat inside me."

"Every woman does. Some are slow to realize it, that is all. It takes the knowing touch of a man to kindle the flame."

"Don't think of kindling anything of the sort, Mr. Worster. I would not welcome it, nor would I think kindly of you afterwards, once you realized you were mistaken about me."

He held his silence for a moment, as if he fought something inside him. Anger, maybe. She could not see Edwin Worster overcome with desire. He liked to talk about it too much.

"You need more time," he said.

"I've had months."

"All of them away from me. Away from safety. Away from propriety. That is why I left Illusion long before dawn to ride out here today. You need someone to advise you. You need a man's common sense."

Maddie thought of several blunt remarks to throw at him. But she wanted very much to avoid an argument; she wanted to be courteous, but most of all, she wanted to be understood.

"What does your common sense tell you I should do? Forget moving into town. I won't do it."

"Even with so many men encamped outside your door?"

"They have behaved as gentlemen." All but one. "I expect them to continue to do so."

"Still, you must be aware of appearances. I have come here with a simple solution, albeit a temporary one. Until matters are settled between us. I suggest you hire a companion; a female, of course, an older woman, respectable, a widow perhaps. If, of course, you have the means. I can provide them if you do not."

"I have the means. I do not have the inclination. Anyway, where am I to find such a woman?"

"Curiously, there are two newly arrived in Illusion. One, Helen Clark, is rather plainspoken and would probably not do. The other, however, Mrs. Brown, is a gentler sort. She has accompanied her grown daughter and family to the town. Until you are in a different situation, she would be a fine chaperone."

Maddie bristled. Already she did not care for either woman, though if she had to choose, Helen Clark would get the job.

"I will take your suggestion under consideration," she lied.

"The way you considered my offer of marriage?"

"I can do nothing more than I have already done."

"Oh, my dear, but you can. You can allow me to kiss you. If you feel nothing for me, then I will leave you in peace."

"What if I'm repulsed?"

He chuckled, but she heard little of genuine humor in his voice. "Dear Madeleine, you do like to consider all the possibilities. Trust me. You will not be repulsed."

She thought the suggestion over. It was not only unappealing, it was dumb. Already, she was a great deal more than simply repulsed. But doing as he asked was probably the quickest way of getting rid of her unwanted suitor.

"A simple kiss," she said. *No tongue*. It was not a stipulation she could put to him. He still viewed her as innocent.

There was only one man in all the world she could tell such a thing. But he did not want to kiss her, and she planned never again to kiss him.

Worster rested his hands lightly on her shoulders, and she tilted her head. Eyes open, she watched his mouth move close.

A twig snapped, loud as a gunshot, and she jumped away. Looking into the trees, she saw Dan Kent in the shadows, sitting high on his Army mount, watching from beneath the low brim of his hat. She had no doubt he had timed the noise for the most inopportune moment possible.

Inopportune as far as Worster was concerned. She did not care.

But neither did she like being spied on.

She put a hand over her pounding heart. "What are you doing here? You scared the devil out of me."

"A storm's coming. I thought you ought to know. In case you were so involved with what you were doing, you did not realize the danger."

"I don't hear any thunder."

In truth, her heart was hammering so hard, she could not hear much of anything. Except Dan.

"You will," he said. He looked at Worster. "You understand the intrusion, of course. You would want your fiancée to be safe."

From her position behind Worster, she could see the redness building behind his ears. He was furious. He must have really wanted that kiss.

She did not want these two stubborn men getting into an argument. She would not take it as a compliment.

"Mr. Worster can take care of me just fine. I'm in no danger. At least I wasn't." *Until you got here.* She knew he got the message.

Dan stared at her. He did not turn red around the ears, in the manner of Worster, but he was angry. She did not know why, except that it was his usual state when they were together.

He flicked a glance at Worster. "You have a long ride ahead of you. You'd best get started. I will see that Miss Hardin gets home safely."

"Actually," Worster said, "I have land north of here. There's a small house on the premises where I had planned to spend the night. I usually do so when I ride out to call on Madeleine."

He looked at Maddie. "But it is not necessary for you to see to Miss Hardin's safety. I can take care of her."

"I can take care of myself." She smiled at Worster to take the sharpness from her words, but only because Dan was watching. "Thank you kindly for the offer, but I know my way. If the captain is right and there really is a storm coming, then I urge you to leave right away."

"But we have unfinished business."

Dan cleared his throat.

"Our business can wait. Please." She put a hand on his arm. He looked at her warmly.

"I can deny you nothing," he said. He did not sound especially sincere.

With a curt bow, he left to get his horse, and within a couple of minutes he was gone.

She looked up at Dan. "How did you know where we were?"

"I've been tracking Apaches for the past week. Following you was simple."

"And unnecessary. Is there really a storm?" She took a deep breath. "Yes, I can smell it. I would have anyway. I did not need your warning."

"Sometimes lovers get so carried away, they forget themselves and everything around them."

He dismounted and walked toward her. "Is that the way it is with you two? Do you forget yourselves?"

I can't forget you.

Nor could she like him very much.

"I have learned never to forget myself."

"That I believe. Maybe it's time you did."

He closed the space between them. She should have run, but she could not move. Tossing his hat aside, he took hers and sent it flying. He pulled at the wisps of hair brushing against her face, loosening the pull of the tight braid, his palms circling against her temple. She closed her eyes and let him gently rock her head, breathing in the scent of him, overcome by his dark, overpowering presence.

He stroked his way across her closed eyes, down her cheeks, outlining her lips with his thumbs, his hands always moving downward, to her throat, to the slope of her breasts, lingering a starkly tantalizing second before moving on.

At last he entwined his fingers in the fringe that hung from the bottom of her vest and pulled her against him.

The air grew thick, so heavy she could taste it, the way she could taste Dan, remembering the warmth of his kiss, the texture of his tongue.

Drugged by his touch, she opened her eyes and looked up at him. She saw desire on his face, but she saw something more. She saw triumph, and something that could very well be revenge. All the passion that had been building inside her exploded into rage.

She shoved him away. The fringe tore, but all she could think of was the harsh light in Dan's eyes.

"Go away. Leave me alone. Go back to Kentucky where you belong."

"Running is your way. Not mine. And even if it were, I've nothing to run to."

He looked beyond her, a savage expression of grief darkening his face for just a moment, as if he stared into his own special hell.

Her rage vanished as rapidly as it had come. She forgot herself and thought only of him.

"What is it, Dan? What's wrong? It's Tom, isn't it? Your brother—"

The grief turned to something hard, something more frightening.

"Don't mention his name. Damn your cursed southern cause."

"It was never my cause. I never chose it."

"Don't take me for a fool. Or maybe you should. Do you want to know my curse? Despite all that's happened, I want you. More than I ever have."

She backed away, terrified, not because he was a man and he was close and they were alone. The terror came because she recognized the hunger in his words. It was a hunger she shared.

"No," she cried out, "no, no, no," all the while backing away, shaking her head, hating the coursing heat that was building inside her, delirious with wanting all the forbidden pleasures he promised with his touch.

"Don't tell me it's because you are betrothed to another man. It did not stop you before, and it will not stop you now. Not if you're honest with yourself."

"You knew about Julien."

"Not at first, of course. It was something you neglected to tell me."

"But you remember him. And recognized me right from the start."

"I remember everything."

But he didn't. He had forgotten the gentleness that existed between them, the courtliness that had been the basis for their getting to know one another. There was no courtliness now. Instead, there was a lack of gentleness so complete it left her breathless.

So much had happened, so much heartache, so much loss. A sudden cold breeze brushed against her, but it could not reach the heat inside. Despite all her protests to the contrary when she had faced Edwin Worster, she could be set on fire. She burned now, transformed into a woman she did not know, welcoming the harshness and the raw desire that Dan aroused. In them lay forgetfulness.

"I hate you for this," she said as she threw herself in his arms. Even as she rested her hands on his face and pulled his lips to hers, she knew it was a lie.

Chapter Twelve

Dan took Maddie's kiss in the way she offered it—fast, hard, hot. Holding her face in his hands, he licked her lips.

"Stop me now, or there's no retreat."

She brushed her tongue against his. "Don't stop."

"Say you want me, Maddie. Say it."

"I want you."

Her eyes were bright as she looked up at him. He saw madness in them, the same madness he felt in himself. It mattered not what she had done or the tragedies that had brought them together. She was Maddie, warm and eagerly loving, and for the moment she was his.

His hands slipped to her throat, then down,

inside her vest, cupping her breasts through the thin brown shirt. Her nipples were hard against his palms. He rubbed gently against the tips. She groaned and dropped her head back, her hands gripping the front of his Army coat.

Looking at her, he forgot all the practiced ease of his lovemaking with other women. He couldn't remember anyone else but her. Slipping off her vest, he fumbled with buttons; she was naked beneath the shirt. Her breasts were full and dark-tipped. She offered them to him as she had offered her lips.

He kissed all that she offered, using his lips and his tongue.

With a cry, she pushed away, catching him by surprise. He waited for the denial, the teasing coyness that she had shown him before, or else the rage that had flared within her today.

What he got was something entirely different.

"Take off the coat," she said. "The weapons, all that you can. I don't want to know who or what you are."

The words were rasped out.

"You've changed," he said. "Far more than I thought."

"You have no idea how much. The coat. Take it off."

Dan was in a mood to do what she asked. But he was not so far gone he forgot where they were.

He kissed her quickly, and then he kissed her

again, making a more thorough job of it. "Wait here."

She stared at him in disbelief. He backed away, but he soon returned, holding the blanket he kept tied behind his saddle. He spread it on a patch of grass beneath the trees, tossed his coat and gun beside it, then pulled her down to him.

She lay looking up at him, her shirt spread wide. Dan ate her with his eyes, then tasted her once again with his tongue. Her skin was warm, and he could feel the pounding of her heart.

He had waited a long time for this moment, and he should savor it, moving slowly, torturing both of them as he sucked out the bittersweet drops of pleasure he found only when he was with her.

But she drove him mad. He could not move slowly.

"I need you naked," he said.

"I need you."

He eased off her shirt, slipping the sleeves from her slender arms, letting his fingers enjoy the texture and contours. It was like touching warm silk.

She unbraided her hair, and the soft strands spread in golden thickness against the dark blanket.

He hardly recognized the woman who lay beside him. She was not the lady of New Orleans, shy and eager at the same time, even while she harbored cruel secrets in her heart. Nor was she the hardened frontier settler she had become.

Today she was a woman of heat and hunger whose hands tore at the front of his shirt.

He covered her body with his, thrusting his erection against her trousers. She jerked once, an involuntary movement that was close to rejection; then she wrapped her arms around his neck and whispered raggedly, "Fast. Don't wait. Don't let me think."

Dan proved himself as awkward in unfastening her trousers as he had been with her shirt, but she helped, and when she was naked, she dug her fingers into his waistband and pulled hard, as if she would tear his clothes from his body.

"Maddie."

"Don't talk."

She was trembling against him. He wanted to do everything at once to her, with her, in her. His hands slipped over soft skin and subtle curves. Each stroke brought him closer to his own explosion. He wanted to go slow, but this was not a time for lazy exploration.

Hers was an urgent, desperate cry for release. The same urge pulsed through him. He slipped his clothes to his knees, but she allowed him to do nothing more. Pulling up his shirt, she kissed his chest, then wrapped her arms around him, her thighs parted, but not enough, not the way he wanted and needed.

"Do whatever you have to do," she whispered. "Show me what to do."

He kissed her cheeks and tasted tears. The dampness stunned him, but there was no holding back, not now. She was worldly and virginal at the same time, surrendering in complete trust at the same time she demanded everything he had to give. He parted her legs wide. When he thrust himself inside her, she was wet and ready, and he met with little resistance.

They pounded against each other, almost enemies, wild lovers who became as one. He felt her tremors; they joined with his, until for the moment he did not know where her pleasure ended and his began. He existed only for her and with her. The climax shook them both. He lost himself in her, holding tight, willing the moment to last forever, knowing as he did so that the world was too harsh for such ecstasy to endure.

She shuddered once, clinging to him with a desperation that matched the moment she had flung herself into his arms. He held her tight and listened to her ragged breathing. It ended with a moan that sounded close to a sob, then she was silent in his arms, her hot skin quickly made slick with sweat from the fierce coupling.

Already he wanted to kiss the skin, to taste the sweat, to thrust inside her once again. As he started to tell her so, he felt a change in her. No longer was she pliant; her body no longer curved into his, but stiffened, as if she would will herself a million miles away if she could.

He did not want to let her go. She gave him no choice.

Rolling away, she sat up and hugged herself, her body curled so that he could not see the intimate parts of her that he knew so well.

Or should have known. They had made love, but he did not know her at all. Nor did she know him. She had held on to him in a manic embrace, she had kissed him and stroked his lips with her tongue. Not once had she touched him intimately with her hands.

She had been his, and at the same time no man's woman, a creature separate from the world, complete unto herself, ashamed because she had shown a human weakness, a frailty to which she would never surrender again.

He sought the same shame within himself. He had hated her. But he could not hate her today. It was hard to hate a mystery. It was impossible to hate a woman who made him feel as she did, who helped him for a short while forget the past.

Thunder rumbled in the distance, and he remembered the storm. Wind rustled through the trees above and around them, chilling the air. Thick clouds darkened the sky and fat raindrops fell on the grassy clearing only a few feet away. It seemed an appropriate ending to the day.

"Maddie," he said, intending to offer his care and protection from the storm.

She whirled on him, and he saw the tears that he had only tasted before. She brushed them away. Her normally brilliant eyes burned dark as the clouds, and he marveled at the power of her, the wild pride and enmity, even as he wanted to thrust her back onto the blanket and make her his once again.

"You got what you wanted. Now leave me alone."

"What was it I wanted that you did not?"

"A southern conquest. You as much as said I was to blame for whatever it is you have lost. Isn't that what this is about? Isn't that what it has always been? Isn't it what all Yankee soldiers—"

She broke off, swallowed, but kept her head high.

Dan stared at her long and hard. Her fine features were set in rigid lines that belied the wildness of her hair and the wantonness of her lovemaking in his arms.

"What happened here had nothing to do with anything except my own weakness. I cannot leave you alone."

"You will have to learn."

"Are you sure? Are you really sure? You liked what happened as much as I. You are a passionate woman. You know it, and—"

He broke off. There were some things he could not say.

"Don't stop," she said. "You were going to say other men know it, too. You were going to say you weren't the first. You could tell, from . . . what we did. After all, I was engaged before. And there's no telling what Edwin and I would have done if you had not got here. If not him, there's always the handsome Lieutenant Jason Leigh."

She threw the names at him like stones.

"Stop it. I make no accusations, not about sex. I've been with other women, and I'd have a hell of a time naming all of them. But isn't there something else you want to confess? Was Julien's death the only reason you ran from New Orleans?"

I was a spy.

He waited for the words. He had never planned to confront her, certainly not like this. But in the midst of the turbulence swirling around and within them, it seemed the time for harsh words.

She looked as though he had slapped her. The rain fell harder, piercing through the trees, hitting the ground around them with increasing ferocity. But she seemed oblivious to the raging weather, fighting another kind of storm, a raging torment inside.

"I have nothing to tell you," she whispered, so softly he barely caught the words. "Believe what you will."

Looking up at him, she shuttered all her feelings from his view, and he knew she was slipping away, to a private place where he could not reach her.

He straightened and fastened his clothes, then gathered hers, dropping the garments onto the blanket beside her.

He did not look away while she dressed. Her limbs were long, graceful, and even in her fury she showed a balletic grace as she thrust them into her shirt, her pants, the boots, and last, the vest with the torn fringe.

She stood to face him. Sometime while she dressed, she had gathered her strength.

"You're right about one thing, Captain. I wanted what happened. To my everlasting shame, I wanted it. But I cannot want it again."

He felt his own surge of anger, of self-disgust, both of them mixed with something she would never understand, jealousy as wild as it was irrational. Despite all she had done, he wanted to ask her who had been the first man to lie with her. Julien? The mocking way she had referred to her Confederate soldier told him the answer was no.

But who? Worse, he wanted to know how many others there had been.

The men had not been gentle, nor had they been very skilled in their lovemaking. He had felt too keenly her almost innocence, and her denial of tenderness.

The rain came down hard. She twisted her hair at the top of her head and pulled her hat down tightly.

"Will this be campfire talk tonight?" she asked.

"Figure it out for yourself." And then, because he could not let her believe otherwise, he added, "No. You can put today in your store of secrets. We wouldn't want your current fiancé to learn what you have done."

"He's not my fiancé. I have no intention of marrying him."

Dan felt a momentary triumph that made no sense. How she lived her life meant nothing to him.

"You might tell Worster."

"I have. I brought him out here to tell him again. Unfortunately, he is a man. He does not listen well."

She whirled from him and darted through the rain to her horse. Already her clothes clung to her, even the vest, and the bank had turned to mud. She moved incautiously, slipped but caught herself, and mounted.

Beneath the floppy hat, her face was without emotion, features carved in marble, eyes straight ahead, giving little hint of what she saw. Without another glance in his direction, she reined the mustang away from him and disappeared into the storm.

He stood for a long time under the trees, listening to the thunder and wondering just what had taken place here beside the fast-rising creek, and more, wondering what he was going to do now.

*   *   *

Maddie rode like a wild woman, not stopping until she came to the front of her house. Owen came out from under the tarp he had thrown over the wagon and took the reins from her. He did not speak, and neither did she.

Inside the house, a fire blazed. Dimly she realized that he must have lit it for her, fed it so that it would welcome her home. There was even a pot of coffee on the hearth, and beside it her mother's dainty porcelain cup from which she liked to drink.

Owen had not stopped there. A cast-iron dutch oven hung from the hook at the edge of the flames. A stew, probably. He cooked them from time to time, when he wanted to use meat he had killed and did not want to name.

Despite the warmth in the room, a chill swept through her. She felt it in her bones. She tore off her clothes, her movements jerky, inefficient, and she threw the damp garments aside.

Naked, she grabbed a blanket from her bed and wrapped herself tightly so that she could see nothing of her flesh. Her traitorous flesh. What had she done? How had she lost control?

Shaking, she sat at the side of the thin mattress and stared into the fire. She had been hot, like the flames, but that was not reason enough for her to abandon everything she believed about herself.

After what had been done to her in New

Orleans, she should have been repulsed by the touch of man. But she had no memory of that earlier time. Despite the attack and having given birth, she had felt virginal. She did not feel virginal now.

Never would she forget the few minutes she had spent lying beneath Dan, giving herself to him in a manner so complete, so personal and searing, she would live with the memory of it the rest of her life.

She had loved him once, in a caring, gentle way, and had loved him through the years. The truth was as hurtful as it was undeniable. She loved him still, though she did not like him very much, no more than she liked herself.

Isn't there something else you want to confess? Was Julien's death the only reason you ran from New Orleans?

Could he know what she had planned to do? It was impossible, but still, she could not get the worry from her mind.

He blamed her for his losses, whatever they were. He proved himself as irrational as she. There was no hope for them. There never had been.

What would have happened had she gone through with her plan and successfully trapped him into marriage? Had he ever figured out the truth, a circumstance that was highly probable, he would have hated her. And she might still have lost Grace.

More than ever, she wished Will was at her

side. He would not question what was happening between her and Dan; he would know, he would understand. Whatever disapproval he felt would remain secret. All he would offer was his quiet strength and the reassurance that she would always have a friend in him, no matter how foolish she was or how mean, selfish, and immoral.

Loving Dan was foolish; giving herself to him had truly been immoral, as well as selfish. But he had been the same, taking what she gave, without question. The questions had come later, after the coupling was done.

Worst of all was the way her skin remembered how he had touched her, how he had kissed. Nothing in her life had prepared her for what she'd shared with him. Embarrassment flooded her, and her cheeks burned. She had acted crazy, but he had not hurt her in any way. For a brief moment in time, he had made her feel glorious. The gentleman officer taking what he could and giving in equal amounts, that was Daniel Kent.

Again, she was not being fair—she had given him little choice—but fairness would not help her to survive.

What they had done was the way babies came into the world. But she had borne the only child she would ever have. She thought of Grace, truly thought of her and no one else, and buried her face in her hands.

The knock at the door was so faint, she barely heard it. The door creaked open. She stiffened. He couldn't have followed her. Even he did not have the insolence to seek her out now. But she did not know for sure. She knew him, but he was a stranger to her in the ways that really mattered.

She watched the door. Brutus thrust his mangy, rain-soaked head inside. She watched as he lumbered over to her on his short, bowed legs, his one ear hanging limp, his good eye downcast, his paws leaving a muddy trail across the wooden floor. He laid his head in her lap. He had never done anything like this before. As heavy as her heart was, she managed a quiet, rueful laugh.

The door closed. Owen was leaving them alone. He was a curious man, but then, she was learning that in their separate ways all men were curious.

A woman alone, she lived in a world of men. That was something she could do something about. The answer to one of her problems came from the unlikeliest of sources, Edwin Worster.

She stood, and Brutus shifted to the edge of the fire, where he could dry his wet hair and be close to the stew. Dropping the blanket, she went to the small chest where she kept her clothes. For the rest of the day she would wear a shirt and trousers, but early tomorrow, once the storm had passed, she would put on a dress and she would go out into the world, specifically into the small town called Illusion.

She would meet Helen Clark and, if they felt a sympathy for one another, or even a tolerance, she would offer the woman employment. Carlos would be returning any day with the vaqueros. She would need help preparing meals, tending the garden, cleaning, sewing, doing all the things a woman was trained to do.

Maddie would have no time. She had a ranch to run. Her dreams of empire had long died, but she would make a home here at the Longhorn. Long after Captain Daniel Kent and his soldiers were gone, she would still be here.

She would survive.

Chapter Thirteen

"I've made this ride into Illusion a dozen times without any trouble."

"All it takes is one bad journey, and you're dead."

"You're exaggerating the possibilities."

"I'm looking at them realistically. If you were sensible, you would see I'm right."

In the light of early dawn, Maddie stared from the seat of the buckboard, straight into Dan's eyes. He stood close to the wagon, in shirt sleeves, his face unshaven, breathing fire.

She had wondered what their next meeting would be like. She should have known it would be an argument, one in which she was accused once again of being wrong.

This time she welcomed the fight. It served to

give her a strength she very much needed. Standing there close by, rudely awakened as he put it, the rascal looked better unkempt than other men did at their formal best. If he had been gentle or caring she might have thrown herself from the seat, right into his arms, and humiliated herself for all time.

But he had not, and she was saved by their argument.

"I've got three soldiers saddled and ready to ride with you," he said flatly, no protests from her heard or acknowledged.

Included in the contingent of three was Lieutenant Jason Leigh. Dan saw her looking at the handsome young man as he rode up to the wagon. She thought about smiling at him in greeting, but she was already too irritated with Dan to bother irritating him more.

"You move fast, Captain," she said, "for someone who just crawled out of bed. Or bedroll. Or wherever it is you sleep."

To her regret, she sounded as if she wanted to know exactly where he spent his nights.

"You give me reason for moving fast."

His voice held a world of meaning.

"I meant in getting the soldiers ready."

"So did I."

But, of course, he didn't. Not entirely.

Dependable stirred in his traces and snorted. In the wagon bed, Brutus perfumed the air with his own brand of noxious fumes. He had eaten most of the stew last night, and the world around him was paying the price. Beside him, Owen sat huddled in his blanket, half asleep, as oblivious to the smell as he was to the angry words.

Maddie gave up. "All right. Send the soldiers. We'll be back tomorrow afternoon."

"I won't be here."

That stopped her cold. For a moment she could not breathe. Dan had one characteristic that drove her especially mad: He could drive her from one emotional extreme to another with a word or a look. He always caught her unprepared.

She tried not to show concern, but she could not bring herself to say she was pleased.

"Tracking Apaches?" she asked, as casually as she could manage, though her heart was pounding beneath her cotton dress.

"It's what I'm here for."

It was not his only purpose. He had come to torment her. In that, he was having far more success than in confronting the Indians.

She refused to think more about what his journey might hold. Nothing had happened to him on his last foray. He was smart, he was tough, and he was cautious. Yesterday, with a storm moving in, he had acted impulsively, but that had been a short-lived aberration. She imagined he regretted his impulsiveness very much today.

As did she. More than he could ever know.

She dared to give him a thorough look. He

was without his sword and pistol, but he had other weapons to use against her, an arsenal of them, against which she had little defense. They included just about everything from his disheveled thunder-dark hair to his calf-high dusty boots. His shirt was unbuttoned at the throat, his sleeves rolled back to reveal muscled, hairy forearms. His trousers fit him in a way that should have been against regulations.

He made the lieutenant look like a child.

She knew so little about what lay under his clothes, and he knew everything about what was under hers. She blushed at the memory.

But embarrassment was the least of her problems. What if she never saw him again?

She looked away fast, lest he see the fear in her eyes. He would think she feared for herself. That, she did not do. She covered the movement by tugging her hat low to protect her skin from the sun.

Without a good-bye, she reined Dependable toward the rutted trail that led to Illusion. She felt Dan's eyes on her. Was he wondering whether he would ever see her again? Probably not. He had got what he wanted from her yesterday. This morning he gave no hint that he wanted it again.

The front left wagon wheel hit a rut, and a grumbled, incoherent protest sounded behind her. She did not know whether it came from Owen or the dog, but it did not matter. Both had been her friend yesterday, when she needed a friend very, very much. She would be more careful at the reins.

The ride took half the day. Lieutenant Leigh rode close beside her, one of the soldiers out of sight on ahead, the other trailing at the rear. Leigh talked for a while about the scenery, but when she did not respond, he lapsed into silence. They stopped a few times, mostly to rest the horses, and the ride was uneventful, as Maddie had known it would be.

She refused to admit that the safe journey might be attributable to the fact that she had made it with an armed escort.

Leaving the escort and Owen at the Grog Shop, Maddie secured the wagon at the far end of the street, left Brutus as its dubious guard, and walked back toward Illusion's general store. Alone behind the counter, the proprietor Ralph Kuntz informed her, without her asking, that Edwin Worster was not in town.

Kuntz, a rotund, talkative husband and father of six, could always be depended upon for conversation. She doubted he talked much around the small family home at the back of the store.

"Worster said he'd be out at his ranch. He's taken to staying out there lately. Must be getting ready for something special. At least that's what folks say. 'Course, you'd know more about that than me."

Maddie let out an exasperated sigh. Apparently dear Edwin had announced to one and all that she was to be his bride.

"I'm not looking for Mr. Worster. Do you know a woman named Helen Clark?"

Kuntz's face darkened. "Sure do."

"You don't sound pleased. Is there something wrong with her?"

Maddie was not trying to stir up gossip, but to check out the woman's credentials. She also knew Kuntz would rather bag flour for a month using only a teaspoon than keep from her what she wanted to know.

"I'm not speaking ill of her, you understand, Miss Hardin. But if anyone's wanting a woman to take charge of things, she'll do mighty fine. She took one look inside the store and started rearranging everything. Suggesting what I needed and what I could let pass by. And there I was, real proud of the shipment I just got in from Corpus Christi. Goods straight off the ship from England, by golly, by way of New Orleans. If the folks in Illusion want to spend money on gewgaws, it ain't no skin off my nose. And it shouldn't be off hers." He added, as an afterthought, "That's what the little woman says, too."

"So the woman is unpleasant."

"Not exactly. Just bossy." He looked as if he was going to say more but stopped himself. "Why you want to know about Mrs. Clark?"

"Is she married? I had gotten the impression

she was single." His eyebrows rose, and she hurriedly added, "Mr. Worster let me think that she was."

"She don't say one way or the other. I'm guessing she's widowed. Probably worked her man into the grave. She came here with one of the new families that're settling in. Mrs. Clark is their hired help, I believe. She's not blood kin." He spread his thick-knuckled hands on the counter and watched her with narrowed eyes. "You ain't told me why you're asking. There's nothing about her I should know, is there?"

She answered him with a smile. "I'll be picking out supplies later today. You be sure to show me those gewgaws. Especially the ones from New Orleans. It could be you will get yourself an extra sale."

The suggestion put Helen Clark out of his mind.

She found Mrs. Clark across the street in the one-room shack that called itself the Illusion Inn. Maddie heard her from the doorway, advising the harried clerk that he ought to hang sheets between the three cots that served as beds, in case his customers wanted privacy.

"You do that, Mr. Ramirez, and you'll have people returning to stay another night."

She spoke in a firm voice that matched her tall, big-bosomed figure. She was dressed in black, including black lace gloves and a black bonnet. The fringed black reticule that hung from her arm looked far too small for the rest of her.

The much shorter, thinner Ramirez, normally a cheerful man with a quick grin, sighed. "Señora, when people leave Illusion, they do not have the habit to return."

"It was just a suggestion, nothing more. But it's a good one."

Ramirez looked beyond her and saw Maddie standing in the doorway.

"Ah, Señorita Hardin, you bring me much pleasure today. Do you sleep in the wagon or do you honor the Illusion Inn by accepting the hospitality that I offer?"

"Unless yesterday's storm comes again, it will be the wagon." She looked at Helen Clark. "Good afternoon. You're Helen Clark, aren't you? I'm Madeleine Hardin. Could you spare me a few minutes of your time?"

The woman looked her over. Trying to look presentable in her wrinkled gown, Maddie took off her unpresentable hat. Her single braid of hair tumbled down her back. Helen Clark nodded once, and with a good-bye to Ramirez, strode out of the inn, leaving Maddie to hurry after. Unmindful of her skirt trailing in the muddy street, she took off at a fast pace. Maddie hurried to keep up, letting her own already muddied skirt trail, too.

In New Orleans she never would have done such a thing. When she went out, she had even carried an extra pair of slippers in case the pair she was wearing became soiled.

New Orleans was a long time ago.

"You are here working for a family, I understand," she said, finally matching the woman's strong stride.

"For a short while. They have terminated my employment."

Maddie's heart sank. She had very much liked the strength and determination of the woman. What had she done to cause the termination? There was only one way to find out.

"Why?" she asked.

The woman did not flinch at the question.

"It's not common knowledge, but it will be soon enough. Though they have only recently arrived, they will be leaving shortly, returning to the family home in Houston, where they will reside with the wife's parents. Illusion is not what they had expected."

"It's not what anyone expected. Are they leaving you here?"

"Where I go is up to me. I can accompany them on the return journey, if that is my choice."

"I detect an accent in your voice. You must be from the South."

"You're an inquisitive sort, aren't you? I was born and reared in Alabama. Let me save you the bother of asking any more questions. My husband died five years ago, and our only son was killed in the war. Being past my prime and even at my best far from a simpering creature, I cannot depend upon finding a man to support me. Therefore, I must support myself. I also have all my teeth."

Maddie had to fight a big grin. Helen Clark might think she was laughing at her, and that was not the case at all. At last good fortune was smiling down on her and, by extension—if everything worked out—on the Longhorn Ranch.

She matched the woman's bluntness. "Work for me. I'll pay you a living wage."

"Doing what? If you are setting up a brothel, you must be expecting strange clientele indeed."

"Me? A brothel?" This time she did grin. "Why would you think such a thing?"

"It's the one disreputable establishment that the town lacks. I expect a thriving establishment to be here long before a church or a school."

"It will have to get started without me. If I had to depend on my ability to serve men in such a way, I would soon starve to death."

"Don't be modest. You're frail and freckled, but I imagine you're quite strong."

"I don't think they would be hiring me for arm wrestling."

"No, but men do like stamina in a woman."

Maddie did not ask how she knew. This had to be one of the most bizarre conversations she had ever had. And that included some unusual ones with Dan.

"When I said work, I didn't mean anything involving the town. I'm asking you to do something far more difficult."

Quickly, she explained her situation, leaving out any mention of her past or present personal problems. Too, she described the ranch, the small house, the hardships that she dealt with every day and the ones she was likely to face, once the vaqueros arrived and she turned her hand to serious ranching.

She also mentioned Indians and outlaws. She even told her about the soldiers who were using the Longhorn as the site of their bivouac, although she did not say a word about the captain who led them. Some things were too difficult to describe, or, if she did get the facts right about him, too exaggerated to believe.

Through all her talk, not once did Helen Clark flinch.

By the time she was done, they were at the end of Illusion's main street. In front of them was the buckboard, its fearless guard dog asleep in the shade underneath the wagon bed. Owen was nowhere in sight. She had not expected him to be. He was still in the Grog Shop acting as host to Leigh and his men.

"I accept," Helen Clark said with barely a glance at Brutus.

The answer came quicker than Maddie had expected, and it startled her. Having proven herself not the shrewdest judge of character, she immediately began to question what she had done. She studied the woman, really studied her, not for signs of physical strength or cleanliness, but for whatever she could read in her face. Her skin was lightly tanned and unlined, though she had to be in her fifties. Mostly Maddie noticed the tightness around her mouth and the wariness in her dark brown eyes as she looked around her.

Helen Clark had lived a hard life. But it had not broken her. She was someone Maddie could understand and someone she could like.

Or so she believed. She reminded herself of one point: Hiring Owen right after she'd met him had worked out fine. Neither was she wrong to hire Helen Clark. But she wanted no mistakes on the woman's part.

"You don't want to think it over?" she asked. "It's a long ride out to the Longhorn. You'll have to be ready to leave before dawn. And you won't be able to return soon, should you change your mind."

"I'll be at the wagon in plenty of time. I don't have much in the way of personal possessions. I lost most everything in the war."

Including her only child. Maddie shared her pain.

"You won't need much—"

Maddie was interrupted by the sound of an off-key, off-color version of "Sweet Betsy from Pike" that Owen was given to sing when he was drunk. She turned and watched him stagger down the street, headed in the general direction of the wagon, though he took several unexpected detours from right to left, lengthening the journey.

She had grown used to his shabby appearance, had even grown comfortable with it. Now she saw him the way Helen Clark must: baggy pants, shirttail dragging, boots run down at the heel, long shaggy gray beard and hair, a sweat-stained hat no better than his boots.

He sported a red-veined nose in the middle of a deeply lined face, and he looked as if a puff of wind would knock him down. He had stamina, heart, and grit, too, but they were not so readily visible. Neither did he call on them all the time.

He managed to make it past the two women, even managed a wobbly salute, then cradled the almost empty whiskey bottle he had been waving around in time to the music, crawled under the wagon, and promptly fell asleep beside his dog.

Maddie had kept her breathing shallow as he staggered by. She hoped Helen Clark had done the same.

"That's Owen," she said. "He claims he's too poor for more than one name. He works for me."

She waited for Helen to turn and run, or at least to sniff in disapproval.

Instead, she turned her back on the wagon.

"You'll be buying supplies, I suppose. Do you mind if I come along and help? Mr. Kuntz needed suggestions on organizing his stock at that strange little store of his. Didn't take to it well. Most men don't. I'm not sure he can find anything anymore."

Chapter Fourteen

When Maddie returned to the Longhorn in the middle of the next day, Carlos and the three workers he had hired were there assembling the adobe bricks for the barn. The soldiers were gone, leaving the area behind her house curiously empty and quiet.

Right away, Owen rolled out of the wagon and made fast for the woods, holding his head and his mouth as he had been doing much of the day. Brutus, naturally, took the same route, tail drooping between his legs.

While Maddie was looking around at her homestead, wondering what Helen must be thinking, the woman was looking at the milk cow staked at the side of the house and at the chickens scratching at the dirt in their coop.

"That cow'll need milking." She eyed one of the soldiers who had been with them on the journey. "Think you can handle it?"

Maddie started to tell her not to bother asking. His captain did not want the men doing any work other than as guards.

But the soldier, as grizzled and hardened as any of Dan's men, was already rolling up his uniform sleeves.

"Yes, ma'am. Pa taught me. That's something you don't ever forget."

Helen turned to Leigh. "You and the corporal there want to help unload the wagon? I've got supper to get on, and some organizing to do."

Maddie looked at the woman in amazement. Every word Helen spoke lifted a weight from her shoulders. She also inspired her to warble a chorus of "Sweet Betsy from Pike."

Instead, she hurriedly changed from her dress into her usual trousers, shirt, and vest. The latter was missing a small section of fringe, but as long as no one asked her how the damage had occurred, she did not care. With Helen taking charge of the house, she went down to greet the men.

Carlos greeted her with a grin. "Señorita Hardin, *buenos días.*"

She answered in her broken Spanish, shaking the hand of each man as Carlos called him by name. She was without her gloves and each man seemed embarrassed by the dirt on his hands. She smiled, and they lost their embarrassment.

His English being better than her Spanish, Carlos let her know he had brought the best workers he could find on either side of the Rio Grande.

"*Bueno.* Good for you, Carlos. I hereby name you foreman of the Longhorn."

He looked at her slyly. "Does this come with *más diñero?*"

She caught his meaning right away. "You will get a raise," she said with a smile.

Mentally, she went through the funds remaining from her mother's legacy. She had been comfortable for a long while, but soon the Longhorn would have to pay.

She proceeded with gestures and a mixture of English and Spanish to let the vaqueros know how she wanted the barn. All the men nodded, as if they understood everything she was telling them, but she got the feeling they were going to construct the building the way they thought best.

She did not care, as long as the walls were solid and the roof did not leak.

Leaving them to their work, she walked on to the pasture where she and Owen had planted corn. After the rain, sprouts had pushed their way through the soil. She went along the rows, coddling the new growth, talking to each plant, glad no one could hear.

Maddie knew about farming from Julien. He had been the one to want crops, while she had been thinking only of horses and cattle. When they were dreaming and planning, before the war, they had spent hours talking soil and seeds and the best time of year to plant, and the time when the harvest would come.

He had not mentioned talking to plants, but she figured it couldn't hurt, especially since his experience had been with wet Louisiana soil, and she was dealing with hard-packed loam.

Besides, concentrating on the corn kept her from thinking about walking on a little farther, and a little farther, until she was in the woods and eventually standing beside the creek. She had met one challenge—talking to Dan again—but viewing the scene of their misdeed would take another kind of strength.

The corn also kept her from far more terrifying topics. How was Dan? What was happening to him? Would he return to the Longhorn soon? Would he ever return?

It was the last consideration that almost sent her to her knees. She tried to think of Carlos and the new workers, of Helen, of the soldier milking the cow.

But the only man in uniform she could bring to mind was tall, dark, and flinty-eyed, and possessed of flesh as vulnerable as that of anyone else.

She did not allow herself to think long of his flesh. Pulling on the gloves she had tucked at her waist, she turned her attention once again to the corn. Enough coddling, both for the plants and herself. There were weeds in her garden. She would work until sundown pulling out every one.

Over the next days, she threw herself into helping Helen rearrange the small house to accommodate the cot purchased from Ralph Kuntz, working in the field, helping where she could with the barn, talking with Carlos about the Longhorns that must be captured before the worst heat of summer arrived.

The first week stretched into the second, and then the third. Rain did not come again, and the sun beat down relentlessly without the intrusion of more than an occasional cloud.

Working alongside her, Owen grumbled that he had forgotten how to spit.

For her part, working from dawn until dusk, Maddie grew skittish, snappish one moment, morose the next. Ever the gentleman, Lieutenant Leigh learned to stay out of her way. He and his men devoted themselves to going on patrol.

It should have helped her disposition that the barn was well on the way to being finished, that despite limited supplies Helen provided the best meals since those her mother had set on the table, that the corn crop held promise, despite the weeks-long drought.

If Helen noticed anything was wrong, she did not comment on it. But she did not know

Maddie very well. She probably thought this was the manner of her new employer, when in truth it was not at all.

For the past two years Maddie had faced the worst of her troubles by keeping her emotions under control, at least when others were around. Not knowing how Dan fared changed all that. She had lost so much, she could not bear losing him, too. Even though he would not be with her for long, she wanted to know he was alive and well somewhere in the world.

It was the way she had felt about Grace. But she could not bear to think of her child, not now when her burdens were more than she could endure.

By way of contrast, Helen never raised her voice or her brow, even when Brutus tracked mud into the house. He did it only once. She firmly escorted the dog back outside, told Owen to take care of the problem, and returned to the mending that occupied part of her time. Included in the stack of clothes were several articles that belonged to Owen, all of them thoroughly washed and dried in the sun.

When she wasn't working frenziedly, Maddie did notice how Owen had changed. He hadn't shaved or given himself a thorough haircut, but he had trimmed several inches off both beard and hair. Every day or so she caught him splashing himself at the pump, and, as far as she observed, he had quit scratching his rear.

Most important of all, he did not drink. She

knew that somewhere he had hidden a stash of whiskey purchased from the trip into town. He rarely looked at Helen, grumbled when she gave him an order, but Maddie knew the woman had to be the cause of his changes.

For one thing, he had developed a powerful thirst for the strong coffee she kept ready by the hearth. When he was in the vicinity of the house, he often dropped in for a cup. He never spoke, never lingered long, but neither did he stay away for more than half a day.

Early one morning, three weeks after the main contingent of soldiers had departed, Carlos began to speak of searching out the wild cattle that would be her first herd. Such talk of Longhorns should have made her excited. Here finally, at least in talk, was the real beginning of her ranch.

But the only excitement she craved was hearing Dan ride up and start criticizing her again. She told her foreman the roundup would have to be delayed. She did not give the reason: She could not leave until she received news of him.

She got her wish that evening. She and Helen were preparing for bed. Her gown was laid out, she had taken off her vest and begun to unbutton her shirt when the sound of hoofbeats sent her running out the front door.

The setting sun had cast long shadows over the front of the house, but still, from the lantern light spilling out the open door, she could make out the front rider. Reining his mount to a halt, Dan loomed high as a mountain in front of her. Her heart sang at the sight.

Anxious eyes took in everything at once: the blanket of trail dust on his uniform, the thick growth of beard that covered much of his face, the gloved hands on the reins, the warm solemnity of his gaze.

There were no missing limbs, no bloody bandages, no splints for mending broken bones, none of the things she had pictured in the middle of every night. She had strength to do nothing but stand there and let relief flood through her. She could not look away from his probing eyes.

She swallowed and started to tell him how glad she was that he was home, even if it wasn't his home and he wouldn't be here for very long.

He gave her no chance. The warmth in his eyes died.

"Do you always run outside unarmed and half naked when you hear someone ride up?"

Her words died on her lips. She must have been wrong about the warmth.

"Always," she said. "It's a South Texas habit I picked up as soon as I got here."

Only then did the *half naked* part register. She glanced down. Her shirt was half tucked in, half unbuttoned, revealing only the beginning fullness of her breasts, but her trousers and boots were still in place. She hardly called that half naked.

Still, just the words on his lips caused a tingle inside her. Shameless woman that she had become, she was in no hurry to button her shirt. Let him look. As long as he did not want to touch.

Look was exactly what he did. Then he shook himself. "I've got an injured man coming along right behind me. Do you think you can get some hot water and bandages? I dug the bullet out and used gunpowder to stop the bleeding, but he needs more than that now."

"Bring him in. We'll take care of him right soon enough."

It was Helen, standing in the doorway, who spoke. She had not yet begun to undress, but she had unbound and brushed her long gray-streaked hair. She made a formidable appearance in the light.

"Who are you?" Dan asked.

"I'm the new help. I could ask the same of you, except I know from what your men have said. You're Captain Dan."

What else had the men said? Maddie had not mentioned him except to tell her of the party of soldiers who were using the Longhorn as a site for their bivouac.

Dan nodded in greeting and reined back toward the fast-falling dark. It swallowed him too soon.

She took a moment to whisper a prayer of thanks, then turned her attention to matters more prosaic than the tears of gratitude that blurred her eyes. Fumbling with the shirt buttons, tucking in the shirttail, she went for the water bucket. She had the water heating at the edge of the hearth when she heard the sound of horses once again, thundering to the front of the house and coming to a sudden halt.

Both she and Helen hurried out to watch as two of the soldiers eased one of their comrades from his saddle. A bloodied section of blanket was wrapped around the injured man's shoulder and arm.

He was as tall as Dan, but much bulkier, and the soldiers had a difficult time managing him with a minimum of jarring. He moaned once, then fell silent. Maddie recognized him as Sergeant Mead Wilcox, the soldier she had seen Dan conferring with most often.

Cradling him between them, the two bearers headed for the house. Wilcox roused himself enough to protest and gesture away from the front door.

"He can sleep outdoors if he's a mind to," Helen said, "but first I'm cleaning and bandaging him in here."

Between the sergeant's groan and the woman's orders, Helen's will won out.

Maddie hurried ahead of them to toss back the covers of her bed. Helen pulled off the top sheet and went for the scissors in her mending basket. Wilcox's feet hung off the end of the mattress, and his good arm fell to one side.

Ordering the other soldiers to set up camp, Dan started to tear at Wilcox's clothing.

Helen waved him from the room. "You've done your bit, Captain. You're exhausted. Get yourself some rest. We'll let you know when we're done."

He rubbed a hand over his beard, then with a curt, "I'll be back," he left, minding her in a way he had not minded Maddie since New Orleans.

The two women worked with little talk, in unison removing the blanket bandage and his shirt and the tattered remains of his underwear. It took the two of them to take off his boots. Helen sniffed once, removed the socks, which were greatly in need of mending, and tossed them along with the boots out the front door.

Wilcox lay still, almost stiff, as if he were done with moaning in complaint. He did not wince when warm water was used to swab out the injury. The wound began to bleed. Helen sprinkled in a spoonful of flour, and the bleeding stopped.

Using dry strips of the sheet, they bound the shoulder and arm tightly. Only when they stepped away did he give any sign of relaxing. Not once had he opened his eyes, but he did so now, looking up at Helen as if he were seeing an angel.

She didn't seem to notice, instead turning from the bed and beginning the cleanup. The sergeant's eyes closed once again. When his breathing became regular, Maddie went outside to tell Dan they were done.

He was standing in the dark close to the door.

She jumped. "I didn't know you were here."

"I haven't left. Your new worker hit me with one of the sergeant's boots."

"He's sleeping right now. Do you need tending, too?"

She had not meant it to sound like an invitation. But of course he took it that way.

"What did you have in mind?"

"A hot meal. Coffee. Bed rest. And I do mean rest."

"Just what a man wants to hear when he's been gone over three weeks."

Too well she remembered the harsh way he had greeted her when she first ran out the door. Men said women were difficult to understand. Bah.

"He might want to hear something different if he's been gone from home. But this is not your home, and you know it. Don't pretend now that it is."

"That's not a mistake I'm likely to make, Maddie."

She could hear the low rumble of voices from the back of the house, and the chirp of insects in the woods. An owl hooted from close by. The moon came from behind a cloud, and a breeze, cool the way it sometimes was in the night, ruffled her shirt. The only disquieting note in the entire scene was Dan's voice and his eyes.

She could look at him no longer. The wagon caught her attention. "Owen. I forgot all about him."

"He and the dog left soon after we got here."

"That's not like him. At least not lately."

"Times change. People change, too."

"Why do I think everything you say is a criticism of me?"

"Sometimes it is. But not this time. I was speaking of myself."

He looked as if he would say more, then backed away.

But she could not let him leave, not yet, even though looking at him and listening to him were torture.

"What happened to the sergeant?"

"Apaches. We caught them about seventy-five miles southwest of here."

"That's a long way from the Longhorn."

"There are settlers scattered between your place and the border. They need protecting, too. One family had already been burned out, and another took some shots in the night."

His words stung. "I did not mean to suggest you should have left them alone," she said.

"You'd be a fool if you did. They were riding on a line that would have brought them straight here. Apaches can't match the Comanches as horsemen, but they're good enough. If they wanted to ride hard, they could have been here in little over a day. They were carrying powerful rifles. We lost one man in a skirmish, and when Wilcox went after the body, they got him, too."

Maddie listened with a growing sense of horror. "Were . . . all of you in danger?"

"Indians don't care about the stripes or bars we're wearing. Yes, we were all in danger."

She hugged herself. "I'm sorry. I know you're close to your men. Wilcox went after the body. I suppose you went after him."

He did not respond. She took his answer as yes. Fear shivered through her, stronger than ever. It scraped at her heart. Dan was here standing two feet away, safe, but she knew he would be going out again.

"What happened to the Apaches?" she said.

"They made it across the river. Orders say we can't go after them into Mexico. Damned fools in Washington. They don't know what it's like on the frontier."

He fell silent, and she knew he was remembering the battle and the death of the soldier. She wanted to wrap her arms around him and give him the consolation that he needed. But that was not the way things were between them. He would misinterpret the embrace. And once she touched him, she would hold on too tight.

Without another word, he left, and she went

back into the house. Later, much later, the sergeant awoke and asked to be taken outside.

"I can't breathe in here," he said.

Maddie went outside to tell Dan. He already had a bedroll spread out close to the fire. He was standing nearby, his coat and weapons tossed aside, his sleeves rolled halfway up his forearms. His shirt was partially unbuttoned, and she could see the shadow of hair on his upper chest.

Half naked, that's what he would call it. So did she. Somehow he seemed more vulnerable this way. Her hands burned to touch him. She kept them behind her back and studied the bedroll.

"You're ready for him. You know your sergeant," she said.

"We've been together a long time. He was in New Orleans before the end of the war, although not in my unit."

She wished she could talk to the sergeant, to ask him about all that had happened to Dan, to talk about the changes in him, about the way he was and the way he had become. She knew she never could.

She went back inside to watch as two of the men lifted their grousing companion and carried him outside and around to the back. Helen, her hair once again tightly bound, went with them.

"I'll watch over him a spell," she said. "You

get some rest. You've been on your feet pretty much since dawn."

Maddie did not give her an argument. Helen had put fresh linens on her bed. There was no sign that Wilcox had ever been inside. She was in her nightgown brushing her hair when the door slowly opened. Helen returning, she thought.

Dan stepped inside. He closed the door firmly behind him. The sound tore her insides apart.

The only light in the room was the flickering fire. It cast shadows across his bearded face, the line of his neck, his exposed throat and chest. She forgot how to breathe.

"Thank you for Wilcox," he said.

"There's no need to thank me," she said, trying to hide her disappointment. It wasn't his thanks she craved.

He watched her in silence.

"Is there something else you wanted?" she asked.

"I didn't get a proper welcome," he said. "I didn't give you a proper hello."

He crossed the room in two strides. Trembling, she looked up at him as he stared down at her, unsmiling, his expression dark and unreadable.

"Welcome back to the Longhorn," she managed.

"That's not what I meant, and you know it. God help us both, this is what I want."

She did not resist when he pulled her into his arms. She was naked beneath the gown. She felt every wrinkle of his shirt, the expanse of hard chest beneath. She especially felt every contour beneath the trousers that fit him far too well.

Cupping his face, she let her fingers play in his coarse beard.

"I'll burn you," he said.

"You already have."

She spoke from a bruised and burgeoning heart.

Chapter Fifteen

Dan kissed her, gently at first, his lips slanted against hers. She grasped the front of his shirt to keep from collapsing against him. He rested his hands lightly against her shoulders, his thumbs stroking the side of her neck.

He trembled once and deepened the kiss, his tongue probing its way past her lips. He cupped his mouth over hers as if he would suck her inside him and keep her there until he was satisfied.

She felt the power of passion within him, and for an instant it frightened her. Too well she knew what men in such a state could do. But Dan was not all men. She was foolish to think otherwise. To prove her trust, and because it came naturally, she leaned her body into his and released herself from fear.

In the doing, his ardor set her blood boiling and her heart pounding until it hurt.

He had taken her fast and hard before. Such lovemaking was too violent for her now. Even as he held her in his arms and she knew he was safe, the harsh images that had tortured her nights while he was gone came to her, flashes of gunfire that were at the same time terrifying and wildly erotic.

She had not known tenderness in his arms, not in a long while. She wanted it tonight. That way she could pretend they lived in a time of peace, that all was well and always would be.

She could tell herself he loved her as she loved him.

With more strength than she had known she possessed, she pushed away from him, ending the kiss, breaking the strong hold he had on her shoulders.

In the flickering firelight, he looked darkly seductive, and it wasn't just the thick growth of hair that shadowed his face, or the depth of his gaze. The image of his pulling her inside him until she ceased to exist as a separate being was more than fanciful. At the moment it seemed all too possible, all too real.

"Don't ask me to stop," he rasped. "Not now."

She touched his lips. "Be gentle. That's all I

want. Show me there's still gentleness in the world"

He stared down at her so long she feared that his ardor had cooled, that he wanted her only one way, that he could enjoy nothing but the quick, hot lovemaking that they'd shared by the creek.

"I don't understand you, Maddie."

"I don't understand you. But understanding is not what we're asking of one another, is it?"

She wrapped her arms around his neck and kissed the edges of beard that surrounded his mouth. Growing bold, she touched her tongue to his lips.

"Give me what I ask tonight, Dan, and I will give you everything that I can."

He eased his hands over his shoulders and down her back, cupping her bottom, rubbing the mounds with his palms, then holding on again, more firmly, pressing her against his all too detectable arousal, his eyes capturing hers.

"I'll do my best." His voice was a growl.

She could not speak for a moment, enjoying his hardness and the coils it tightened in her belly. Whatever fear she had harbored melted under his heat.

"Your best is very good," she whispered shakily. "But there's one thing more."

"Name it."

"I don't want to be the only one naked."

His eyes burned. "I like the way you think.

There's only one thing I would like to add. You don't have to be gentle with me."

But she did. He would not understand how much she needed to touch him, to kiss him, to stare at his strong body. His strong, uninjured body. She needed to know that he had returned to her whole. Such an exploration could be made only with tenderness and with love.

Unbuttoning his shirt, she tugged it open and kissed his nipples and the expanse of hair on his chest, taking her time, letting the taste of salt and sweat and the long, hard ride tingle on her tongue. His body was warm, his flesh taut against muscle and bone, and she felt his heart pounding beneath her lips.

He was alive. Tears came to her eyes. She blinked them away. Tonight was not a time for crying. It was a time for admitting to joy. She had thought it was an emotion she would never experience again. How satisfying it was to know she was wrong.

When she fumbled with his shirt, he helped her take it off. When she did the same with the placket of his trousers, his hands covered hers.

"No," she said. "I'll probably go slow, but eventually I'll get what I want."

She brushed her fingers against his erection, then fumbled some more with the buttons.

"You could teach the Apaches about torture," he said.

She smiled to herself. He tortured her

equally with nothing more than his presence. If he thought she was truly inept at the undressing, he did not know her very well.

Which, of course, he did not.

Her fingers started the brushing again. He moaned deep in his throat. Out of mercy—and her own sense of urgency—she hurried along, tugging the trousers and underwear down his slender hips, hesitating when the waistband hugged low on his hips, then lower, until his sex was released.

Her embarrassment surprised her. For a minute she could not look at him, and then, after a short while, she could not look away. What she had felt before with her body, she experienced with her eyes. It was a new sensation. Looking at his manhood, she felt more like a woman than she ever had.

Slowly she raised her eyes to his. They were black as night, wild, captivating her with the raw desire she saw in their depths.

The tension of the moment became unendurable.

Miraculously, she managed a laugh. "I didn't know you brought your sword."

"For you, Maddie, I am always armed."

The sight of his nakedness, the hunger in his eyes, the throbbing power of his presence—everything about him overwhelmed her. She turned away and looked into the fire.

"You'll have to finish. I'm not as bold as I thought."

She listened as he undressed, his boots dropping one after the other. Her imagination filled in what her eyes would very soon see. While she listened and imagined, she unbuttoned her nightgown, slipped it from her shoulders, and let it fall in a whisper to the floor. Smoothing her hair, she pulled several strands over the rise of her breasts, letting them curl around the hard, pointed tips.

At last she turned to face him. She had not the strength to look into his eyes again. Somehow, that would seem too personal. Too revealing. Through her eyes he would see into her heart, into her soul.

She studied the rest of him, the strong arms and powerful legs, the broad chest she planned to kiss once again, the narrow hips. Everything but his sex. How she could possibly have turned shy, standing naked in front of him while he stood naked in front of her, she did not know. She did not tell him how she felt. He would understand no better than she.

"You have a small scar on your side," she said. Inane. Foolish. But it was an observation that was as necessary as anything else she saw to understand who he was.

"It's an old wound."

"Did it hurt?"

"I suppose so. I don't remember. Please do something for me. Turn around. No, slowly. I like the way the light kisses your skin."

He asked much of her—too much—but he

promised much in return. He did not speak while she did as he asked. Moving slowly was hard. Even harder was keeping her hands at her sides when she wanted to cover herself everywhere that she could. She was not proud of her body. It had changed since giving birth, hips wider, breasts fuller, though she was still far too thin.

She thrust all thought of the birth from her mind. Closing her eyes, she grew dizzy and had to open them again. She had to fight not to run for the bed and dive under the covers. The trouble was, a woman's body had so many places for potential flaws, so many places that were private, that once upon a time she herself, as a child and then as a young woman, had not wanted to look at.

But in the course of her life, the last days in New Orleans and the months after she left, she had been forced to look and know. And now Dan looked, too.

"You have no scars, Maddie. Your skin is beautiful."

Dan forced her to think of the unthinkable. Worse, with the offhand comment, he came close to destroying all the desire that had been building inside her.

I have scars, far worse than yours. They still hurt. But they do not show.

She would never know him well enough to confess the truth.

"Hold me, Dan. Kiss me. Make love to me."

She went into his arms. The brush of his skin against hers was electric. She shivered against him.

He stroked her arms and back. "Are you cold?"

"I'll never be cold again."

Both of them knew she lied, but it was an idea that went with the night and the time that brought them together. She rubbed her breasts against his chest. Again his hands trailed down her back.

"The bed's stronger than it looks," she said.

"But narrow. I want room, Maddie. Lots of room."

He let go of her long enough to shove aside the table and bench, then drag the covers to the floor in front of the fire. He kneeled in the middle of them, staring up at her, taking a long time to get to her face. Could he see the embarrassing way her body was reacting to him, the full, hard-tipped breasts, the throbbing, the moisture between her legs?

He was not an inexperienced man. What he did not see, he understood.

She dropped to the floor beside him. They stretched out side by side, and she explored him as she had wanted, touching, kissing, stroking, at first needing to know he had returned to her whole, then needing to touch him for no other reason than she loved him and touching felt very good.

He did the same for her, and she knew what

she had missed by the creek. Tonight, in Dan's arms, she managed the impossible. She existed in a void, where there were no judgments, no time, no hurts, where the only space that existed was on a small pallet in front of a glowing fire in the middle of a nowhere land without threat of harm.

They were two lovers without a past or a future. They had only now.

He took her through the nowhere land on clouds. When she thought she could soar no higher, he lifted himself on top of her with an unspoken promise of grandeur yet to come. This time she knew to part her legs wide. She went farther. She wrapped them around his hips, urging him with tight tugs to join his body with hers.

He did what she wanted, a dozen thrusts, a million, her heart pounding with such ferocity, she thought she might die. In the brief, blinding apex, he brought her to the edge of death and gave her glorious life.

Maddie woke with a start and sat up. Daylight streamed around the edges of the thin rawhide that covered the window close by her bed. The embers of last night's fire glowed at the edge of the hearth. It was morning. She was naked. She was in bed alone.

She tried to remember last night, not the way it had begun—Dan's entrance was burned in her mind, along with most of what happened afterwards—but the manner of its ending.

The only thing she could recall was his holding her close to him on the floor in front of the fire, both of them listening to the pop of wood and the settling of burnt logs into ash. Hours had gone by, or so it seemed. She must have fallen asleep. He had lifted her, covers and all, and laid her on the bed. He had managed the feat without waking her.

He was a very strong man.

Pulling the covers close to her chin, she lay on the mattress and with eyes closed remembered exactly how strong.

"Good morning."

Her eyes flew open. Helen was sitting at the side of her cot, already dressed for the day, braiding her hair into the knot she wore at the back of her head.

She had forgotten all about the woman. She had forgotten everything but Dan. She wanted to pull the covers over her head and tell the world to go away.

Retreat was not an option. For Maddie, it never was for long.

She glanced about the room. The nightgown she had discarded so hurriedly last night was folded on the bench. Dan had straightened everything neatly when he left. There were no signs that he had ever been there.

The signs were all inside her.

Guilt rushed in, and with it embarrassment. Helen knew what had happened last night. She must think her new employer no better than the whore she had first thought her to be.

How could she explain the way things were between her and Dan? She couldn't, not even if she used a million words.

"I kept you from your bed last night," she said.

Helen thrust the pins in her hair, securing the knot in place. "Sergeant Wilcox was restless. I stayed outside with him for a long time. You didn't keep me from anything."

The woman spoke matter-of-factly, with no hint of judgment or censure. Maddie wanted to hug her in gratitude, but given her naked state, she chose to thank her with a nod.

Helen stood and spread the covers neatly over her cot. "I imagine you're hungry this morning. I am. I'll put the coffee on and gather some eggs."

When she had water heating in the coffeepot, she paused at the door. "You take your time about getting dressed this morning. The work'll be waiting when you get up."

Work wasn't the only thing that would be waiting. She would also be dealing with Dan's presence, his memory, his eyes. Before she could begin to devise a plan to cope with them all, Helen returned with a bucket of water.

"One of the soldiers is milking the cow.

There's plenty of eggs, looks like. You have any objection to sharing them with the men?"

Maddie shook her head. "Did you see Owen?"

"Nope. Nor the dog. I suspect that nag of his is gone, too."

"I hope nothing has happened to them."

"I doubt it did. He took the whiskey with him."

Maddie did not ask how she knew. Helen seemed to know everything that was going on around her. If she suspected Caesar II was not staked out with the rest of the Longhorn horses and mule, then that was the way it was. She could probably have described much of what had happened last night in front of the fire.

Again, Maddie wanted to pull the covers over her head. Instead, with Helen gone back outside, she got up and bathed, rubbing the washcloth quickly over her body, almost ruthlessly, refusing to think of where Dan had touched, where he had kissed. When she was once again dressed in her work clothes, she set to braiding her hair.

Helen returned, set the skillet at the edge of the fire, and while it was heating, poured each of them a cup of coffee. The hot brew burned Maddie's tongue, but she scarcely seemed to notice.

She sat at one end of the bench and stared into the cup. "The captain and I knew each other in New Orleans."

She hadn't planned to mention Dan, but the words came out on their own. She did not regret saying them. Helen had a right to know as much as Maddie could bring herself to tell.

"I thought that's the way it was." Helen spooned a dollop of butter into the skillet, then cracked the eggs over the sizzling fat and began to stir. "Before the war ended?"

"He was part of the occupational army. I was engaged to someone else at the time, someone fighting far away for the Confederacy."

"You broke off the engagement."

"I was going to. But he died in battle."

"Guilt's been haunting you ever since."

Helen had no idea how much. But Maddie had confessed all that she could, all that she would ever reveal, and she let silence be her answer.

Helen reached for one of the inherited plates that Maddie valued so much. Usually they ate off tin, but this morning seemed an appropriate time for fine china. How Helen understood that, she did not know.

"Cold biscuits, hot eggs, and a glass of warm milk. That'll get you started."

Maddie sighed. "I'm not sure I want to get started. That means I'll have to go outside. I'm not ready to face what's out there."

Helen fixed herself a plate and sat on the bench beside her.

"He's already ridden out."

There was no need to ask the identity of *he*.

Maddie set down her fork. "He's not gone on patrol again, has he?"

"Not far. That's what one of the men said. He took a couple of soldiers, said he was going to check out the Longhorn. One of the families they came upon said there were outlaws on the move across the Strip. And the Indians they chased across the river weren't the only ones around." Helen's voice softened. "You didn't pick a garden spot to grow roots, did you, dear?"

The *dear* brought tears to Maddie's eyes. No one had addressed her in such a manner since her mother died. This was a morning not only for coping with an awkward situation, it was also a time for sentiment.

But Maddie's sentiment always came mixed with hard truths.

"I bought the Longhorn without seeing it. The man who sold it to me in New Orleans claimed to be a friend of my brothers. I'm guessing now that he heard stories about them, but they never actually met."

"You've got brothers?"

It was the most outright personal question Helen had asked.

"Two. Cal lives a couple of hundred miles east, in Victoria County. Cord, the middle one, has a big spread west of San Antonio. They're both very successful ranchers."

"So you bought land and came here after the war thinking you could have you a big ranch, too."

"Am I so obvious?"

"I'll bet they both have families."

"Big ones. Happy ones."

Maddie knew she should abandon the subject of families, of Cal and Cord and their loving wives and the half-dozen children they had sired between them. But she felt a need to talk.

"I wanted a family, too. But I had troubles. Physical problems. It doesn't seem I'll ever have a husband and children. So I'll get myself that big ranch. It'll just take longer than I planned, and require a lot more work."

"What about the captain? I know I'm prying, but sometimes that's the only way to find out things. Let me know if I go too far."

"You're not. Dan and I have a complicated relationship."

"Love can be that way."

"Love would be simple. What we share is definitely not love."

"Humph."

"We aren't in love. We spend all our time arguing."

Helen raised her brows.

"All right, most of the time. We didn't argue last night." She thought over what they had done instead, and her heart warmed. "I admit I have feelings for him. They are not returned, not in the same way. Out here in the middle of nowhere, I'm a very handy convenience."

"If you think that's all you are, you'd better start thinking different."

"That's one of my problems. I do too much thinking."

"And here I am causing you to do more."

"You're doing nothing I don't want you to do, not if we're to understand one another."

"Then you'll pardon an old woman one more question. About Owen. How did you get hooked up with him?"

"He was squatting on the land when I got here. The man I hired to lead me down from San Antonio and help get me started had ridden away. I offered Owen a deal he couldn't refuse."

"Money for whiskey."

"You spook me," Maddie said. "You know what I'm going to say before I say it."

"It's a gift I have with some people. My late husband did not appreciate it overly much."

"Were you married long?"

"Twenty-two years. Which was about twenty-one too many."

Maddie forgot all about herself and her problems. The tightness around Helen's mouth, and the wariness in her eyes, both traits she had noticed when first they met, were more in evidence than ever.

"You weren't happy."

"I gave him a son. When I could not give him more to help on the farm, he was not kind."

The women looked at one another. So much was left unsaid between them, yet so much was understood.

"Men," Maddie said.

"Men," Helen said with a knowing nod.

But Maddie could not let the harshness remain in her voice, not after what had passed between her and Dan last night, not with all the glory of the hours still warm in her heart and in her mind.

"I have more than just simple feelings for the captain. I love him very much."

"Have you told him? No need to answer. You had trouble telling me."

"He would not care. Like most everyone else, in the war he lost something, or someone, that mattered to him very much. He won't talk about the loss, yet he manages to blame me."

"Could be that's his way of keeping you at arm's length."

"Arm's length is not particularly where he wants me."

"I was speaking in a figurative sense. But if you think his feelings are not involved, you are wrong. You didn't see him walk out of here last night."

"That's the point. He walked out. He did not choose to stay with me until the light of day."

"All I know is, he had an unsettled look about him, like a man who doesn't know whether to be grinning or searching around for someone to shoot."

"I know the look. He's directed it at me a few times. I'm more inclined to duck than to smile."

Helen stood to clear the table.

"Mark my words, Miss Madeleine Hardin, you've given the captain some things to think about. I suspect while he's out riding the perimeter, as he put it, he's doing more thinking than looking. You give a man something to ponder and he's liable to become downright dangerous."

Chapter Sixteen

When Maddie finally went out to face the day, Sergeant Wilcox was sitting on his bedroll, looking as if he could bite the paw off a bear.

He wore his shirt over his good arm and shoulder. Someone had buttoned the other half over his wound, and the empty sleeve hung limp at his side.

He was the only soldier in sight.

Maddie remembered the look Helen had described on Dan's face, as if he didn't know whether to grin or shoot somebody. She felt the same way.

She concentrated on the sergeant. Beneath his beard, his face was pale. For a big man, he looked almost gaunt.

He glanced once at her, then looked quickly away. The movement told her the worst. Like Helen, he knew what had happened last night between his captain and the woman in the house. If Wilcox knew, everyone knew.

At least he did not leer.

Maddie held her ground. She was embarrassed—it was a feeling she was getting used to—but she felt no shame.

"Can I get you some water?" she asked.

"You women must think I'm dry as dust. All I get is water. What I need is a stiff drink of whiskey."

Ignoring his gruffness, she knelt beside him. "I'm sorry you were injured. I know it must hurt."

"Bullet chipped a bone, best I can figure. I'll live."

"But you won't be moving around for a while. You're pale. You lost a lot of blood."

He shifted on the blanket. She caught his brief wince.

She studied her hands. "I owe you an apology. I wasn't very gracious when you first got here and set up camp. Ever since, you've been out risking your life for me and others like me."

He looked away, as if she embarrassed him.

"Man's got to pass his days somehow. Tracking Indians is what I do."

"That doesn't mean it's ordinary work. You and . . . all the men lead dangerous lives."

"You keep talking like that, you'll get me to worrying so much I'll turn yellow and start wearing a skirt."

"I doubt it. I don't. Wear a skirt, I mean."

He raised a hand and again winced.

"I didn't mean no offense. Those trousers of yours are right fine by me." He grimaced. "Not that I noticed 'em or anything like that. Cap'n Dan warned us we better not—"

He broke off fast.

Maddie's heart quickened, the way it always did at the mention of Dan.

"Go on. Better not what?"

Wilcox lay back on the bedroll and closed his eyes. "I'm plumb tuckered, Miss Hardin. I'll get me some shut-eye. You tell Miz Clark I may be needing attention before long. She better stay close to the house."

"I think she's already planning on doing that."

As much as he was capable of doing so, the sergeant looked pleased.

Maddie went down the hill to find Sunset bounding about the corral instead of staked outside in the nearest stand of trees with Dependable and the mule. The sight came as a surprise. Was one of the perquisites of sleeping with the captain getting her horse better care?

Best not start thinking that way, or else she would be overinterpreting everything that happened around her, right up until the day he rode away for good.

Waving at Carlos and his men, who were working on the barn, she saddled the mustang and set out for the pasture where she planned to graze her cattle. She had chosen acreage in the southern part of the ranch, near the small pond that could serve as a primary source of water for them.

With the sun beating down and rain becoming a distant memory, the ground was cracked and dry, and the grass was turning brown. The pond was down, too, alarmingly so. It was still May. The worst of summer had yet to come, and she was beginning to feel real concern.

She had never experienced drought in Louisiana, but the dry wind that brushed against her face was something she faced in Texas every day.

She was at the edge of the pasture when she saw Dan and four of his men come riding in her direction. She reined to a halt and watched their progress. Without glancing at her, the men rode on by.

Not Dan.

He had shaved since she last saw him. His smooth cheeks made him look very young, very vulnerable, and her heart turned. She wanted to rub her face where his beard had burned, in remembrance of last night. Instead, she held tightly to the reins and watched as he stopped beside her, taking in everything at once without seeming to see anything at all.

Finally, when she could no longer stand the

growing tension, she forced herself to look right into his eyes. They were shadowed by the brim of his hat, but then, so were hers. He would have to guess at her mood the same way she was guessing at his.

"Are you all right this morning?" he asked.

Hello, my darling. I want to thank you for the most wonderful evening of my life.

She hadn't expected such a declaration, but it would have been welcome. Instead, she got, "Are you all right?"

"I'm fine."

Lifting her hat, she wiped her sleeve against her brow, smiled to show him that she spoke the truth, then dropped the hat back in place.

"And you?" she added. "I hope you got some rest."

She shouldn't have said that last part. He would think she wanted to analyze what had happened between them. As little as she knew of men, she doubted they liked to talk about a sexual encounter except while it was going on. Even then, if Dan was any example, they did not say much.

He looked around the pasture and settled on a stand of mesquite and scrub brush twenty yards away.

"Let's get out of the sun," he said, and without waiting for her assent, spurred his horse toward the shade.

She should have gone in the opposite direction the minute she saw him riding toward her. If she had any pride, that's exactly what she should be doing now. Instead, she followed, as he knew she would.

He dismounted and waited for her to do the same before he spoke.

"We need to talk about last night."

They were words to chill her. She had been wrong about him, as she so often was. Curse him, he wanted to talk.

"No, we don't need any such thing."

"I can't stay away from you."

He took her by surprise, and she barely managed a small, "Oh." She had to think before she could come up with something else to say. "I assume this is a problem for you. Are you asking if it's a problem for me?"

"Maybe. Hell, I don't know."

Maddie could have told him that she didn't mind in the least, but something perverse deep within refused to let her make this confrontation easy for him. If he expected her to simper and throw herself at his feet, he was very wrong.

She also doubted he expected much simpering. He might not know much about her, but he ought to know that was not her way.

"I did some figuring while I was riding around." She glanced around her, then slowly returned her gaze to him. "You've been at the Longhorn one month. Exactly one month yesterday, as a matter of fact. We've been together twice. I suppose you understand what I mean by together."

He nodded, continuing to stare at her from beneath the low brim. She had his complete attention, the way she usually did when they were lying side by side.

Only now they were standing. And she felt more in control.

"How much longer do you plan on being around?" she asked.

"What's your point, Maddie?"

"It's not a difficult question. How much longer will you bivouac on the Longhorn?"

Was he gritting his teeth? It certainly looked so.

"My orders are open-ended. As long as it takes to make sure the Strip is safe."

"It will never be completely safe."

"So I ask you the same thing. How much longer will you stay in this godforsaken place?"

"The rest of my life."

"That might not be so long. You ought to be back in New Orleans."

"Never."

"That's a long time."

"I know. But there's nothing for me there. Not now."

An awkward silence fell between them.

Maddie turned down a different path. "What if I told you I never wanted you to touch me again?"

He looked at her for a long time before he spoke. "I would ask if you meant it."

She crossed her arms across her chest and stroked up and down on one arm. "I'm trying to be as completely honest with you as I can." *As honest as I dare.* "I don't know what I want. We said harsh things to each other by the creek, but that did not stop us from . . . being together last night. What we did was wrong in the eyes of most people. Not that I care what people think. I gave that up a long time ago. Except where your men are concerned. I don't want them laughing at me behind my back. I don't want you talking to them about me."

"Do you think that is what I would do?"

"I don't know. I don't know you very well, no more than you really know me."

"Then you'll just have to trust me to honor you when you're not around. I told you once before that I would."

"And when I am present? Will you honor me then?"

"Of course."

"I meant when we're alone. No witnesses. Just you and me."

He thumbed his hat to the back of his head. His eyes burned with a familiar light. She wanted to jerk the brim back in place. Only then could she breathe.

"No promises there. Unless by honor, you mean this."

He took her in his arms so fast, she had no chance to turn and run. Her hands fell to her sides, and a sense of helplessness swept over her, of inevitability. When he kissed her, she felt no inclination to do anything but kiss him back.

They parted, as if by mutual consent. But he stayed so close, she could count the tiny lines edging his eyes.

"While I was riding this morning, I kept wondering if you would be wanting an apology when you saw me," he said. "I barged in on you last night and I left without saying good-bye."

"You didn't apologize after the first time."

"Last night seemed different."

"Less spontaneous."

"Something like that."

It had been different in other ways, too. She had been different, and both of them knew it. A new fear struck her. What if he understood the truth of how she felt?

She would have died on the spot rather than have him catch even a hint of her love.

Backing away, she kicked at a rock and sent it flying. "You say one word about being sorry, and you'll find I can use that rifle I carry with me."

His mouth twitched. He wasn't a smiling man, but he almost smiled now.

"Maybe I'm wrong about you. Maybe you don't belong in New Orleans."

He stepped toward her. She raised a hand.

"Don't get any ideas, Dan. You kissed me once. That will have to be enough."

"One kiss is never enough for us."

"Please don't talk that way. I'm having a hard time not feeling cheap. Or at least thinking that's how you regard me."

The smile in his eyes died. He started to speak, but she shook off whatever he planned to say.

"I was worried about seeing you today, too, thinking about how awkward it might be. We got over the awkwardness. Now we're going to have to get over the urge to paw each other every time we're alone. I've got years to travel through and so do you. They don't run along the same path. Both of us know it. You go about your business and I'll go about mine. If we're together again, then we are. If we're not, that's something we'll both live with."

She put as much finality in her voice as she could. When she turned to mount Sunset, she wondered if he would come after her. He could grab her right now, tell her he would go down any path she chose, that he would follow her for the rest of his life because nothing else held any value for him anymore.

But he kept his distance. He did not say a single word. He had no idea how he broke her heart.

Over the next few days she did not see him often, and when she did, they were never alone.

The man she saw most often was Jason Leigh. He was as friendly as ever, though a little more reserved than he had been in the past. She knew exactly why.

A couple of times she caught Dan watching her as she talked to the lieutenant. He had a way about him that could wall off anything he was thinking or feeling. All he did was watch, then look away.

Sergeant Wilcox continued to mend, though Maddie thought he required an overabundance of Helen's attention to do so. She and the woman did not have another private talk like the one in which they had revealed glimpses into their respective pasts.

They were both essentially private women. Maddie decided they had told all they could and were now regretting that maybe they had said too much.

Owen did not return. He had been gone for as long as three weeks before, but somehow this time seemed different. She suspected that Helen was involved, but she did not know how. She didn't know if Helen suspected the same thing.

The vaqueros completed the barn, and Carlos announced that they were riding out to look for a band of wild mustangs that were in the area.

"You've seen them?" Maddie asked.

"The men feel the hoofbeats in the ground."

"I ought to go with you."

She could see he did not like the idea at all.

"I would consider it a great honor if you would trust me to capture fine mares and a stallion who will bring many colts and fillies to your remuda."

He had a very diplomatic way of saying he would rather she stayed at the ranch and kept out of his way. In that respect, he was a lot like Dan.

"Will you show me sometime how to capture them?"

"Such will be another honor."

The day after they left, she moved the milk cow to the shelter of the barn and introduced Sunset and Dependable to their respective stalls. In celebration of the move, the soldiers who were not out on patrol were invited to a dinner of roasted venison and potatoes. The meat came from a deer Wilcox had shot while he was out practicing the use of his injured arm. In gratitude for the nursing he had received, he slaughtered his game and offered everything, even the hide, to Helen.

Because of the cramped conditions in the house, they ate outside around a low fire. The sky was cloudless. Maddie watched the sun spread itself into a red-gold band against the horizon. She watched the first stars poke through the gray-blue sky. She watched the men stack their plates when they were done. She studied the dust on her boots.

She looked everywhere but at Dan, who sat

on his heels across the dying fire and ate in silence. He was in his shirtsleeves. His collar was unbuttoned. If she looked close enough, she could see the brown skin that pulled tight across his throat.

She tried very hard not to look.

She had taken the plates inside and was returning to look around for more when he stopped her at the front door. How he managed to get her alone when there were so many others close by, she did not know. It was a talent he had. He had not used it for more than two weeks. She wondered why he chose to use it tonight.

He kept a distance of two feet between them.

"The sergeant is pretty much healed," he said. "We'll be riding out again tomorrow."

Her heart dropped, but she kept her voice light.

"I don't suppose you know where you're going or how long you'll be gone."

"We're going north to begin with, but after that the tracks take us where they will. As for time, it could be weeks."

"Of course. Take care."

"Don't go riding out alone, Maddie. With the vaqueros and Owen gone, you women need to stay close to the house."

His advice rankled, not because it was bad, but because she had wanted to hear something else. She was wearing her hair loose tonight and she had put on a dress. He had not given a single indication that he noticed.

She flipped back her hair. "Are you leaving the lieutenant to watch over us?"

"Do you want me to?"

"Until this moment, I hadn't thought about it one way or the other. The nights can get lonely here. He would help to pass the time."

"Is that what he did before while I was gone? I must ask the lieutenant how he managed it."

"Why don't you ask me?"

"All right." His voice was low, barely audible, and she felt a tingle down her spine at no more than the sound of it. "You tell me how he does it."

"He looks at me. He talks to me. He smiles and occasionally he even laughs. A few minutes ago he even told me I looked lovely tonight."

She lied. He hadn't said a word about her appearance. But he had looked.

Dan halved the space between them.

"When you walked out, you don't know how close you came to being thrown over my shoulder and carried into the woods."

She stared at his lips. "Is that the same as being called lovely? Somehow I don't think so."

He reached out and touched her hair.

She did something she never should have done. She grabbed his hand and kissed the palm. Then she dropped it as if it were on fire.

She was on fire. He was going away again,

and she burned with fear and lust, too far gone to put a more subtle name to what she felt.

She turned from him, but he whirled her back around to face him. He kissed her long and hard, thrusting his hands into her hair, holding her head in place, taking her lips as his, giving her no choice but to kiss him the way he was kissing her.

When he broke the kiss, he rested his forehead against hers and she counted his heavy breaths.

"Take care, Maddie. We're riding out before dawn. I won't see you again until we return."

He left quickly, before she could answer, before she could tell him to take care, too. She stood in the twilight swaying from the dizziness of wanting and worrying, one emotion no stronger than the other, the combination of the two almost lethal in the way they drove her to despair.

The next morning she rose early to watch from a distance as the soldiers broke camp. She stood at the edge of the trees, keeping to the shadows, and followed Dan with her eyes, absorbing every movement, every turn of his head, every spoken command.

They rode away fast, and she watched the dust in their wake until it settled back upon the dry ground. When daylight came, she rode out to her crop of corn to harvest whatever she could, then went back in to clean the cobs and grind the kernels into meal.

Two days later Carlos returned with a dozen mustang mares, two of them full-bellied with new life, and a magnificent white stallion who kicked down a portion of the corral and had to be tightly hobbled while the damage was repaired.

With admiration, she watched as the men tamed the wildness from the mares, using gentle firmness instead of whips and spurs, gradually bringing them to submission. They left the stallion and the two pregnant mares alone.

A week after Dan had ridden away, she told Carlos it was time to go after the Longhorns.

"This time I'm riding with you."

He did not give her an argument.

Next day, over the protests of Leigh and the two soldiers, she, Carlos, and two of the vaqueros headed southeast toward the brush country where the Longhorns could most readily be found. The lone remaining vaquero would remain at the ranch to ride herd on the mustangs when they were let out of the corral to graze.

The stallion was kept penned in, with feed and water brought to him.

The destination Maddie had chosen, after conferring with Carlos, was the public land that bordered the Longhorn along its southern rim. There, thousands of unbranded cattle were waiting to be caught and claimed. On the spot they would brand them, castrate the calves, then drive the herd to their new home.

She could not register them at the county seat, Dimmitt County being thus far without such a luxury. But they would be hers, according to legislation newly passed in Austin.

Maddie had done some investigating of the Longhorns during those dark days in San Antonio when she had been struggling with grief over her child, thinking of Will, arranging to travel on. She had learned all she could about the stock she planned to capture and raise, and the markets where she might offer them for sale.

Longhorns, she had discovered, were the descendants of Spanish cattle brought in a hundred years or more before and the more recent English breeds. The interbreeding had occurred while their owners were away fighting for the Confederacy. They were mean beasts, truly wild, but they would be the basis for her holdings.

Chapter Seventeen

From out of the thicket, the bull stared at Maddie with round black eyes. She could swear fire was coming from his nostrils. Three scant feet separated them. She was on foot. She was without her gun.

He was long of leg, brown, and round-bellied. An L-shaped horn extended from each side of his narrow head, their points sharp as knife tips. Her only weapon was a lariat. Throughout the past week on the trail she had been practicing her roping, carrying the lariat everywhere she went.

Unfortunately, she still wasn't very good.

"Nice bull," she said soothingly, but the animal was not impressed. The sound of her shaky voice terrified her all the more, especially when she viewed his indifference.

He lowered his head. The points were aimed at her. He pawed the ground. She let out a circle of rope and held it in front of him, her gloved hands moving slowly, awkwardly. The muscles of his powerful shoulders bunched. Simultaneously, she screamed, threw her hat at him, and jumped aside. He thundered past, shaking the ground. The hat went flying, the rope caught around the horns, and she found herself bouncing over the ground after him, dragged over rocks and cactus, her legs in front of her, bootheels leaving ridges in the dirt.

She was saved by a tree. The bull went one way, she went the other, and somehow the rope tangled and pulled him up short. He bellowed, waved his mighty head in the air, but he could not break free.

A lifetime too late she let go of the lariat. Hunched over, she fought for breath. The more she breathed, the steadier her heartbeat became, and the more she hurt.

Carlos and the two vaqueros rode toward the tree. More ropes flew, and the bull was secured. Carlos dropped to her side.

"Señorita Hardin, are you all right?"

She took a moment to answer. She was covered in dirt, her bottom was stuck like a porcupine with cactus needles, and where she wasn't stuck, she was stone-bruised. Over the next few days she would be so sore, she would not be able to move without wanting to cry.

But she had the bull she had not expected to capture, nothing on either her or the beast was broken, and even the pain was encouraging. It proved she was alive.

She grinned. "Yep."

Hovering over the captured animal, the two vaqueros glanced sideways at her. They must think she was crazy. Carlos knew better. He flashed her a smile, his teeth white against his brown skin, his dark eyes bright with what she decided had to be admiration.

"On this ride," he said, "we were not going after a bull."

"I saw him and changed my mind."

He knew she lied. She had been in the thicket to relieve herself. Thank goodness she had finished her business. The bull had surprised her as much as she had surprised him.

"He will sire many fine steers," Carlos said.

"I certainly hope so. He needs to get something out of being caught by a woman."

One of the vaqueros drew near and held out her hat. It sported a hole through the side where the bull's horn had pierced it. He had been aiming for her gut. She took the hat, cradled it against her breast, and allowed herself a small shiver.

Her bottom began to smart mightily. Shaking the top layer of dust from the hat, she

Evelyn Rogers

plopped it on her head. Carlos helped her to stand. She would have thanked him, but she was too busy groaning in pain.

"Does the señorita wish her horse?" Carlos asked.

"I would prefer not to sit for a while. Camp's not far. I can walk."

Walking wasn't easy, but it was better than bouncing against the fancy leather-and-silver saddle her foreman had purchased for her months before.

A torturous hour later, she was lying on her stomach in the shade near the campfire, listening to the sizzle of the branding iron against the bull's flank, hearing his answering bellow, feeling not the least bit of sympathy for him. Carlos had already talked about the pen that would be built for him and, in broken English and with much embarrassment, discussed the manner in which he would be bred to the cows.

The bull, which she promptly dubbed Brasado, Spanish for the brush country that had been his home, was headed for a good life.

The return ride was held up two days while she alternately pulled cactus needles out of her rear, practiced stretching her sore muscles, and, at last, gingerly lowered herself into the saddle and rode cautiously around the herd.

On the third day she pronounced herself ready to go home.

It was only then that she allowed herself another torture: worry about Dan. She admitted that she had been lucky thus far not to have suffered Indian attacks or brushes with the outlaws and bandidos that roamed the Strip. But he might not have been so lucky. If he wasn't, if something terrible had happened to him, nothing else mattered. She could celebrate the success of the roundup only after he was with her to celebrate, too.

She thought about the ways he would choose, the details of which kept her from losing her mind. She could hope that her bruises were healed enough for her to respond with half the fervor she had shown before. The one thing she would not have was the same suppleness. She had never felt stiffer in her life.

Carlos estimated that with the cattle slowing them down, the ride back to the Longhorn would take five days. One of the vaqueros rode on ahead to let the others know they were coming and to give orders for Brasado's pen. He returned to report that there had been no news of the soldiers. Maddie told herself that was not necessarily bad, but she did not believe her own assessment.

When they were on her land but still a day's journey from the house, the second vaquero rode in to report their arrival, returning at night with the same news: no word had been received concerning Dan and the patrol.

Maddie felt near panic. Until now she had been patient, worried but outwardly calm. No more. She could not face her small stone house without Dan nearby. It mattered not that he wouldn't be there for long. She wasn't being reasonable, but she was a woman in love.

"Tomorrow morning you and the others ride on in, Carlos. Owen's still gone. I need to do some hunting if we're going to have anything to eat."

Carlos protested.

"I'm all right. I'm sure Lieutenant Leigh and the soldiers have kept a sharp watch over the Longhorn. I'll bet there aren't Apaches within fifty miles."

He continued to protest.

"I'm not going to take long. I'm a good shot. And you know what I can do with a lariat. When I have to, I can lasso a bull. If I get lucky, I could be back before you."

They faced one another on horseback. He said a few things in Spanish; she answered him in French, neither understanding precisely what the other said, but at last she won. She was the boss, and he had to concede.

He and the other vaqueros were not an hour gone when she ran out of luck.

The gobble of wild turkeys drew her into the thicket. She guided Sunset slowly through the brush, riding deeper into the shadows until the open land over which she had been traveling was far behind.

The click of a trigger behind her sent her grabbing for her rifle.

A gun roared, and a bullet kicked up dust on the ground six inches from Sunset's front right hoof. The horse reared, and Maddie fought to get him under control.

"Hold still, lady, and no one will get hurt."

She turned her head toward the speaker.

"The gunshot must 'a deafened you a mite. I said hold still."

She looked back at Sunset's twitching ears and did as he asked; all the while her mind raced as she tried to figure out whether the man was alone.

She did not have to figure for long.

"Gawddamn it, shoot her and be done with it. That's a fine horse and saddle she's got. I've done enough walking over the past week to last 'til Judgment Day."

"That ain't no way to talk in front of a pretty lady. Besides, I done promised she won't get hurt."

The way he said *lady* made her skin crawl.

Listening to footsteps coming up on her, she tried not to breath. She cast her eyes down to the ground to her right and saw a pair of worn boots and tattered trousers moving past her. When the man stood in front of her, she dared to raise her eyes and look at him.

He was a stranger, short and scrawny, the rest of his clothes as worn as the trousers, his eyes dark and beady and hard as rocks in a narrow, grizzled face. Mostly what she looked at was the pistol he was pointing at her.

Another man, bulkier, taller, but just as worn and dirty, came up on her left. He was carrying a shotgun the way he would carry a satchel, loose at his side and careless, but the eyes that studied her were just as dark and just as hard as his companion's.

The pair could be twenty, or they could be forty. She couldn't tell. However old they were, they had been riding a long, hard trail for most of their lives.

The men stood in front of Sunset and grinned. The grins sent a stab of fear to her gut.

"So what d'ya think, Abner?" the first speaker, the small man, said.

Abner spat through the gap in his mottled front teeth. His eyes left her face for only a minute, to take in the rest of her. He scratched at the belly hanging over his gut.

"She'll do."

"Do, hell. She's prime."

"She's trouble, Jack. Ain't I told you a thousand times, we don't need woman trouble when we're running from the law?"

Maddie eased her hand a quarter inch toward her rifle.

Jack pulled back the hammer on his gun. "Get the rifle. She won't be no trouble. Leastwise, nothing that won't be worth it."

Maddie's terror took control. Pulling back on the reins, she ducked as Sunset reared. A gunshot roared over her head, and ruthless hands tugged her from the saddle. She landed hard on her back and started kicking and flailing out with her fists.

Abner dropped his bulk onto her, smashing his bottom against her twisted arms, and back-handed her across the cheek.

Her head reeled and her eyes blurred from the pain. Worse, all the aches from her recent encounter with the bull returned in excruciating torment.

The outlaw put his face close to hers. His rank breath made her want to puke.

"You show too much spirit, lady, and you'll find yourself dead."

She closed her eyes and stopped breathing. She was probably already dead. She just wasn't free yet of the pain.

He rolled off her and jerked her to her feet. Jack had caught Sunset's reins and threw her rope to his partner. After binding her arms in front of her, Abner towed her through the thicket the way Brasado had been led. She stumbled, but righted herself.

"Camp ain't far," Jack said, as if she would be soothed by the information.

She tried not to think what would happen to her after they reached their destination. The cruelty of it all was more than any woman should have to bear. This time she would not have the blessing of unconsciousness. Jack and Abner would like to hear her screams.

Maddie had a hard time staying on her feet. For the first time in her life, after all that had happened to her, she truly gave up hope.

"She did what?"

Dan was practically roaring.

Carlos shrugged and lapsed into Spanish. Dan had picked up enough of the language to translate his response.

"She is a stubborn woman. She would not listen to my warnings."

They were standing by the Longhorn corral. Dan had ridden in, expecting to see Maddie, planning on exactly how he would greet her, wondering exactly how she would greet him.

Now he found she was out hunting for supper. In the woods, alone. It always worried him when she rode out by herself. For reasons he couldn't put into words, he was worried far more today.

Hell, he was ready to tear up a tree.

He looked past Carlos to his lieutenant.

"What have you got to say for yourself?"

"We followed them the whole time they were gone," Leigh said, shifting his eyes from right to left, up and down, anywhere but at his captain. "They didn't know we were there. We didn't want Miss Hardin to feel hemmed in. We missed it when she dropped back and left the herd."

Dan cursed some more. When he rode up a

half hour ago, he had felt bone weary. All the weariness had fled.

"See that I have a fresh mount," he barked at Leigh.

"I'm riding with you," Wilcox said from behind him.

Dan wanted to protest. The sergeant had not totally regained his stamina since being shot. After the long ride back to the Longhorn, he was drained of color.

But Wilcox was a stubborn soldier. It was one of the things Dan admired most about him.

"Leigh, against my better judgment, I'm taking you, too. Along with the men I left here. Be ready to ride in ten minutes. No, make that five. Carlos, you take us to where you last saw her, then come on back here. Too many of us, we'll be shooting at one another."

"Besides," Leigh said, "she's probably all right. Miss Hardin is a resourceful woman."

"You'd better hope you're right, Lieutenant. She's resourceful, all right, but she's still a woman. That's something she sometimes forgets."

He looked past the young officer to see Helen Clark waving to them from the back of the house.

"I've got fresh coffee ready and waiting. Come on up and help yourselves."

A quarter hour later Dan, Wilcox, Leigh, and

the two soldiers headed out toward the south, following the trail set by Carlos. He took them no more than a couple of miles, then gestured toward the thicket that acted like a fence to the east.

"We last saw her riding in this place," he said.

Dan studied the landscape. He listened to the rustle of the hot wind and to the call of a bird. He looked at the cloudless expanse of sky. No buzzards. He cursed the fact that he had thought to look.

When Carlos had gone, he gave terse instructions to the men.

"Spread out and go in slow. Chances are nothing has happened to her. She's probably in there cleaning a couple of wild turkeys. We don't want to startle her. She's a good shot. She's liable to put a bullet between your eyes, not knowing who you are."

He didn't believe a word he said, and the men knew it. But no one gave him any argument.

Dan took the center path. He rode in slowly, studying the ground and the surrounding shrubs, looking for trampled earth, broken branches, anything to show that she had ridden this way. A hundred yards into the brush, he found signs of a struggle, the cartridge of a bullet, footprints, imprints of pounding hooves. His blood ran cold.

Dropping to the ground, leading his mount, he followed the tracks left by three pairs of boots, two down at the heel, one worn set deeper, indicating a heavy man. Two bastards had her. With cold efficiency, he checked his pistol, loosening it in its holster, then did the same to the rifle strapped to the front of his saddle.

There was no way he could summon help without alerting Maddie's captors, and so he walked on, carefully placing one boot in front of the other, moving silently through the brush and the scattering of oak and mesquite.

He heard them before he saw them. He picked out two gruff voices. No woman's voice. Not at first. Then he heard her insistent, "No."

Whatever she was saying *no* to had not terrified her into silence. She was alive. She was strong.

He felt his own fear fall from him. He would do her little good if he let emotion control him now. He was a fighting man. He had been riding for weeks doing damned little of it. It was time he got busy and earned his pay.

Tethering the horse, he draped his saber over the saddle horn, slipped the rifle from its scabbard, and went to save her. As best he could make out, her captors were grumbling, arguing back and forth, while she held her silence. When he came upon the three of them, he pulled up short, keeping to the shadows. She was sprawled on the ground, her hands tied in front of her with a thick rope, the end of the rope wrapped around a tree.

Two men stood over her, the scrawny one punching his fatter companion in the stomach to make a point. Dan got the drift of their conversation. They were arguing over who would take her first. The prospect of enjoying their spoils had them so engrossed, they did not hear as Dan crept to the edge of the clearing.

But Maddie saw him. Her eyes widened and she shook her head twice, fast, then looked away, as if he were not there.

Smart woman. She did not give him away.

He stepped into the clearing, the pistol in one hand, the rifle in the other.

"Put your hands up," he ordered.

The men whirled.

"Gawddamn," one of them shouted.

They went for their guns. Dan caught one in the stomach with the pistol and the other in the heart with a fast rifle shot. The front of the man's chest exploded. The other gripped his stomach, bent forward, and dropped to the ground.

The shots reverberated in the woods and shook the trees. Dan went over and kicked at the two bodies. It was an unnecessary precaution. Both men had died before they hit the dirt.

Dropping his weapons, he kneeled beside Maddie and stroked her hair. Except for one reddened cheek that was beginning to bruise, her face was pale, her eyes stark with disbelief that he was there. A shudder went through him when he thought of what had happened to her and, worse, what had almost happened.

Then he put himself to the task of untying the rope. He was barely aware of the sound of thrashing in the thicket as one by one, the men he had brought with him rode into the clearing.

Wilcox was the first to get there; Leigh was the last. By the time all were crowded into the small clearing, he was standing with Maddie at his side, his arm around her holding her close, the echoes of the shots dissipated in the afternoon air as if they had never been.

"It's over," he said. "She's all right. Take the bodies out of here and bury them. See if there's any identification. I doubt you'll find much."

"Abner and Jack," Maddie said shakily.

Dan stared at her.

She blinked her eyes and looked away from him, from the bodies, from the men who surrounded her.

"That's all I know. They called themselves Abner and Jack. Abner's the big one. They were running from the law."

She fell silent and closed her eyes, her body leaning against his for support. She did not say another word, not until the bodies were dragged into the thicket, not while anyone other than Dan was near.

When they were alone, she looked up at him.

"You're all right," she said. "You made it back."

"In a lot better shape than you, Maddie. Let me know if you're too weak for this."

When he kissed her, she did not push him away. He held her against him, supporting her lest she fall. When he lifted his lips from hers, she smiled up at him and fainted in his arms.

Chapter Eighteen

Maddie opened her eyes to the sight of Dan leaning close, his face unshaven, smudges of dirt and sweat across his brow, his eyes bloodshot and sunken.

He was the most beautiful creature, man or beast, that she had ever seen, although, at the moment, he was looking more like a beast. She did not mind. Right now he was *her* beast and all was well.

On the edge of her consciousness ugly memories lurked, but for just a while she held off reality. Dan was all the reality she needed. Dan, alive, warm, well. Stirring slightly, she smiled at him and took assessment of her surroundings. She was lying on thick blankets in the shade of a live oak tree, its branches blocking out much of the sky and all of the bright sun.

And of course, Dan was kneeling beside her and bending close.

"What happened?" she asked. "The last thing I remember is that you were here and holding me and then . . . nothing."

"You passed out on me. Glad to see you come to."

She managed a smile. Never in her life had she been so happy, but never, she was forced to admit, had she been so sore.

He lifted her head and held a cup of water to her lips. She drank, then drank some more, suddenly struck by a thirst that matched her pain.

He set the cup aside, then turned his full attention to her. The bloodshot eyes turned hard, and his lips flattened into a grimace. Maddie shuddered. The reality she had been holding off was approaching fast.

"I ought to turn you over my knee and give you a good spanking."

She thought of the cactus needles and bruises from the rocks where the bull had dragged her in his last run for freedom.

"I'd rather you didn't."

"Then I'll give you a tongue-lashing."

Even as he said the words, she saw the tightness around his mouth begin to soften.

"Can't you think of anything better to do with your tongue?"

"I can think of it, all right. There are times I can't think of anything else."

"Talk's cheap, Captain."

"It's costing me a lot right now."

"Meaning?"

"Meaning I would rather be doing a lot more than talking. I just don't think you're up to it. Besides, I'm not feeling kindly toward you at this moment."

"Yes, you are. Let's see what I'm up to."

She tried to sit up, but the world moved in and out of focus. Dan gave her the needed support, but she had to hold onto his sleeves to remain even halfway upright.

He kissed the rope burns at her wrists, then stroked her cheek, so lightly it was like being touched by a feather, but she still felt the touch with something besides pure pleasure.

"They hit you."

"It's the only thing they had time to do before you got there."

"I'll bet you were cussing them out at the time."

The ugliness moved so close, it clawed at her mind.

"It's hard to remember what was going on at the time. I think I was trying to get to my gun."

He rubbed at his eyes and wiped his brow. "You could have been killed."

"It's a consideration I have not ignored."

"You should have thought about it before you rode off on your own."

"I didn't realize it then, or I would have."

He picked up her hat from beside the blanket and poked a finger through the hole in the side.

"How about this?"

"The bull did that."

"The bull?"

"Maybe I ought to tell you about that later."

"Maybe you should."

He fell silent, for which she was grateful, if criticism was all he planned to level at her.

She studied the gauntness of his face. "I'm not the only one who's been through some hard times."

"I guess we both ought to be glad we're alive."

Their eyes locked, and she saw the anger and the concern heat to something entirely different, something she was feeling low in her stomach, something that was causing her heart to pound.

They were all physical reactions she understood very well. She had been threatened with a terrible harm, worse than in New Orleans, though the ending had been far better. This time Dan had rescued her. The least she could do was show how grateful she was.

"You want to start out for the ranch now?" he asked.

"No."

"You've been roughed up a bit," he said. "Surely you're hurting."

"Not so much."

She wondered if she would regret the lie. No, she decided as she dropped her gaze to his lips. She touched his bristled cheek. "The beard's not so heavy this time."

"I shaved a day or two ago, I forget when."

"Did you have any encounters this time? Was anyone hurt?"

"No, thank the Lord. The worst part was the frustration. We seemed to get to areas right after the Apaches had been there. They're stealing cattle and horses, then moving them across the river. Somebody's buying them. They don't have use for all that stock. But they do have use for money. And guns. That's probably how they're being paid."

"Who supplying them? The Mexicans?"

"I don't think so. I've got ideas, but nothing I can prove. I've sent a dispatch to General Sheridan reporting what's going on. I've asked for some information that may help."

He looked pensive for a moment, lost in thought, lost to her.

"So we both have problems," she said.

His expression hardened. She should have kept quiet.

"Some are worse than others. The most excitement we had was when we got back."

"Don't start getting angry again."

"It's just that I don't know what to do with you."

"Keep thinking. You'll come up with something."

"Here? Now? I'm not such a brute."

"Then just hold me and kiss me."

She knew him well enough to understand that he wouldn't keep to simply holding and kissing for very long.

He didn't. With his lips covering hers and one arm holding her in a gentle embrace, he touched her breast.

He broke the kiss. "Does that hurt?"

She shook her head. He had picked one of the few places on her body that was uninjured.

"Try the other one," she said.

He did.

"Still fine," she reported.

He moved to her stomach, circling his palm across her abdomen. "And here?"

She caught an edge in his voice.

"Are you asking if I'm hurting?"

"Not exactly. Do you have anything to tell me I ought to know?"

She held still for a moment, experiencing a different kind of pain.

"I'm not expecting a child, if that's what is bothering you."

"Not yet, you're not."

Not ever. Through his probing, he had found an aching part of her, but not with his hands. His words had twisted her heart.

She put her arms around his neck. "Don't stop what you're doing. You make me forget."

What she said was true. But he also made her remember. Too much, far too much.

He eased his fingers between her legs and rubbed against the seam of her trousers. She let out an involuntary sigh. With that simple touch, she truly did forget everything but how much she loved him and how joyful she was to have him in her arms.

Moving slowly and then more quickly, they explored one another, most of their touching done through their clothes, but finally the clothing became too much of an impediment. They stripped from the waist down, each helping the other, though Maddie did not object to Dan's doing most of the work.

When at last he settled himself on top of her, she ordered him to go fast. Pain and pleasure were so mixed in her, she knew she would cry out. She wanted him to believe it was a cry of pure ecstasy.

He moved his body in and out of her.

"Don't tease me," she said.

"Does it feel good?"

"It feels good."

"Then I'm not teasing. I've never been more serious in my life."

Biting her lip, she wrapped her legs around him and pinned him inside.

"Fast," she ordered.

He started to protest, and then she felt his whole body stiffen and the movements grow quick, the tempo increasing to match her own throbs. She climaxed first, but he was soon to follow. He rested himself on top of her and she felt the shudders as strongly as she felt her own.

She would have liked to hold on to him forever. Today, forever lasted a few sweet minutes, and then he rolled over to lie beside her and stare at her profile until she thought she would scream.

From start to finish, their lovemaking had taken no more than a quarter hour, the length of time some couples might need to get through the amenities of a friendly greeting.

But she and Dan were not friends. She did not know what they were.

"Marry me."

Maddie was certain she had heard wrong. She rubbed at her head. "I must be worse off than I thought."

"You heard right. I asked you to marry me."

She dared to look at him, but only for an instant. He wasn't grinning, and he looked as sane as ever, if maybe a couple of degrees more intent.

She stared through the overhead branches and on to the clear blue sky. He frightened her. What was he doing? Did he understand how she would have sacrificed all that she owned, all of her old dreams, to know that he was serious?

But Maddie was not used to getting anything close to what she wanted. She knew that the things she valued in life did not come easily. They came with a terrible price.

"Why?" she asked, then added a quick, "Don't answer that yet. I'd rather be dressed. I'd rather both of us be dressed. I can think better that way."

She rolled away from him and managed to stand, doing a pretty good job of keeping her winces to herself. Too, with a little shifting and turning, she hid her shaking hands.

"My God," he said in a none too flattering voice. "What the devil happened to your backside?"

It was not a romantic response to the view she offered of her nudity.

"Does it look bad?"

"Not bad. Never bad. But it's an interesting color. Or I should say colors."

"The bull."

"Again? He got your hat and he got your—"

"He got my attention. But I got him."

She dressed as fast as she could manage, hearing nothing but the rustle of clothing and the natural sounds of the woods.

Marry me.

He gave no indication that he planned to repeat the suggestion. He must have changed his mind. Ardor cooling, he was probably regretting having said the words. She came close to a sigh of relief. Dealing with disappointment was more familiar to her than dealing with hope.

Her braid was a mess. Quickly she undid it, knowing the crinkly look of her hair, combing it with her fingers as best she could, smoothing it against her shoulders.

At last, taking a deep breath, she turned to face him. They stood on either side of the folded blanket. Like her, he was dressed.

"Marry me."

She took a deep, steadying breath. "You haven't told me why you asked."

"After what just happened, you can't figure it out?"

He did not sound like a man who was about to declare his undying devotion.

"I've had a bad day. I'm not thinking clearly."

"I never do when I'm around you. You yourself once told me we can't keep our hands off one another. You said you're not with child, but you could be after today."

"No."

"Be sensible. Of course you could. You're a good woman, Maddie. We'll be good together. I still own land back in Kentucky. You once told me to go back there. I'm asking you to go with me. We can have a good life."

"You're asking me to leave the Longhorn."

"You will anyway, eventually. If you don't, something will happen to you here. It already has. Today. It's not an isolated incident. You've been lucky nothing like it has happened before."

He started across the blanket. She held up her hands.

"Let's just talk, please. I can't think when you're close."

"I know."

"Weeks ago, when you first got here, you were very angry with me, though you pretended to be otherwise. The anger returned when we were by the creek. You cursed what you called the southern cause. Why aren't you angry now?"

"I changed. I quit trying to blame you for my brother's death."

His honesty stunned her. She knew the anguish that lay behind his words.

"I thought he must have died. Nothing else could have hurt you so much. Was he killed in battle?"

"Such glory was denied him. He died in Andersonville."

Tears came to her eyes. She had heard about the hellish Confederate prison, about the squalor, the inhumanity of the captors, the thousands of Yankee prisoners who had perished in the midst of its wretchedness.

His beloved Tom had been one of those thousands.

Her heart caught in her throat. "I'm sorry, Dan. Truly sorry."

"The news killed my parents."

"You lost them, too."

"The world became too cruel for them."

"And you blamed me."

"I blamed everyone in the South. For a while. After you left New Orleans so suddenly and I found out about the death of your fiancé, it didn't take me long to figure out what you had been doing."

"What are you talking about?"

"Let's not go into this now."

"There's no time better. You said you figured everything out."

But how could he? Had he really known she was expecting a child? He could not be standing here like this, talking about blame, and all the while carry with him the knowledge of the assault on her. Dan was not that kind of man. Or so she had believed.

It had been wrong of her to consider trapping him into marriage. But she had been desperate. Surely he could understand.

"There were lots of spies in the South. You were doing what you thought was right."

His words blocked everything else from her mind. She could do nothing but stare at him.

"The questions you asked, the friendly way you had when we were together. It all fell into place. And then, when your fiancé died and you had no one to receive your messages, or maybe you just did not care to send them anymore, you left. I was the enemy. It was something I had allowed myself to forget."

"What if I deny your accusation? What if I tell you you're wrong?"

"Do it. If I have a choice, I would rather believe otherwise. Tell me you weren't trying to use me. Let me hear you say the words."

But of course she couldn't. She had been trying to use him, but not in the way he thought.

"Do it," he said again.

"I can't."

"It's all right. I don't care anymore, Maddie. I understand."

"You forgive me."

"If you insist on putting it like that."

She turned from him and squeezed her eyes closed to her tears. His forgiveness was a knife in her heart.

Dan knew nothing about her. Nothing at all.

She felt the same utter despair and loss that she had felt when Grace was taken from her. Never had she thought to feel such pain again. She felt it now.

Worse, a blanket of guilt enveloped her, a blanket woven of threads sharp as a razor's edge.

She ought to tell him the truth. He was trying to be honorable. He did not love her, but he was willing to give her his name. Because they were good together. Because she was a good woman, despite what he had figured out about her. Because she needed rescuing. Because he could not leave her alone.

Another woman might have found these reasons enough. But Maddie had been through too much, lost too much, to accept the life he offered. It was a life of lies, one that both of them would very much come to regret.

She wanted a man willing to sacrifice everything for her because he loved her and could not exist without her. What she got was *I don't care anymore.*

Her dream of a complete and abiding love was as foolish as her illusion about the Longhorn Ranch.

He feared she might carry his child. That, she could have told him, was impossible.

But she could not bring herself to tell him anything that would clear up his misconceptions about her. He would hate her for the real way she had tried to use him, he would pity her for her infertility, he could very well wonder whether she had in some way caused the young soldier to attack her, had given him hope she would accept his advances, the way he thought she had encouraged Jason Leigh.

"I can't marry you," she said.

"You'll change your mind. Don't answer me right away."

"I won't change my mind." She bit the inside of her mouth and welcomed the sharp pain. But it could not come close to what she felt when she turned to face him and looked into his eyes.

"We don't love each other, not in the way we should if we're to build a life together."

She felt him draw away from her, though he

did not move. Neither did he speak, and she went on.

"I'm not leaving the Longhorn. I've worked too hard to walk away. I know you don't understand, and I don't understand it completely myself. But I had a dream when I was a child, to be the equal of my brothers, to have what they had, to live the life they lived. I can do that only in Texas. If I die here, then that's the way it is."

In truth, she had already died inside. What he did not understand was that in remaining in the Nueces Strip, with its isolation, its drought, with its outlaws and Indians and absence of anything approaching civilization, she was not sacrificing anything.

She had nothing left to lose.

Over the next few days, Maddie and Dan were rarely alone, and when they were, they spoke only of the weather, of the cattle, the dying field of corn.

Dan was most animated when he viewed the mustangs Carlos and the vaqueros had brought back to the ranch. He paid particular attention to the white stallion, who had yet to be tamed.

One morning early, he took his saddle and walked down to the corral. Only the stallion was within its confines, the other horses having been let out to graze. The vaqueros, the soldiers, Maddie and Helen, all walked down the hill to see what he was going to do.

Taking off his uniform jacket, he tossed it over the fence along with the saddle, and with only a rope bridle in his hands, slipped through an opening in the fence. The stallion whinnied, eyed him nervously, and trotted around the perimeter. Dan talked low to him all the while, his words indistinguishable to the onlookers.

No one watched more carefully than the men who had captured the splendid animal. Except Maddie. Here was Dan as she had never seen him before, quietly confident, masterfully in control. And very, very much at home.

He walked and talked for over an hour, and gradually the stallion quit his pacing. Dan stood in front of him and looked him in the eye. The stallion bent his head as if to smell him, whinnied, backed away, then returned to smell him again.

The day wore on. No one left. Eventually Dan was able to get the hackamore over the stallion's head. Eventually he was able to lead him around the corral. Finally, he slid onto him, bareback. The horse bucked, but Dan stayed on.

Later, after he slid to the ground, he took a quick break for food and water, but the stallion was not so lucky. He returned to get the blanket from the fence, and then the saddle. Twilight was descending by the time he had the horse saddled and tolerating the weight of a rider.

When Dan at last dismounted and unbuckled the girth, easing the leather trappings and blanket to the ground, the mustang stood in the middle of the corral, head high, his pride unbroken though his spirit had been tamed to a man's will.

Dan slipped through the railings close to where Maddie stood. Around her she heard the vaqueros whispering excitedly in Spanish, and the soldiers set up a low cheer. But his attention was directed to her.

"That was beautiful, Dan."

"I'm a horseman, Maddie. It's all I've ever been."

He tossed his uniform coat over his shoulder. She watched as he walked up the hill, his gait strong and steady, though he must have been exhausted. He hadn't asked for an audience. She didn't think he particularly liked the fact that there had been witnesses to his remarkable feat. Having accomplished what he set out to do, he wanted to be alone.

She was filled with pride and with love for him, although he had never seemed so distant.

The next day Owen returned with Brutus and Caesar II. Shuffling up to the front of the house, trailed by horse and dog, he looked a little scruffier than when he'd left, thinner, more bleary-eyed, but otherwise unchanged.

"Welcome back," Maddie said, going out to meet him.

She wanted to ask him where he had been the past few weeks, but she knew he wouldn't answer.

"You've been missed around here," she said when he did not respond right away.

His bloodshot eyes shifted to the front door, where Helen was standing. "Don't know how long I'm staying."

"You're a drifter. I know. Drifters drift. But sometimes they find a reason to stay."

"Sometimes they find a reason to leave, too. A place gets too crowded, it's time to move on."

After another glance at Helen, he crawled beneath the wagon and fell asleep.

Before joining his master, Brutus came over and rubbed the side of his head with the ear against the leg of her trousers, as if he was honoring her with his good side, showing he could be polite. Like his master, he seemed thinner; he had definitely lost a few tufts of hair.

Helen carried food and water out for the dog, Maddie took charge of Caesar, and later she saw a canvas bag beside Owen that she assumed to be food. From Helen, she was sure.

As glad as she was to see Owen, his return did not lift her spirits. Like the soldiers, like Dan, he would be moving on.

On the same evening, she had another visitor. She had gone out to get water to wash the supper dishes. She saw a tall, broad figure riding toward her, slowly emerging from the dark into the spill of moonlight that fell across the front of the house.

She was vaguely aware of others joining her to see who it was.

Her heart began to quicken. It was the first time she had felt its strong beat since the terrible day when Dan had proposed.

She started running toward the visitor before he had finished dismounting. Tears streamed down her cheeks.

"Will," she cried.

Wrapping her arms around his middle, she burrowed her head against his chest and welcomed his comforting warmth.

Chapter Nineteen

Maddie had a thousand questions for Will. It took all her restraint to hold off while he took his carpetbag from behind the saddle's high cantle, handed the reins over to one of the soldiers who volunteered to care for his horse, then reluctantly accepted her offer to come inside her home.

"It's not much," Maddie said.

Will looked over the front facade. "It's built of stone. That's what you was told."

"It's the largest stone house in the county."

"Could be it's the onliest one."

"You figured it out as quickly as I did." She touched his arm, needing to know he was not an apparition. "I've missed you. You have no idea how much."

Helen met him at the door with a cup of coffee in her hand.

"I'll be taking this outside," he said.

"Nonsense," Helen said. "You'll come in and sit down. You carry a lot of weight, and you've been on the road. That's two reasons to sit. If you can think of a reason why you shouldn't, don't let me hear it."

"You heard her," Maddie said. "Around here no one argues with Helen Clark."

"I been in parts of Texas—Illinois, too, for that matter—where I wouldn't be invited inside."

"You haven't been on the Longhorn Ranch," Maddie said.

He followed Helen inside, continuing to watch her, and Maddie could see he was still uneasy.

Helen must have realized it, too. "I was born and bred in Alabama," she said, "but I never owned no one. Never wanted to. Except for some unfortunate marriage vows, no one ever owned me."

She dragged a cast-iron pot to the edge of the fire. "Sit there on the bench. I'll have you a plate of food shortly."

When he was seated, Maddie joined him, easing herself down gingerly, and looked him over with greater care. He was wearing a dark suit and shirt, both streaked with trail dust, and he had on boots, something she had not seen him wear before. There were lines of gray in his black hair, and he had picked up some lines in his face. He was thinner, too, but still massive, still powerful-looking enough to make most men step cautiously around him, no matter what color they were.

"Will came to the family when I was just a baby," she explained to Helen. "I've known him all my life."

"What she means is, her mama bought me and my sister, then set us free. Later, Cinda went north and married. I stayed on with Miss Maddie. Until she settled down here."

"How is Cinda? How are her boys?" Maddie asked.

"They're fine, jes' fine. Husband's fine, too. Got himself a good job in a lumber mill."

"And Illinois?"

"There're some good folk there, and some bad. Same as most places."

He was answering perfunctorily, as if where he had been held no importance in comparison to where he was now.

He looked around the room. His attention settled on the china-faced doll resting on the shelf over Maddie's bed.

"You still got it. I remember when your mama gave it to you. You was a happy child." He looked back at Maddie. "She'd flail you if she could see how you was dressing now and how you let the sun turn your skin all brown."

"Mama never touched me in anger."

"She was gentle, all right, but she could flail you with words."

"Without ever raising her voice."

"She had that way about her."

Loneliness welled in Maddie, so strong it almost spilled out in tears.

"I miss her, Will. And I've missed you." She took his hand. "It's been more than a year since you left San Antonio."

He looked at the hand holding his, at the blunt, short nails, the brown skin, the calluses.

"A long, hard year, it looks like."

"I don't mind the work. I love it. But it's as if my life has been divided in two separate parts, the years in New Orleans, the years after. You're the bridge between those two parts. You help me feel more like myself, as if I know who I am again. That probably doesn't make much sense, but it's the closest I can come to describing what's going on inside me right now."

"You're giving me a powerful lot of importance."

"Deservedly so. I'm happier than you can know that you're here. But I can't help wondering why. Did anything happen in Illinois? Anything bad?"

He shook his head, glanced at Helen, then looked quizzically at Maddie.

"Say what you're thinking," she said, trusting there was one topic he would avoid.

"I got to worrying. Something was telling me you might be needing ole Will."

"It was a long way to come just because of a worry."

"I weren't thinking of the distance. I come most of the way by stagecoach; then when I crossed into Texas, I got myself a horse. Took a while to get the hang of riding all day, but I got it. I come straight here, straight as I could."

The stubborn tears welled a little more, and her eyes blurred. She looked away. She did not want to cry. She did not want him to worry more than he already had.

Helen set a plate in front of him. "Leftover stew and cold biscuits. Leftovers all right?"

"I'm much obliged."

He ate fast and drank two cups of coffee. Maddie waited until he was done to continue her inquisition.

"How did you find me?"

"I had the general directions in my mind from when we was in San Antonio. A Señor Ramirez in Illusion pointed me on the exact trail. He said there was soldiers here looking for Apaches. He said they was led by a cap'n name of Kent."

"That's right, Will," said a voice at the door. "Dan Kent. It's good to see you again."

Maddie stiffened. For a few minutes, she had forgotten Dan—an impossible feat, she had thought. She tried to relax, tried to look unmoved for one imperative reason: Will was looking at her instead of at Dan. He already knew part of what was troubling her. He had been with her when she said good-bye to Grace.

If she showed any signs of distress, he would know it all.

Smiling, she glanced over her shoulder. "It's a nice surprise, isn't it, Will being here?"

"For a godforsaken, waterless hellhole in the middle of nowhere, the Longhorn draws a lot of people," Dan said. "Why do you suppose that is?"

Maddie tried to look innocent. "Because it's actually a beautiful land that offers opportunities unheard of anywhere else?"

"Try again."

She turned her smile, stiff though it was, onto Will.

"The captain and I disagree as to the wisdom of a woman living out here and trying to make a success of the land on her own."

"Maddie tends to overlook things like Apaches, outlaws, drought, and rattlesnakes."

"I don't overlook them. I just don't let them frighten me into running."

Will took a turn. "It's good to see you two getting along, now that the war's over and all."

Maddie's smile died, and she looked into the fire, aware of Helen's quiet presence and Dan's angry stare. Why had he come in criticizing her

311

the way he had? Probably to enlist Will's help in getting her to leave.

Not even her old friend could do that.

"It's late and you must be tired," she said. "I need to find you a place to sleep."

"Don't worry yourself about me, Miss Maddie. I got some blankets that make a fine bed. I've been sleeping out in the open, building me a little fire close by. I'll be jes' fine."

"There's an army tent you can use," Dan said.

"I've got a new barn with fresh hay on the ground," Maddie said. "At least it's almost fresh. You'll have to share it with some of the stock. They're friendly without being too much so. And they stay in their stalls."

Will looked from one to the other. "Man can't ask for more than you two are offering. Guess I'll take the barn."

Maddie took his decision as a victory. When she looked toward the door in triumph, Dan was gone.

Dan waited for Will in the dark down by the barn. He caught him before he could go inside the double wooden doors.

"Will," he said, stepping into the moonlight.

"Cap'n Kent," Will said with a nod. Opening the doors, he set his carpetbag inside, along with the lantern he had carried down from the house.

"Is there nothing that surprises you?" Dan asked.

"Not no more."

"Maddie probably could, if you were around her long enough."

"Miss Maddie is predictable. All's you got to do is figure out what any other woman would do, and look for her to do the opposite."

"Is that the way I ought to handle her? Compare her to other women?"

Will frowned. "That'd be right forward of me to suggest. It ain't my place to ask, understand, but I thought you was in the business of catching Apaches, not handling Miss Maddie."

"She needs help. You know it, too. When I saw you tonight, I decided that's why you're here."

"She didn't send for me. Not in the usual way. But I been sensing that child's troubles ever since she was a baby. It ain't something ole Will's gonna ignore."

"Old Will, is it? How old are you?"

"Some days it seems like a hundred."

"You're not yet forty."

"Close to. They been hard years. Not with Miss Maddie. She always treated me right fine. It's been the times."

"She's having some hard times. This place isn't what she expected. But she's stubborn. She won't give it up. It's going to kill her one day."

"You seem mighty concerned."

"I asked her to marry me and come back to Kentucky. She turned me down."

"Why'd you do a thing like that? Understand, it ain't none of my business, and you don't have t'answer ole Will."

Because I can't stay away from her or keep from kissing her or wanting to do a hell of a lot more. Because if I leave her here to the dangers she's facing, I'll never know another moment's peace.

If he told Will all those things, the man would probably come back with another why. And Dan didn't have answers, either for Will or himself.

"I lost a great deal in the war," he said. "So did she. We can help each other make up for the losses."

Will studied him for a minute. "She tole you?"

"I learned about the death of her fiancé after she left New Orleans. Life's not turning out the way either of us wanted. But we can still have a good marriage."

"Miss Maddie maybe wants more than jes' a good marriage."

"She doesn't want any marriage at all. I'm not the only one to propose to her. She turned down a man in town. He owns land north of the Longhorn. By marrying him, she could probably increase her acreage by at least a third, but she told him no."

"You think she should'a said yes? For her own protection, that is, since you seem mighty concerned about the danger and all."

Dan thought about Edwin Worster holding Maddie, kissing her, doing more.

"It's best for Worster she didn't. I don't like the man. I would have hated to shoot him."

He was only half joking. Will looked as if he knew it.

Will looked back up the hill to the house. "Are you asking me to get her to marry you? I don't rightly know how to go about that."

"I'm asking you to convince her that she needs to sell out and settle some place else. As to marrying me, that's something I'll have to take care of myself."

He held out his hand. Will took it.

"I'm glad you're here," Dan said. "She doesn't know it, but her army visitors will be pulling out in a few weeks, as soon as the orders arrive. It would be unsightly for an army captain to ride back to Louisiana with a woman hog-tied and thrown over the back of his saddle. I'd rather she rode out on her own."

Leaving Will standing in front of the barn, he started back up the hill toward the army encampment and his tent pitched in the trees away from the others. There he would set up his nightly vigil of watching the house and thinking about one of the women sleeping inside. He would be thinking about her most of the night.

Too, he would be trying to answer the why of his marriage proposal. He had told Will the truth, that they had both suffered losses and could help each other through their grief.

He had told Maddie the truth, too, though with her he had added the part about wanting to have her every time he saw her.

But there were other truths as well, reasons he had yet to understand himself. She had stirred something in him that had never been stirred before. He liked looking at her, even when he couldn't touch her. He liked listening to her, even when they were arguing and she was driving him mad.

He liked knowing she was safe, away from harm. It was more than just a like. It had become essential to him, the way breathing was.

Maybe that was love. He did not know. After the war, after all the cruelty and the misery he had witnessed, after all the foolish waste, he had decided he could never bring himself to care for another human being in the manner that some people called love.

He had loved his parents and his sister, and he had loved his young, innocent brother. The loss of love had hurt too much for him to admit to caring in such a way for anyone again.

Yet he was going to spend the night on hard ground, staring through the darkness at the shadow of a small rock house, and he was going to think of the warm, passionate woman lying inside.

He was going to imagine holding her in his arms. He was going to think about how he could keep her safe.

Chapter Twenty

Over the next two days, Maddie took Will on a tour of the Longhorn. He did not say much, just looked, and she had no idea whether or not he was impressed. He was not a rancher, had never lived outside a city in all his life, but she wanted him to understand where she lived and who she had become.

On the third day, with the vaqueros divided between watching the cows in the south part of the Longhorn and guarding the horses in the north, she decided to ride into town for supplies.

"Brutus and I'll hang around here," Owen said, casting a cautious eye toward the house.

She wasn't surprised. Since his return, the farthest Owen had strayed was down to the barn to milk the cow. Unlike his previous disposition, he had taken an interest in caring for the chickens, gathering eggs, tossing them corn, even digging up bugs for them to eat, as if they couldn't manage hunting and pecking on their own.

He had also gone back to splashing himself with water every other day.

He must have gotten very lonely during the weeks he had been gone. He talked about drifting on every now and then, but his heart didn't seem in it.

She mentioned the observation to Helen, but all she got was, "Humph. Men."

She turned to Will, asking if he would ride in the wagon with her.

"You sure you want me going with you into town? When I rode through there on the trip down, Señor Ramirez was the onliest one didn't look like I'd come to steal someone's child."

"I want you with me."

"That's enough said."

The person she didn't want was Dan. So, of course, he declared he would serve as her army escort throughout the time she was gone.

"It's an overnight ride. I usually stay in the wagon. There won't be anywhere for you to sleep."

"I'll think of a place," he said.

She was certain he would. If that place was the wagon bed, he would have to think again.

Armed with a list of supplies Helen had requested, wearing a dress, the floppy hat, and boots, she set out the next day at dawn. With a minimum of stops, she pulled up in her usual spot, the shade of the big oak tree at the end of Illusion's main street.

Dan was close behind.

Will dropped down from the wagon seat. "I'll take care of your horse and watch over things here, Cap'n. You do what you have to do."

To Maddie's dismay, that meant staying close to her. Things had changed between them since he had asked her to marry him and she had turned him down. They had not changed for the better.

She wanted him so much, she could scarcely think straight. She wanted to touch him, she wanted to smile at him, she simply wanted to talk about things that were on her mind. But she hadn't the right. He had offered her his name, the greatest gift a man could give a woman, and she had turned him down.

Besides, the offer wasn't really the greatest gift, not to Maddie. She needed to have his love.

On the walk down to the store, she caught sight of a new tent off to the side. She strayed closer. A large, crudely painted sign out front said: VISITORS WELCUM. NO MUDDY BOOTS ALOWED. NO HORSESHIT. NO SHOOTING GUNS.

Dan, who was following her closely, stared at the tent with what looked like appreciation.

320

"Illusion's turning into a real town, I guess. It's got its first fancy house."

"It doesn't look so fancy—oh, I see what you mean. Good. If a man gets an itch, he has a place where the women are willing to scratch."

"If you refer to me, there's only one woman whose scratching I'm interested in. And she's not in that tent."

He stepped close, lowering his voice. "And if you mean you weren't willing to do a little of it when the chance occurred, you have a very convenient memory."

She dared one quick look at his eyes. They were about what she had expected: so warm, he rivaled the sun.

Her stomach did a couple of somersaults. Picking up her skirt, she hurried on her way. In the general store, she turned over Helen's list to the proprietor, Ralph Kuntz.

"You and Miz Clark getting along all right, I suppose," Kuntz said. "The missus always says two women under one roof is one woman too many."

His smugness irritated her, and she spoke without thinking. "How many women are there in the new tent?"

He flushed. "I wouldn't be knowing about that."

His flush said he lied.

"I'll bet you've heard rumors."

"I heard talk of two. Rosella and Christina." He flushed some more, as if he had revealed something he didn't want Maddie to know. "If you gotta know, they came in here buying food."

"Were they pretty?"

"How would I be knowing a thing like that? They were . . . I guess the way you'd say it was ripe. Like those peaches I got from the coast last week."

"I'm surprised you waited on them."

"Their money was good as anybody else's, I said to the missus. When I told her what they spent, she agreed."

Maddie wondered how much of that money had come from Ralph Kuntz. When she glanced sideways at Dan, she got the feeling he was thinking the same thing. She almost smiled. That would have been a weakness. She caught herself just in time.

A shadow darkened the door.

"Maddie, it's good to see you again."

Her heart sank. Edwin Worster had returned from wherever he had been traveling. She hadn't seen him in more than two months.

"Mr. Worster," she said with a nod, well aware that Kuntz and Dan were watching and listening.

"Sorry I've been gone so long, but it was necessary to leave the county on business. I'd like to talk to you. Now, if you've got the time."

Standing squarely in front of her, the way he had the day he moved in for his undelivered kiss, he didn't give her much of a choice. Leaving the list with Kuntz, she walked outside.

She stopped in the bright sunlight, shifted her hat to get maximum protection, and said, "Okay, talk."

"I'd like some place a little more amenable."

She started to suggest the new tent, but Worster might take her up on it. For all his pleasantness, she really did not know him very well.

"How about the Grog Shop?" she said.

"Ladies are not usually found inside."

"They were there to welcome the new year."

"That was a special occasion," he said, but when she headed out for the town's drinking hole, he followed without further protest. Naturally, so did Dan.

She walked through the tent opening, and on to the wooden addition at the back. Two men sat at one of the tables, and a lone drinker was leaning against the plank that served as a bar. They and the bartender watched the procession.

"Where's Owen?" the bartender called out. "Ain't seen him for a spell."

She did not answer. Choosing the table at the far back, she sat down before either of her escorts could pull out a chair. Thumbing her hat to the back of her head, she rested her hands on the table and looked at Worster.

"Talk."

Worster glanced at Dan. "I would rather we were alone."

"The captain thinks I need protecting. I can't get rid of him, so he has to stay. Unless you can figure out a way to get rid of him."

Worster's pale blue eyes flicked from her to Dan and back again. The movement reminded her of a snake. She half expected to hear rattles when he moved.

Worster set his hat on the table. In imitation of her, Dan thumbed his hat away from his face, leaned back in his chair, and rested his hands on his thighs, but he remained silent. Maddie studied her own hands to keep from looking at his.

Worster cleared his throat. "Have you reconsidered what we discussed when we were last together?"

"Are you talking about your proposal of marriage or your suggestion that we kiss so I could find out whether I liked it? In either case, the answer is no."

His face reddened. "You're a plainspoken woman." He sounded angry. She would have been surprised at anything less.

"I also tell the truth." Usually. "On several occasions you have mentioned marriage, and I have told you I am not interested. Put it out of your mind, Mr. Worster. I'm not marrying anyone."

The latter was directed at both of her would-be suitors, a stranger pair she could not imagine. A more optimistic woman might have told herself that she had universal appeal. But this was Texas. Women were rare. Maddie knew her charm was in being available.

"As you know, we're experiencing a terrible drought," Worster said.

He did not seem the least bit heartbroken over her denial of his suit. Maybe she should have accepted him. Living with a man who did not care for her and for whom she held no affection would be far less taxing than hitching herself to a man for whom she would move heaven and earth if she could.

"You want to talk about the drought?" she said.

"I've discussed it with several ranchers in the area. They say it's likely to continue on into the fall."

She nodded and waited for the rest of the bad news he seemed eager to impart.

"Bad weather brings out bad people. And Indians. They feel the dryness as well as we do. Your stock will die. Plants will wither. And for what? So that you can call yourself a rancher? You won't be able to handle it. No woman living alone can."

That did it. Maddie shot to her feet. "We're done. I've heard all the criticism I ever want to hear."

"Hear me out," Worster said, still seated. So was Dan. She wanted to dump the table over on the pair of them and leave. But she sat and drummed her fingers on the table.

"I want to buy you out," Worster said. "I'll pay double what you paid."

She stopped the drumming. "You're out of your mind. I paid too much. Way too much."

"Nevertheless, my offer is sincere."

"What about the drought? The stock will die. The plants will wither. You told me so yourself."

"I'm gambling that in a year or two the weather will change."

"A year or two?"

"I have the resources to wait that long. I doubt that you do."

He was right. His superiority made her all the more determined to stay, which was exactly what she told him, in words even Worster could understand.

His earlier anger was nothing compared to his fury now. He turned so red, she imagined smoke coming out his ears.

"Don't be stupid."

"I'm a woman. It's all I can be."

"You're making a terrible mistake."

"Probably. I've been told that before." *By a far better man.*

His voice turned mean. "You'll regret this."

Dan sat up straight, but one hand stayed on his thigh, close to his gun. "Are you threatening Miss Hardin?" he asked.

Worster looked at him as if he'd forgotten he was there.

"I'm telling her the way things are. If you care more about her than just getting in those pants she likes to wear, then you'll advise—"

He got no further. Dan launched himself across the table and socked him on the chin. Worster went backwards over the chair and landed with a crash on the floor.

He reached inside his coat, but Dan already had his pistol cocked and ready in his hand.

Maddie scrambled out of the way.

"Out," Dan snapped.

Worster rubbed his jaw, already bruised and swollen. Standing, he brushed the sawdust from his suit and straightened his coat.

"That was unwise of me. And ill-bred. I apologize." He spoke to Maddie. She was not impressed.

"Out," Dan repeated.

Worster continued to look at her. "My enthusiasm for settling here got the better of me. Such a scene will not happen again. The offer remains. Please do not reject it because you have rejected me."

Slicking his hair back from his face, he put on his hat and left. Maddie did not watch his departure. She had seen all of Edwin Worster she cared to see.

The sudden display of violence shook her, and she dropped back in her chair. Dan did the same, just as the bartender arrived with a glass of whiskey and set it in front of him.

"On the house," he said. "Never did like that man. Anything for Miss Hardin?"

"Water," she said, wondering if it was too late in life for her to take up whiskey.

"We ain't got any. It's the drought, understand. Whiskey's easier to come by."

"Then bring her a whiskey," Dan said.

"You're trying to get me drunk," she said.

"I'm trying to get some color back in your cheeks. You have the damnedest way of getting into trouble. I never know what to expect when you're around."

"This is trouble I did not ask for. If you'll recall, he got really nasty only after he brought you into the conversation."

It was, she thought, a pretty good riposte, given the circumstances and the humiliation Worster's comment had brought her. Dan looked ready to come back with his own when a shadow fell across the table. She looked up to see the man who had been standing at the bar.

He was wearing a long frock coat and a paisley vest, and his white shirt sported a long string tie at the neck. He was tall and thin, with long gray hair, a drooping mustache, and a pair of twinkling brown eyes. In his hands he held a top hat and a cracked black leather valise.

Nothing about him looked new, not even the twinkle. His face, lined and leathery though it was, gave off the impression he smiled a great deal.

"Miss Hardin, pardon my intrusion, but I could not keep from overhearing your conversation with the angry gentleman. A Mr. Worster, I believe. Strange as it may seem to you right now, I believe I can help with your problems."

Maddie looked away, wondering what part of the conversation had interested him most. The part about Dan's wanting to get in her pants was something she never wanted to think about again.

"Do you know Miss Hardin?" Dan asked.

"No, sir, Captain. The gentleman who serves bar identified the two of you. I am being bold, I know, but I mean no harm."

"You're selling something," Maddie said.

He lifted the valise. "A service. For a not inconsiderable sum, I admit, but you pay me only after you are fully satisfied."

She could tell Dan was about to shoo him away, which made her not quite so reluctant to hear what he had to say.

She gestured toward the chair opposite Dan. He sat. "My name is Isaiah Jones," he said.

"Isaiah," she said, "like the prophet."

"Like the prophet. I, too, am a predictor. I can lead you to the water you very much need."

"You're a water witch," she said.

"I prefer the term diviner. I have the gift of

finding water, sometimes far, far below the surface of the ground. I know something about this country. I can help you find what you need. I can even advise you in the purchase and erection of a windmill."

"A windmill?"

"It's a tall wooden structure that harnesses the wind and uses its power to pump the precious water to ground level. It was invented a few years back by an enterprising young man in the East, but it is in the West where it will serve the best. I predict that one day windmills will rise like trees across this arid land."

"I've seen a few of them," Dan said, "but not where Indians and outlaws roam. You go out on your own in this country, and you won't last long."

"I have lived around such people. The Lipan Apaches know I have special powers. They will not interfere with my wanderings. The outlaws are a worse breed, but I go on foot, I am careful, and I have nothing of value to take. They view me as a harmless eccentric. It has been my experience that they are as eager to avoid my company as I am to avoid theirs."

"This windmill . . ." Maddie said. "It sounds too good to be true."

"It is both good and true."

He sounded sincere, he looked kindly, but she had been fooled by men before.

"You've got a gold mine for sale, too?" she asked.

"I have found in my travels that women are far more skeptical than men. What I have in my valise is a forked peach switch. Sarah has served me well through the years of my travels."

"Sarah?"

"The switch. I am, as you can understand, given to biblical names. We diviners trace our special ability back to Moses himself."

Maddie's whiskey arrived. She offered it to the diviner, who shook his head. She took a sip, coughed, then took another. The second went down easier, but she shoved the glass aside. One more swallow, and Isaiah Jones might begin to sound sensible.

She was ready to thank him for his interest, then send him on his way, but Dan spoke first.

"Miss Hardin isn't interested."

Her eyes narrowed. In assuming his place as her spokesman, her most precious love had made a tactical mistake.

Warmed by the whiskey, she leaned across the table toward the diviner.

"You say I don't have to pay you unless you find water for me," she said.

Jones looked back and forth, as if trying to determine which of the two he should listen to.

"I own the Longhorn," Maddie said. "Free and clear. You lay out what you can do, what you will charge, tell me a few things about this windmill, and then I'll make up my mind."

The diviner did as she asked. An hour later,

after another two sips of whiskey and despite Dan's hard and skeptical gaze, she said to Isaiah, who was now on a first-name basis, the two words she hoped would change the fate of her land:

"You're hired."

Chapter Twenty-one

The whiskey sent Maddie to bed early, burrowed down with the supplies in the back of the wagon. Will slept in a bedroll on the ground, the way Owen usually did.

She had no idea where Dan passed the night. He could very well be checking out the ripeness of Rosella and Christina. After the way he had argued over the diviner—"You're throwing away good money, and you know you're not going to stay for long in this part of Texas"— she had even suggested the bordello as a place for him to bed down.

The wagon pulled out early the next morning. Dan was there before she had finished eating the cold biscuits and bacon Helen had packed. With Will on the buckboard seat beside her, the diviner tucked in the back with his valise and an extra carpetbag of supplies from Kuntz's store, his top hat rising high on his head, and with Dan riding close to the side of the wagon, she cracked the whip over Dependable's rump and the journey back to the Longhorn was begun.

Every time she looked sideways at Dan, which was far too often and totally unnecessary, her irritation grew. He had intruded on the journey, tried to take over her dealings with Isaiah Jones, taken advantage of every chance he could get to comment outright about how the life she had chosen for herself was wrong.

But irritation was the bandage she had put over a far more serious wound—the deep hurt of knowing he was leaving her. His going would be soon, she suspected, and this time when they parted, she would never see him again.

If she dwelled on the hurt too long, she would find herself crying and declaring her love and in general making a fool of herself. She preferred being vexed. She knew that he would approve of her choice.

Two miles from the ranch house, the diviner called her name.

Reining Dependable to a halt, she looked over her shoulder to see him crawling out over the back of the wagon, valise and carpetbag in hand.

"I might as well get to work," he said as he walked up beside her.

"You don't want to leave from the house? I can get you a hot meal and a place to sleep, and you can start out early tomorrow."

"If you start out at all." It was Dan, interfering again. He looked across the rolling landscape of scrub brush and gray packed dirt. "I get the feeling all isn't well here."

"You always have that feeling," Maddie said.

"Sometimes it's stronger than others."

"I thank you for your concern, Captain," the diviner said. "But Madeleine and I have a business arrangement." He looked at her. "The sooner I get to work, the sooner you can order yourself that windmill. Word will spread. I will have more business in these parts than I will be able to handle."

He lifted his valise. "Besides, I can feel Sarah quivering to be released from her prison. It would be cruel of me to keep her locked away in the dark for much longer."

With a smile and a wink, his eyes merry as ever, he took off away from the trail, walking past shrubs and green-gray mesquite, angling up a long rise, then disappearing down the far side. She half expected him to click his heels before he dropped from view.

Leaning against the pommel of his saddle, Dan watched, too. When he looked at her, there was nothing merry in his eyes. He seemed ready to say something, then shrugged and reined his horse on ahead of the wagon for the last short portion of the journey.

They arrived at the house by midafternoon. Lieutenant Leigh and three soldiers were there, along with Helen. All came out to greet them.

"I sent Owen out to look at the horses," Helen said. "Man kept getting underfoot. It seems he knows only two ways to live—staying or going. What he needs to understand is, a woman appreciates a little of both."

Maddie disagreed. Dan's staying would be fine with her, but he was standing close by and she did not want him to hear her preference put into words. He had never offered to stay, and she could never ask him, mostly because he would turn her down. Whatever affection he held for her was not enough to keep him in Texas.

Will helped with the unloading, while Dan went back to talk with the lieutenant. When he returned, Maddie was just coming out of the house for another armload of supplies.

Right away she saw the worry on his face.

"You still think something's wrong?"

"More than ever. Sergeant Wilcox felt it, too. Indians, probably. He took a patrol due west early this morning. But this is such a damned big country, even a tracker as good as he could miss them by a mile."

He looked at the sky, blue with puffs of drifting white clouds. The sun was a hot yellow ball in the western sky.

Walking away from the house, he made a slow circle, watching, listening, studying the landscape as he had done on the ride to the house.

"Did you hear something?" he asked.

She shook her head.

Leigh joined him, along with the remaining soldiers. One of them, a grizzled veteran of the Indian wars, spoke up.

"Gunfire, Cap'n Dan. To the south."

Maddie clasped a hand to her throat. "Carlos is down there with the cattle. So are the other vaqueros."

"I'll need a fresh horse," Dan said.

"Take the stallion. You'll make better time."

He looked ready to protest.

"He might as well be army property. You're the only one who can ride him."

For once he did not give her any argument.

"Lieutenant, get the men mounted," he said.

"Cap'n Dan, rider coming!" the veteran soldier barked.

They looked to the south. In the space of a half dozen heartbeats, a distant speck took the shape of a horse and, gradually, a man slapping reins, like a rider out of hell headed straight for the ranch house.

"Carlos!" Maddie cried and ran out to meet him.

337

He reined back, his horse lathered in sweat, and dropped to the ground in front of her.

"Apache," he said between gasps. *"Ganado.* The cattle." He gestured to the south. *"Un vaquero . . . muerto,"*

Maddie reached out for Dan, but he was staring past Carlos, looking as if he could see across the miles, as if he was to blame for the attack, and for the death. Helen came up and wrapped an arm around her.

Leigh and the soldiers disappeared behind the house. Almost instantly, the lieutenant returned at a run, trailed by Owen on Caesar II.

Owen looked at Helen, then at Maddie before dismounting.

"The horses ain't there. Vamoosed. Only the stallion down in the corral is left. I got out to where you had the rest of 'em staked, and they was every one gone. I seen lots of tracks. Must'a been a dozen rustlers. Don't make sense. There's wild mustangs that can be caught and broke.

Some folks'd rather steal than take a gift."

"Apaches took them," Maddie said.

Owen turned pale beneath his beard. "I must'a missed 'em by no more'n a couple of hours."

Helen hurried toward the house, shouting, "Coffee's coming."

But Dan was already going down to the corral to saddle the stallion. Maddie went after him, keeping her distance, watching him, so scared her heart missed most of its beats.

When he pulled himself into the saddle, she could tolerate the distance no longer.

Hurrying to him, she brought herself up short. "Don't do anything foolish. I'm not worried about the stock."

"They may not be content with killing one vaquero."

She put a hand on his leg and felt his solid warmth. "Be careful."

He leaned down to wrap an arm around her waist. Lifting her off the ground, he kissed her, fast and hard. When he set her down, she backed out of the way and watched as he rode away, too frightened even to cry.

Her head reeled from all that had happened, so fast, too fast.

Brasado, the captured Longhorn bull, pawed nervously in his pen by the barn. Maddie watched him for a while, then shook herself and hurried back up the hill to begin the long nightmare wait.

"It's been three days," Maddie said, throwing herself onto the bench.

Helen nodded and worked her hands into the biscuit dough.

"That's a long time."

"It can be," Helen said.

"There ought to be something I can do."

"I'd say go hunting for wild berries so I can make a cobbler, but with Owen out guarding us, the chickens, the bull, and just about everything around here that breathes, and with Will stalking and staring when he's not out practicing with your rifle and scaring every living thing Owen's protecting, and with the vaqueros making a regular circle around the house, there's not much else we can do besides wait."

"And count the days."

"It's still three."

Maddie rubbed her eyes. If she could get some sleep, she might cope with waiting better. No, sleep would make her feel fresher so that she could worry all the harder.

"You know what bothers me the most?"

"What?"

Maddie almost smiled. Helen knew. She had heard the answer to the question a hundred times.

But Maddie told her again anyway. "Dan and I have passed nothing but harsh words between us recently. A thousand lingering words and one quick kiss. I wish it was the other way around."

The door creaked open. Maddie jumped to her feet as Will entered.

"Is there—" she began.

"No, Miss Maddie, there's no sign of a bluecoat or Apache leggings or anything you'd be wanting to know about."

He leaned her rifle against the wall by the door. "I've done wasted all the ammunition I plan to. If anybody comes around bothering you or yours, I can't guarantee I'll hit 'em, but neither will I be shooting off my foot."

Maddie started to reply when she saw a look pass between Helen and Will, a questioning look on his part, a quick shake of the head on hers.

She sat up straight. "What's going on?"

"Nothing that has to do with the cap'n," Will said.

There was only one other subject that could bring a look of such solemnity to his face.

Maddie felt as if a fist had hit her in the stomach. "Grace." The name came out a whisper.

"I don't know for sure. Miss Helen found a letter tucked down in the supplies we brought back from town. Mr. Kuntz must'a put it there and forgot to tell you. It's from San Antonio, that's all I know. We've been waiting for the right time to give it to you. Didn't seem to be a right time. Since it was sent out more'n a month ago, didn't seem no urgency about it."

Maddie's mind raced with possibilities. "Maybe one of my brothers sent it. Cal and Cord wrote me in New Orleans. They could have found out where I'm living now and written me here."

"Sounds real possible. There ain't no other name but yours on the outside."

Helen wiped her hands and came around the table. "Will told me what happened to you in

New Orleans. He didn't mean to. It just came out when I showed him the letter." She sat and took Maddie in her arms. "You dear, darling girl. You've been through the worst things a woman can suffer. I love you like you were my own."

Maddie returned the embrace, but she couldn't let it go on long, or she would break down completely.

"Can I see it?" she said.

Will pulled it from the pocket of his shirt and handed it to her. It had been folded, refolded, and handled by many hands, but the seal was intact. The handwriting on the outside was unfamiliar to her. Holding on to it tightly, she left the house, nodded at Owen standing guard by the front door, and went around back where she could be alone.

Saying a prayer, she broke the seal, read the terse message hastily once, and then twice more. She looked up and stared out at the expanse of land that was the Longhorn, and then at the early afternoon sun.

Folding the single piece of paper, she slipped it into her pants pocket, then hugged herself and lifted her face to the sun. She felt pulled and crushed, all at the same time, like a dozen people occupying one inadequate body—a novice, bungling rancher, an employer responsible for the well-being of people besides herself, a sister keeping foolish secrets from those who could care for her best, a woman trapped in an unrequited love—and more, much, much more.

Everything came together in the letter. The few words pointed the way to what she must do.

Except for Dan.

Her heart wrenched. She thought about the letter. She wanted to laugh and to cry, to shout the news and huddle in the shadows while she considered what it meant.

But she could do nothing until she knew about Dan.

For once, fate seemed to hear her plea. Even as she stood on the hard-packed ground that had been the soldiers' camp, riders slowly emerged out of the distant trees and galloped across the pasture, and around the corral.

Fate was cruel. The stallion galloped with the others, riderless, the rope around his neck held by Sergeant Wilcox. Dan was nowhere to be seen. Her knees gave way and she collapsed, still hugging herself.

And then she saw the two riders on one horse, and her heart began to pound. Pulling herself to her feet, she ran down the hill, unable to breathe, unable to think. Stopping short, she stared at the tall, straight figure of Lieutenant Leigh. In front of him in the saddle, head bent, was Dan.

"He's hurt," Leigh said.

"How—" She couldn't bring herself to finish the question.

"Shot. He's lost blood."

Like Wilcox. She told herself that the sergeant had survived.

Leigh urged his mount up the hill to the house, moving slowly, leaving the others behind to care for the horses. Maddie ran on ahead to prepare the bed for Dan. She knew what to do. And the sergeant had survived.

But her hope was fragile. She had gotten a good look at Dan's face, drained of color, drained of life.

Helen was already preparing for her latest patient. Using his massive strength, Will took Dan from the horse and carried him inside. She heard one low moan, and then silence. She swallowed a cry. She would do Dan no good by falling apart.

Will slowly laid Dan onto the narrow bed and began to undress him. Helen offered to help, but he shook his head. Maddie thought of how he had undressed her after her troubles in New Orleans. Like Dan, she had been unaware of what was happening to her. She had survived. Wilcox had survived. So would Dan.

It became her litany over the next two days. His wound was in the side, near the scar of an earlier wound. The bullet had passed on through, but the skin was torn. He would bear another scar, this one far worse—after he survived.

Maddie scarcely left his side. A fever took

hold of him. She bathed him with a cool, damp rag, she spooned sips of water through his lips as often as he would let her, she watched him, she listened to the ravings as he fought once again the battle with the Apaches.

The heat in the cabin was oppressive. He lay naked on the bed, as pale as the sheet beneath him. The fire in the fireplace was allowed to die, and Helen cooked out of doors.

The chill came on the third day. She covered him with blankets, but his shivering only grew worse. Stripping off her clothes, she crawled beneath the covers beside him, took him in her arms, trembling when she accidentally brushed against his bandaged wound.

At last, during the night, he fell into a peaceful sleep, and she allowed herself to cry.

Early the next morning she bathed herself, put on her best dress, a simple blue cotton frock, brushed her hair, and sat on the bench beside the bed.

His eyes fluttered open.

"Hello," she said. "Welcome back to the Longhorn."

"I must be in heaven. I'm looking at an angel."

"I thought you were through hallucinating. Never in your life have you thought I was angelic."

"A man can change his mind."

"I'm going to remember you said that."

He looked solemnly at her, at the cabin, then back at her. "I didn't get the cattle or horses back."

Anger flared. "Do you really think that's what I've been worried about?"

The anger immediately gave way to guilt.

"I'm sorry," she said. "I didn't mean to snap at you."

He managed a weak grin. "You're angry. Good. That means I'm back in the real world."

"The real world means you have to eat and sleep and drink, and you need to get lots of rest."

She turned from him long enough to get a bowl and spoon from the table.

"Helen made some chicken broth."

"You sacrificed one of your chickens?"

"It was an old hen. She gave her life willingly."

Propping his head up, she spooned the warm liquid through his dry lips. He took two sips, fell back, and went to sleep. When he woke again, she was ready with the spoon, and so it went for much of the day. That evening, with Will's help, he stood and shuffled slowly around the room. By now he was wearing his long underwear, and Maddie thought he had lost at least twenty pounds.

But he was alive and he was getting his color back. She allowed her heart to rejoice.

She also allowed herself to remember the letter. The rejoicing died.

Over the next week, he got up more often and walked farther, and complained about being treated like a child. He also told her about joining up with Wilcox and his patrol, the skirmish with the Indians, about a captured Lipan warrior, about what they had learned from him.

"Have you ever heard of the Comancheros? I thought not. They're mostly out of New Mexico. They're the ones who have been trading guns to the Indians in return for rustled stock. They've been selling the animals down in Mexico. But not animals from here, not anymore. The Indians say there are too few ranches in the Strip. They plan to ride farther to the west."

To Maddie, the news meant the county was safe from them. Dan would probably put up an argument about safety being a relative term, so she kept her opinion to herself.

"Any extra grub you've got, pass it on to Jason Leigh. He behaved bravely. All the men did, but that was no more than I expected. Leigh surprised me. He's the one that caught me when I was hit. He also saved your horse."

"I was really worried about that horse," she said, but she was silently deciding to give the lieutenant a big kiss of thanks. Along with the extra grub.

The gradual returning of Dan's strength brought Maddie to the decision that she had made in her heart the moment she read her letter. In the hours he rested, she kept herself busy talking with Helen, with Owen, with Carlos and the vaqueros, getting things settled, in the end feeling better about what she had to do.

She was left with only one more unattended matter. If she could take care of it. If Dan could give her a little help.

When he felt well enough to ride, the two of them went to the creek.

"Remember what happened here?" she asked as she dropped to the ground.

"Remind me."

"I'll remind you as much as you can handle."

When their horses were tied close to the thin trickle of water and were cropping grass, she spread blankets in the shade, choosing the exact place where he had placed blankets for her once before.

They stretched out beside one another, and she kissed him.

"Lie back," she said. He did not argue.

Slowly she unbuttoned his shirt, kissing the line of exposed skin as she moved down his long, blessedly solid torso. Not once did he grimace, even when she freed the shirt from his trousers and eased the sleeves down his arms.

A fresh bandage covered the puckered crease of skin that had once been an open wound. She kissed the bandage, lightly, then around it, and down to the waistband of his trousers. She felt him stiffen.

"Let me know if I'm hurting you," she said.

"You're torturing me, but you're not hurting me."

His eyes were dark, and so was his voice, but there was nothing frightening about him. With his cooperation, she was able to undress him completely, and then she showed him with her hands how much she loved him, unable to tell him with her words.

He stopped her before she could complete what she had set out to do.

"Not like this," he said. "You've been a good doctor. Let me show you just how good."

With her help, he undressed her. He took his time, studying and touching and kissing each area he exposed, as if he had never done so before. He made her feel precious; he made her feel beautiful.

She settled her body over his.

"Are you ready?" he asked.

"I've stayed ready since the first time we met. I just didn't realize exactly what my feelings meant."

With excruciating care, she lowered herself over him, taking his erection inside her, slipping it out, taking it again, until he laughed and moaned and grabbed her backside, holding her down so that her sweet torture of him was drawn to its natural conclusion.

She had wanted this moment to last forever. The final thrusts took no more than a few glorious seconds, and then, unwilling to put even her slight body weight on him longer than necessary, she fell beside him, one leg wrapped over his hip as the last sweet moment of pleasure shivered through her.

She put her palm against his chest to feel the powerful heartbeats that were a sign of life.

They rested awhile. Because of the drought, there was no ripple of creek water to listen to, only the rustle of wind in the trees and the sound of Dan's easy breathing.

They dressed slowly, as they were doing everything. Back at the small stone house where she had planned to spend the rest of her life, she ate with him, she kissed him, she smiled, she even talked about the Comancheros, but she did not reveal anything that was in her heart.

Nor did she tell him what she planned to do.

He slept soundly. Before dawn the next day, as she and Will had planned, they took their belongings and the food that Helen had prepared, and they went down to the pair of horses that Owen had saddled and waiting.

"I haven't heard from Isaiah," she said, "but I've left money for him with Helen. He gets it whether he found water or not."

"What if he did it? What if he found a big old underground spring?"

"Dan will point out the unlikelihood of that."

She hugged him good-bye, quickly, surprised at the glistening in his eyes. With Will beside her, she reined Sunset to the north. She did not look back. If she did, she might decide what she was doing was too hard.

For months she had been waiting for Dan to leave her. But once again, as she had in New Orleans, she was leaving him.

Chapter Twenty-two

Dan woke up late for a change, feeling at home lying in Maddie's bed. He looked over at the cot where he was used to seeing her. She wasn't there.

Sitting up, he remembered what she had done yesterday and what he had done, and he diagnosed himself as completely well, or, if not completely, as well as a man needed to be to participate in the greatest joy in life.

Maddie was joy. This morning he had things to tell her. Things he should have told her a long time ago. Tugging on his uniform trousers and shirt, barely feeling a twitch in his side, he went out to find her.

Helen met him at the door.

"She's not here."

Dan's disappointment fought with irritation. "If she's out riding after Longhorns again, or mustangs—"

"She's not."

Helen looked away, then back at him, and he felt the inside tightness that he had come to expect when bad news approached.

"I have a letter for you. Before I hand it over, she wanted me to get your promise about something."

The tightness choked the last remnants of joy from him.

"What kind of promise?"

"The kind a man would make on his mother's grave. She wants you to promise that after you read what she wrote, you'll tend to your army business."

"Instead of bothering with her."

"More or less. She may have said worrying instead of bothering."

Dan let out a long, slow breath. He would do more than bother her. But he had to find her first. Helen was a formidable woman, but he figured even with his recent weakness he could wrestle her to the ground and find the message that had been left for him.

He almost wished he was the kind of man to do just that.

"The letter," he said.

"It's hidden, and not on my person. I need the promise first. I've given her my word. You have to do the same."

Dan gritted his teeth. "I promise."

Helen shook her head. "You don't sound overly sincere. She says you're a man of honor, and maybe you are. But it's been my experience that men tend to find a way to do what they want and reason their way around the honor part."

"She wanted a promise, she got it. I'll tend to army business. Now the letter."

She went inside the house and returned shortly with a small piece of folded paper. Without ceremony, Dan pulled it from her hand and read Maddie's message fast. She was gone, asking him not to follow her, not spelling out exactly where he could find her should he try.

This first part he had expected. It was the second part that sent a fist to his gut.

I love you, Daniel Kent. I have since the first time we went out riding in Louisiana. I always will. But some things are not meant to be. For once trust me to be right.

He glanced up at Helen and on to Owen, who had walked up behind her. "Do you know what's in here?"

"I can guess," Helen said.

"Will's with her," Owen said.

"That doesn't make her safe."

"You go back on your word," Helen said, "and you'll hurt her more than you know."

He stared at the two people facing him, Maddie's line of defense—a matronly widow and a scrawny, gray-haired drifter half her weight. The light of determination in their eyes would make an Apache shiver.

He was vaguely aware that his men had begun to gather around. He focused on Helen. "You haven't told me everything. What's going on that I don't know about?"

She looked away. "I've said all I'm going to."

Owen hitched his trousers. "Same goes for me. Except for one thing. She said when you leave Texas, you should take the stallion. She said it was thanks for risking your life to keep her safe."

Dan did some silent cursing. If he had her within reach, he would turn her over his knee—

Hell, that's not what he would be doing. He would be holding her tight and whispering to her, choosing words of such sweetness that if she truly loved him, she would never be able to leave again.

She had him lassoed. Hog-tied. Corralled. Damned if he wasn't beginning to think in terms a Texas rancher would understand.

One of the soldiers looked over his shoulder and craned his neck to see around the side of the house. "Someone's coming."

Maddie. She had changed her mind.

"It's the foreman, Carlos. He's riding fast."

Maddie! Something had happened to her.

Shoving her letter into his pocket, he set out at a run. He intercepted Carlos at the base of the hill.

"Señor Captain. Quickly," Carlos said breathlessly. "There has been trouble."

"Where is she? Is she all right?"

"No, not the señorita." In Spanish he told of finding a man badly beaten, close to death. He described the diviner, Isaiah Jones.

He added a curious detail. Someone had cared for Jones after the beating, cleaning the wounds, making him a bed of leaves and a blanket of thick branches. Even more curious, he had been taken to a place away from the site of the beating, to an area of shade beside a trail frequently used by the Longhorn vaqueros.

"The Apaches," Dan said.

"This is what I believe," Carlos said. "It is as if they wish no harm to come to him."

Jones had said the Indians were convinced he had special powers. In caring for him, they were protecting themselves against those powers. Maybe. Dan could not begin to understand the Apache mind.

Any explanation he came up with did not tell him who had beaten Isaiah and left him for dead. He had to believe that the beating was somehow connected to Maddie. To hell with the promise. She could hate him all she wanted once she was safe.

Owen hitched Dependable to the wagon, prepared to go after the diviner, while Dan saddled the stallion. A quarter-hour ride took them to the injured man. The two vaqueros were standing guard over him, each one of them armed and watchful.

Jones lay on a bed of leaves, just as Carlos had described. His frock coat and paisley vest were ripped and stained, his gray hair and mustache matted with blood, his long, thin face a mass of bruises and cuts.

Dan knelt beside him. "Can you hear me, Isaiah?"

The diviner's eyelids fluttered. His cracked lips opened wide enough for him to whisper one word. Dan had to lean close to make it out.

"Sarah."

"We'll look for the switch. Who did this to you?"

At first Dan thought the question had gone unheard. Jones stirred, rousing himself enough to give him the answer he needed.

"Worster."

Dan caught Owen's eye and read the same question he was asking himself. Why would Worster have wanted to hurt a harmless old man like Isaiah Jones?

But Isaiah was more than that. He had special abilities that Worster might consider a treat.

Dan helped Owen and Carlos get the diviner into the wagon, placing him carefully on a bed of blankets that Helen had tossed in, making sure he was covered and warm. Isaiah's eyelids fluttered and his hand went up as if he would hold on to someone. Leaning over the side of the wagon, Dan leaned close enough to hear the diviner's last message before lapsing into unconsciousness.

Things were beginning to make sense. Worster had coveted Maddie's land. Now Dan understood why.

He stood and looked in the direction of Illusion. If the bastard had brought any harm to her, he would hang him from the town's one good tree.

He mounted the stallion. "I'm going after him."

Owen nodded once. "The way she talked about him, she seemed right fond of the water witch. Don't think even Helen'll take objection to seeing justice done."

"Wilcox and a couple of the men have gone to town for a brief leave. Tell the rest of them where I am. Tell them to stay here. I won't need any help."

He set out fast, keeping up the pace as long as he could, resting the stallion, then heading out again. The mustang had heart. He seemed to sense the urgency of the ride.

Halfway to Illusion, he met Wilcox coming the other way. Quickly he relayed the mission he was on, dwelling on Worster, leaving out any mention of Maddie.

Wilcox had news of his own. "Here's the dispatch from the general you've been waiting for.

Somehow it got delivered to town instead of the ranch. That's why I left, to bring it to you."

Dan took the leather packet, leafing through the pages quickly until he found the particular message he was looking for. It was the best bit of news he'd had in a long time.

He took time to look back through the rest of the dispatch. Someone on the general's staff had been thorough. The information he had requested in a dispatch sent weeks ago was clearly laid out.

Carefully he refolded the packet and returned it to the sergeant.

"The unit'll be pulling out soon. Give these papers to Lieutenant Leigh. He's in charge now. I've got the discharge I requested."

Wilcox shook his head. "I ain't liking it, but I ain't surprised. How the hell are we gonna get along without you?"

"The way you always do. Go easy on Leigh. Give him the same cooperation you've given me. He's a good man."

He had already reined away when one last thought occurred.

"Tell Owen and Mrs. Clark about the discharge. Tell them I've taken care of all the army business that I can."

Dan found Worster at a table at the back of the Grog Shop. Intent on nursing a glass of whiskey, Worster didn't see him until his shadow fell across the table.

"She ain't here," he snarled. "A few hours ago she passed through here with that man of hers, headed out for San Antonio." He grinned nastily. "I guess she prefers dark meat over white."

Dan debated over smashing him in the mouth now or later. He flexed his hand, while Worster watched.

"I've got two words for you, Worster. Isaiah Jones."

"Never met him."

"Sure you have. The diviner. You must have seen him talking to Miss Hardin at this very table a few weeks ago. Or if you didn't, you heard about it."

Worster sniffed. "You mean the old fool who bragged about finding water with a stick? She was fool enough to think he could do it. Women should be kept under lock and key."

"You believed him, too. But you made one mistake. You should have stayed around long enough to finish the beating. He's still alive."

Fear flashed through Worster's pale blue eyes. He downed the rest of his whiskey and poured another glass from the bottle sitting on the table.

"I don't know what you're talking about. I never touched the man."

"He identified you."

"What are you talking about?"

"I'll put it in simple terms. He said you beat him. If he dies, you'll hang. If he lives, you'll spend a long time in jail."

Worster rubbed his nose. "You can't prove I did it. It's his word against mine. Why would I harm a crazy old coot like him?"

"Because it's in your nature. Or maybe there are more serious reasons."

Dan pulled out a chair and sat. He did not try to keep his voice low. When he spoke, his words carried to the half-dozen men in the saloon.

"You might be interested in news about your wife Elizabeth and your son Samuel."

Worster knocked over his glass. A dark stain of whiskey spilled across the table.

"Damn, look what you made me do."

"You must be excited to hear their names again."

"I don't know what you're talking about. My wife's dead. So is the boy. You're a bastard to bring their good names into a place like this."

"They were abandoned, yes, but they're not dead. Your wife found refuge with her parents in Richmond. They went there after you deserted them. Of course, you had to leave town fast, didn't you, considering the law was after you. Crooked land dealings, wasn't it? That seems to be your specialty."

Worster poured himself another drink. His hand shook. Most of the whiskey missed his glass.

"You're crazy, too. You're all crazy. You don't know what you're talking about."

"Everything I've said is all laid out in the

army dispatch I got today. Texas authorities know where you are now. So does the army."

"Those charges were lies. I've done nothing wrong here."

"The United States takes a dim view of its citizens trading in guns and rustled cattle with the Comancheros and the Indians. That's what you do when you're gone for weeks at a time, isn't it? You trade. It's an occupation you picked up when you deserted the Confederate Army and ran to Mexico."

Part of what Dan said came from the dispatch, part from what he knew about the Comancheros, but the main part was instinct. The story he laid out made perfect sense.

"Shut up," Worster hissed, then shouted, "Shut up!"

"Poor Isaiah. He didn't know you put your money into waterless land, that you knew the Longhorn was sitting over underground springs. You're not a stupid man. There are signs for someone who knows where to look. The plan seemed simple enough. Marry Madeleine Hardin, a greenhorn if there ever was one, and take over—"

Worster sprang to his feet, in the same motion shoving the table against Dan and reaching inside his coat. Dan was ready. He shot him in the heart. Worster fell backwards, crashed onto the floor, and with a sudden, fierce jerk stared sightless at the crude open-beamed ceiling of the saloon.

The roar of the gunshot subsided, but the smoke and the smell of lead lingered. Men who had dropped to the floor at the blast stood and slowly, one by one, made their way back to the table.

One of them nudged the body with his foot. "Dead. Good. I liked the water witch. Can't say that about many who pass through here."

"He had no call to say that about Miss Hardin," another said. "She's a good woman. A lady, too, even if she does wear pants."

Dan nodded. He leaned down to take the small pistol that Worster had been trying to grab. Tossing it on the table, he looked at the bartender.

"Do you have any suggestions as to who should be told about this?"

"You're army. You're as official as we got around here."

"Not anymore. As of today, I'm discharged. I'm no more official than you."

The bartender scratched his head. "Then damned if I know what to do. This is the first real shooting we've had, leastwise the first one where someone got killed. We got us whores, got plans for a church, and now it looks like we got crime. Next thing you know, we'll get us a sheriff. Illusion may turn out to be a real town after all."

"The weather's right hot," someone said. "Let's plant him fast and worry later about what ought'a be done."

"I know one thing," Dan said. "He should have money hidden away somewhere, along with the deed to his land. All of that ought to go to the widow and her boy." He looked around the room. "Anyone got an idea who's honest enough to make sure they get what's coming to them? Lieutenant Leigh out at the Longhorn can supply the details about how she can be reached."

"Ralph Kuntz."

"Ramirez over at the inn."

The suggestions came simultaneously.

"We'll make them a committee of two," the bartender said. "That way they can watch out for each other."

"Sounds like a good plan." Dan settled his hat firmly in place. "I've got a long ride ahead of me, and I'd better get started."

"You going to San Antonio?" one of the men asked.

"As fast as I can."

"Good for you. We've been making bets about whether you and the lady would be getting hitched. Soon as we hear about the nuptials, we'll be settling up."

"I'm sure the new Mrs. Kent will be passing around announcements."

He lied. When the Mrs. Kent in question was Madeleine Hardin, he couldn't say for sure there would be anything to announce.

Outside, he made a stop at the general store. The army uniform had served him well—it had

brought him to New Orleans and to Maddie—
but it was time to set it aside.

A man going courting, especially when the
intended was as reluctant and stubborn as his
was, needed to look his very best.

Chapter Twenty-three

The knock at the rental house door came at three in the afternoon. Maddie was in the kitchen taking a loaf of bread from the oven. Startled, she dropped the hot pan on the table. She had been a week in San Antonio. Except for Will, no one had come to call.

Immediately she began to think of the bad news that could be behind that knock. One worry in particular soared to the top of the list.

Taking off her apron, smoothing her hair and dress, she took a deep breath and went to the door.

She had guessed correctly. Dan stood on the porch, staring down at her with such intensity, she knew she had done something very right or very wrong.

She decided on wrong.

Too late, she tried to close the door. One step and he was inside. She backed up. "You're supposed to be taking care of army business."

"A promise is a promise. I took care of everything I could."

Suddenly she realized what he was wearing: an open-throated white shirt, a red bandanna at his neck, black trousers, black boots, a black hat pulled low over eyes as deep as night. He looked gorgeous. He also looked as immovable as her house.

"Where's your uniform? Why the civilian clothes?" She could have added that he wore them very well. In truth, everything about him was as wonderful and terrifying as she had ever imagined.

"I can take them off if you prefer."

Maddie's heart leapt to her throat. "You would, wouldn't you?"

Looking at him took too much courage. She turned away. Her gaze fell on the closed door that led from the parlor to the lone tiny bedroom of the house she was temporarily calling home.

For a moment she had forgotten what was behind that door. The heart that had been pounding wildly turned cold and weak.

"I gave my promise and I kept it," he said. "Otherwise I would have caught up with you on the road."

"There's trouble at the ranch."

"Not exactly. Your diviner found water. Lots of it. The Longhorn sits on a web of underground springs."

Any other time, she would have laughed with joy and thrown her arms around him in happiness. But the ranch was not uppermost in her mind. She could not look away from the door.

"It's time to play fair and give a promise to me," Dan said. "Anything I ask you, you will tell me the truth."

Listening to him, she knew without doubt the path she must take. He was right. It was time for the truth, and not just in part. He needed—he deserved—to know everything. Whatever the telling cost, she had no choice.

"I promise." She turned to face him. "I haven't really lied to you, Dan. Not ever. But I kept things to myself. Important things. I can't do that anymore. No matter what it costs."

"Why did you leave?" he asked.

"Which time?"

"I know why you left New Orleans. We've already settled that."

"You settled it. I did little more than nod."

He tossed his hat on the table by the door and ran a hand through his hair. "What in the devil is going on? I've never considered myself a particularly stupid man, but where you are concerned, I am lost."

Maddie's head throbbed. She pressed her fingers to her eyes, then looked at him. "You're not stupid at all. You're so smart, you frighten me. I knew I couldn't keep my secret from you so I ran away."

He stepped toward her.

"No," she said. "Please stay back. This is hard enough. If you touch me, I'll never say what needs to be said."

"What secret, Maddie? The spying—"

"I wasn't a spy. Such a thing never occurred to me."

"But you admitted it. You said you were using me."

"Not in any way you could ever imagine."

She looked once again at the bedroom door. A month ago she would have felt trapped by this moment. Now she was glad it had come to pass. At last, she felt freed.

"Come with me. But please, be as quiet as you can."

She walked softly to the door and opened it slowly. The room, facing to the east, was dimly lit in the afternoon, and with a breeze drifting in from opposite windows, surprisingly cool for an August afternoon. A large bed took up most of the floor space.

The small child lying on her side in the middle of the high mattress, clutching her grandmother's doll, looked lost under the covers, her white-blond hair tangled against the pillow, a tiny hand pressed against her mouth. She did not suck at her thumb for comfort, but instead chose the middle two fingers, one of the thousand endearing traits that over the past days Maddie had been taking to her heart.

She felt a shiver of happiness and surprise, the way she always did when she looked at Grace.

"She's my daughter." The words almost choked her. She had never said them before, except to herself. She got no response.

The silence of the room was broken only by Grace's shallow breathing. Dan stood close beside her, his attention on the child. He brought a new element to this delicate haven for a mother and a little girl, a masculine presence that filled the space, overwhelming and completing it at the same time. She wanted very much to take his hand, but she could not bring herself to do so much as look at his expression.

She did not have to. She knew what he was thinking. It was what any man would want to know first, the identity of the father.

It was time he knew.

He followed her out of the room, and she quietly closed the door. "She takes a nap every day about this time. She'll be waking soon."

Dan kept his silence.

"Would you like coffee? Tea? I can make either. I even made a pie. The crust is terrible, but it was wonderful having fresh apples and sugar to put in it."

"Maddie—"

"I know. I'm stalling, but only because I've got so much to say and I want to say it right. You want me to name the father. The trouble is, I can't."

Talking, telling took all of her strength. She fell into the small rocking chair that Will had found for her in the Mexican market near the Alamo. Instead of sitting, Dan went to the front window, stared outside, then gave her his full regard.

"I know little about children, but she looks very young," he said.

"Twenty months. Almost. She's small for her age. As I said, you're smart. You know Julien could not have been responsible for her birth. He had been gone too long. Besides, in our moments alone, even when we said good-bye, we did nothing more than kiss, and that very few times."

"You don't have to tell me all of this. I haven't asked."

"But you will. Eventually. Besides, I want to tell you. You have a right to know."

Maddie took a deep breath, folded her hands in her lap, and closed her eyes for a moment, letting the words come quickly, naturally.

"When I said I couldn't identify the man, it wasn't because there were so many of them, I simply didn't know the particular one. It was because I saw him only twice and never knew his name. The young soldier, the private who came to my house—he saw me on the way home from the riverfront market."

She stared at her hands, but that was a cowardly way to tell him, and so she looked into his eyes.

"He raped me."

"My God," Dan said. He started toward her.

"Please, no. I'm all right. It was a long time ago. Anyway, I didn't know what was happening. I had fallen and struck my head. Later, when I woke and realized what he had done, I thought God had abandoned me on that day." She looked toward the bedroom. "I was wrong."

She felt his fury across the room. Once, she had felt it, too.

"You should have told me right away."

"And made my disgrace public? I couldn't bring myself to do it. Telling would not have changed anything for the better. It would have made things worse."

While she had the strength, she told him briefly how the attack had occurred, how Will had rescued her, how he had tracked the soldier to his death.

"Several weeks went by before I knew of my condition. By then, all I could think of was my unborn child. You were there, being so attentive, leading me to believe that you cared. What if we . . . did things together? You would believe the child was yours. I wanted my baby to have a father, to have a last name."

"What stopped you?"

"You did." Her voice softened for a moment. "I fell in love with you. When I learned of Julien's death, I saw how I was betraying you both, even though I had long ago decided to break off the engagement when he returned. I could not marry him while I loved another man. The best thing to do, the only thing, was to leave."

"Ah, Maddie, dear, dear Maddie, how I hated you. Or tried to tell myself I did."

She looked up, startled.

"You were right. I had begun to care deeply. You fascinated me. You charmed me. I felt things I had never felt before. But I didn't know you, didn't trust you. It doesn't mean a damned thing against you. You needed me and I let you down. Where did you go? What did you do?"

"Will and I managed to get to Shreveport, for the birth. I made up stories about my husband being away at war, and nobody doubted anything I said. She was born a week after Christmas. I named her Grace because to me, regardless of the manner of her creation, she was born in a state of grace."

For Maddie, one of the worst parts was yet to come. She brushed at her eyes, more from regret than grief.

"The birth was not easy. I was damaged. She

was born sickly. I thought she would die, and at the time, I wanted to join her. But we both managed to survive. Most of my money had gone to the purchase of land in Texas, so Will brought us to San Antonio. I stayed here for weeks, hoping time and boundless affection would help my baby gather strength, but they didn't. A childless couple who had traveled with us fell in love with her. They had little in the way of funds, but they were good people. I knew they would provide the care she needed, as well as a last name."

"Are you sure I can't hold you now? I am strongly in need of it. And so are you."

"This is so hard. Let me be done. I . . . paid them to take her into their home, while I claimed what was supposed to be my grand and glorious land. I always planned to come back for her. She was my strength and my reason for going on. But—"

Her voice broke, and it took a moment before she could continue. Always she was aware of Dan's presence, of his watchful eyes.

"They left," she said, barely above a whisper. "Before I did, without a word, and I had no idea where they had gone. I gave her up for lost and told myself I had done the right thing. My heart knew otherwise."

"Somehow you found her and got her back."

"I wish I could say that were true. As in most of the important areas of my life, the decision was made for me. I got a letter from the couple.

Indians to the west drove them back to San Antonio. The woman had learned she was with child and insisted they abandon their new homestead. She loved Grace dearly, but she was not strong. Even in the safer home in town, she could not handle a new baby as well as the active little girl that Grace was becoming."

"And so you left without telling me."

She hugged herself. "I had to. Surely you can see that. I knew I would be gone a long while. I talked to Helen and to Owen, to the vaqueros, too. They will be there when I return. No matter how long it takes. Even Owen swore it. But I knew you would be leaving soon."

"Remember, you're supposed to tell me the truth. You still did not trust me."

"No, no, you're wrong. I feared what you would do. I had burdened you enough with my choices and my problems. You had done more than any other man would have done. Since I was obviously incapable of caring for myself, you had even asked me to be your wife. But I couldn't let you make that sacrifice. It was why I turned you down. As for taking in another man's child, such a thing was unthinkable. You deserve far, far better."

"Better than you?" His voice was thick and soft. "Tell me where to find such a woman. I don't believe she exists."

It took a moment for Maddie to realize what he had said. A stillness settled inside her, so fragile she feared it would shatter, and with it, all the implications of his words.

She leaned back in the rocking chair and looked up at him. He remained by the window, but she could feel his warmth and she could see the stark emotion in his eyes.

"I love you, Madeleine Hardin. I'm insane with it. I can think of nothing else. When you left me again, a darkness descended that is only now beginning to lift. But I need one thing to know that I am completely in the light. I need to hear the words that you wrote."

"You mean it, don't you? You love me."

"I can say it again if you like. I love you. I want to help you through whatever troubles come. I will regret always that I did not help you through the troubles of the past."

She was unaware of standing, of going to him, but suddenly she was by his side, staring up at his strong, lean face, losing herself in his deep, dark eyes.

"I love you, Daniel Kent, so much it frightens me."

"Ah, Maddie, I once said you were not sensible. I have not been a very lovable man."

He took her in his arms and cradled her face, brushing his lips against hers, kissing her eyes, the corners of her mouth, returning to her lips. She felt him tremble, as if he held back an overwhelming urge to kiss her hard, to kiss her long, to do far more.

"Marry me," he said.

"You know why I can't. For one thing, you're an officer with commitments."

"You asked about the civilian clothes. I requested and received a discharge from the army. I can go wherever I want."

Any other time, the news would have brought her joy. But not now. She, too, had commitments.

"You know the army was not the only reason. You said you wanted to help me through my troubles. It's not my troubles that bother me now."

"Grace? You don't think much of me, do you, if you think I'm incapable of loving her, too."

"I'm afraid, Dan. Wanting something and having it are so far apart for me. You said yourself you didn't know much about children. You certainly don't know her."

As if on cue, a small cry came from the bedroom. Maddie pulled herself from his arms.

"She's still so unfamiliar with where she is."

"But not with you."

"No." Tears glistened in Maddie's eyes. "No, miraculously, not with me. Not after the first couple of days. She even calls me Mama. Each time I hear it, I have a hard time not bursting into tears."

"Then take me in and introduce me to her. You said yourself a child needs a father. The sooner she and I get to know one another, the sooner I can get her on my side."

Maddie's heart was so full she feared it might

explode. He started for the door ahead of her. She hurried to catch up. When they entered, Grace was sitting in the middle of the bed rubbing her eyes, the doll still lying under the covers.

"Hello, sweetheart," Maddie said and sat beside her, brushing the hair from her eyes.

Grace burrowed her head against her mother, then turned her head to look sideways toward the door. "Who's he?" she asked.

"A friend. A very, very dear friend."

"He's big."

"He's tall, but he's gentle. And very, very nice."

Maddie stood and took her daughter in her arms. Grace was light, far too light for someone approaching two years of age. But she had an amazing ability to express herself in words and in her very brief life had already proven her resiliency.

"She's got your eyes, Maddie. Big and blue. She's beautiful."

"She is, isn't she?"

Keeping her arms around her mother's neck, Grace whispered a request into her mother's ear.

"She wants you to know her name is Grace Adrienne Hardin. She wants to know the name of the big man."

"Daniel Robert Kent."

That seemed to satisfy her. "I'm hungry, Mama," she said, loud and clear.

"You're always hungry. Let's take Mr. Kent into the kitchen and see what we can find to eat."

When she was passing Dan, he stopped her. "You go on. If Grace Adrienne Hardin doesn't mind, I'd like to carry her and find out what she likes to eat."

Without waiting for an assent, he took Grace into his arms. She looked smaller than ever against his massive strength, but Maddie was tearing up so much, she was having a hard time picking out details.

The last thing her daughter needed was to see her cry.

They were in the living room when the front door opened and Will stepped inside, a flour sack of food and supplies in his hand.

Maddie grinned at him, Dan grinned, even Grace smiled.

Will's look of surprise turned to a smile, and then a scowl.

" 'Bout time you got here," he growled.

"You knew I was coming," Dan said.

" 'Course I did. Miss Maddie's the onliest one with any doubt. When she hasn't been loving on that pretty child of hers, she's been moping around here like she didn't know if she could live."

"She'll live, all right." He looked at her and smiled. "Right here in Texas. I'll have to stay, of course, to make sure she comes to no harm. You may have noticed she has a way of getting into trouble that will require all of my attention. When, of course, I'm not helping her build that godforsaken land she bought into the empire of her dreams."

Maddie could contain herself no longer. Hugging Dan and Grace, she looked up and smiled through her tears.

"Okay, you win. I'll marry you. On one condition. You never say a negative word about the Longhorn Ranch again."

"You ask a great deal of a man," Dan said. "I'll do my best to comply. But know one thing. I'll be wanting something from you, too. Often. By the creek. In front of the fire. There's no telling where I'll be wanting it."

Maddie blushed.

Will set down the flour sack. "Come to me, Miss Grace. 'Pears your mama and her man got some kissing and talking to do. Let's go out in the kitchen and see what we can find to eat."

Maddie watched them leave, grateful when Will closed the door, leaving her and Dan truly alone. She felt weightless, giddy, and young, and as completely happy as a woman could ever feel. She wanted to laugh and to dance around the room, but such actions would require leaving Dan's arms. That was one thing she definitely did not want to do.

She looked at him out of the corner of her eye. It was about as close to coy as she could get, especially when he was looking back at her with eyes that could melt a woman's bones.

"You spoke of wanting something from me," she said.

"I believe I did."

"So show me what you had in mind."

He did as she asked, repeating a few touches and kisses to make sure she understood.

Wrapped in his embrace, Maddie put her hands and tongue to work and showed him right back.

Epilogue

They waited for Maddie's family to gather in San Antonio before holding the wedding ceremony. Dan's sister and her family were too far away in Kentucky to attend, but he wrote a letter promising to send a daguerreotype of his wife and little girl.

Helen and Owen remained at the Longhorn, taking care of the place and helping Carlos and the vaqueros as best they could in the gathering of a new herd of Longhorns, and in the construction of several adobe houses that would augment the small ranch house.

Dan was already talking about knocking out one of the stone walls and building on.

In gratitude for what Isaiah Jones had discovered lying under the hard-packed Longhorn soil, Maddie invited the newly recovered water witch to the wedding, but word had spread about his success and he told her that with Ruth, his new switch, twitching away, he needed to tend to his growing business.

The wedding was held in the small chapel where, eleven years earlier, her brother Cord and his wife Kate had been wed. As before, the reception was held in the adjoining hall.

Maddie told the rest of the Hardin brood exactly what Dan told his sister about the child who was now legally known as Grace Adrienne Kent: nothing. She and Dan had met and fallen in love in New Orleans, but the war had separated them. They had not found each other again until a few months ago.

She knew the story raised a thousand questions in everyone's mind, but no one put them into words. They simply congratulated the happy couple on their good fortune.

Maddie's worst confrontation with her brothers came not over the out-of-order birth-then-marriage. Their concern lay in the way she'd come to Texas. As soon as the wedding was over and the celebration begun, they let her know how they felt.

While her beloved bridegroom was meeting and greeting the rest of the Hardin clan, they took her aside and lit in.

"You sneaked onto your land," Cal said.

"You didn't trust us to help you out," Cord said.

Both were tall, handsome, strong-willed men who ruled successful cattle empires—as much as their loving, strong-willed wives let them rule. But Maddie had the same Hardin blood flowing in her veins. She refused to be intimidated.

"Which of you had help when you came here?"

Cal, his dark hair streaked with gray but his Hardin blue eyes determined as ever, spoke first.

"I wasn't trying to establish any kind of ranch. I had a couple of rascally uncles who wanted to settle here. I planned to move on as fast as I could. Then I met Ellie, and the next thing I knew we were joint owners in the Crown of Glory."

"Still," Maddie said, "you were a loner. You wanted to do things for yourself. Until Ellie."

His eyes twinkled. "Yep." He looked across the room to where his lovely, fair-haired wife was laughing at something Dan had said. "It's hard to believe she's going to be a grandmother in a few months."

Maddie switched to Cord.

"You came here the same as Cal. You had business to take care of, and then you were gone, or so you thought. Kate changed your mind."

A smile broke Cord's usually dark, serious expression. "You're a tough woman to argue with."

"I'm a Hardin. My problem—if that's what you want to call it—was that I loved you two so much. You were my heroes, and I wanted to show you that I could be as successful as you. I had to do it on my own."

"We started out with better resources," Cord said.

His Lone Star ranch was located in a lush area at the edge of the hill country west of San Antonio. Cal's Crown was to the southeast in a rolling landscape of rich grass, rivers, and creeks.

"You're referring to the quality of my land, I suppose." A new thought occurred to her, and she eyed them critically. "Or is it the fact that you are men and I am just a woman?"

The two men glanced at one another, then back at her.

"The land," they said in unison.

"If I ever used that phrase *just a woman*," Cord said with a shudder, "it was before I saw Kate for the first time, standing on a hilltop and leveling a shotgun at my heart."

Maddie sighed. "You're right about the Longhorn. I didn't know how bad off I was until I got here. When I bought the place, I thought I was dealing with an honorable friend of yours. I figured out on my own that he had done a great deal of lying."

"All of us have truths to admit. We needed Ellie and Kate," Cal said. "You needed Dan. None of us can make it on our own."

Both Hardin men had already told their baby sister that they heartily approved of the man she had chosen. Their approval did not come as a surprise. What she could have told them was that choosing was not exactly what she had done. Fate had paired her with Daniel Kent, and she had finally learned not to fight her destiny.

She looked across the room at her husband, resplendent in a morning coat and white shirt. As if he read her mind, he turned from talking to Ellie and the beautiful red-haired Kate and looked at her. He smiled. Maddie's heart hit the floor and bounced back to her throat.

"You're right. I needed Dan. But you know what? He needed me, too."

"And your beautiful daughter needs both of you."

"You two made pretty great fathers. Three children each, one grandchild on the way. Dan shows every sign of being the same."

She watched as her husband walked across the room toward her, sidestepping a group of girl cousins who were giggling and chattering. One of the girls held Grace. In her pink lacy dress, the child looked like an angel. She also looked totally absorbed in what was going on around her, as if she was taking lessons on what it was like to be an adolescent girl.

"Gentlemen." Dan said with a nod to his brothers-in-law, "I need to steal my wife away from you for a few minutes. Hope you don't mind."

"I don't think it would matter if we did," Cal said.

"No, I don't think it would."

Dan took her by the hand and led her outside, where the shadows of twilight formed a convenient area of privacy between the hall and the street.

He didn't waste time. Pulling her into his arms, he kissed her. "How much longer is this going to last?" he whispered against her lips. "You've got a wonderful family, but we've got only a couple of nights together before we need to head south. I don't want to squander a moment of either one."

"You're insatiable."

"I haven't spent more than a few minutes alone with you since you promised to be my wife. I've been a saint."

She ran her fingers across his cheek. "I love you."

"I love you."

"And you really do care for Grace."

"She's the real reason I married you. I was afraid you wouldn't let me keep her unless we were man and wife."

Maddie fell silent.

"What's wrong?" Dan asked.

"How do you know something's wrong?"

"Because you are a part of me. That's the

only way I can put it. Long before today we were truly one."

"Remember how I told you that Grace's birth was difficult? I also said the doctor felt certain I could not have another child."

"Remember I told you I didn't care? I meant it. You and Grace are all I want in life and more than I deserve."

"I was afraid you would say that."

"Okay," he said. "Maybe we're not one, not completely. Right now I don't have any hint about what's in that imaginative mind of yours."

"The doctor was wrong." She spoke in a small voice, and waited for Dan to understand.

It took him no more than a few seconds.

"You're expecting another child."

"I have all the symptoms. I waited until I was sure to tell you."

"You were afraid to tell me."

"I considered different ways you might respond."

"You're doing it again, Maddie. You're not trusting me."

He sounded almost angry, but he brought joy to her heart.

"You're not upset?"

"When you married me a couple of hours ago, I thought nothing could make life more complete. You just did."

She buried her head against his chest, welcoming the feel of his strong arms around her, then looked up with glistening eyes into his smiling face.

"I guess it would be silly of me to do somersaults down the middle of the street."

"In your condition, it would be more than silly. Besides, remember you're wearing a dress instead of trousers. And a very pretty dress it is. I can't wait to take if off you so I can get a better look."

"All right," she said, enjoying the anticipatory thrill that ran through her, "somersaults are out of the question. I'll just have to think of another way to tell you how much I love you and trust you and how happy you have made me."

"And Grace."

"Oh, yes, definitely Grace."

"Let's go in and bid everyone good night," he said. "They don't need us to continue the party. We've got a half-dozen nannies for our daughter, including her Aunt Ellie and Aunt Kate. We stand a good chance of being alone."

Maddie linked her arm in his and turned toward the door just as Will came outside.

"Figured I'd find you two out here," he said.

"We were just coming in," Maddie said.

"I've got something to tell you. This is as good a time as any. Soon as you head south, I'll be heading north."

"You can't," Maddie said. "The Longhorn is your home."

"It's yours, Miss Maddie, and a right fine one

it is. Or will be. I got faith. But no, it ain't mine. See, I didn't tell everything about what was going on in Illinois. I got a woman waiting. We're gonna get married soon as I get back. She's got herself a little boy, cutest tyke you ever saw, calls me daddy sometimes. You don't need me now, Miss Maddie, not with Mr. Dan close by, but she and that child sure do."

The two men looked at one another, and Maddie got the feeling they were passing something from one to the other—the care of her from Will to Dan.

"Accept what he says, Maddie," Dan said. "He's like me. He's got a new family and a new life."

"You be happy for me, same's I am for you," Will said.

She managed a smile, though she suspected it looked forced. "You don't give me much choice."

She broke away from Dan to give her old friend a big hug. Then it was back to her husband's arms.

"I am happy," she said, "it's just that it'll take a little while to separate it from the regret."

"I'm gonna be leaving now," Will said. "I 'spect I'll see you two in a couple of days. Then we can say our real good-byes. For now, let's make it jes' good night."

With a nod at them both, he turned and headed down the street to the room he had rented at the edge of town.

Maddie watched until he was swallowed by the dark.

"You're right," she said. "We need to go inside and say our good-byes, then get to that hotel room you've got waiting. I feel a strong need to be comforted, and there's no one who can do it better than you."

Dan started working on the comfort right then and there. His lips got involved, and his tongue, and he even used his hands to show her a little of what she could expect at the hotel.

"Oh," she said when he finally let her come up for air. "Let's make it very quick."

They did, accepting the well-wishes, taking time to tell Grace good night and, in Maddie's case, to leave Ellie and Kate with a dozen last-minute instructions as to her care.

Outside, Dan picked her up and cradled her close to him.

"What are you doing?" she asked. "I can walk."

"I'm getting you to that wedding bed without another interruption. For the rest of the night, Mrs. Kent, I am in charge."

Maddie nestled her head against his chest and grinned, but she kept her thoughts to herself.

So you're in charge, are you, Mr. Kent? I'll bet before very long you will be welcoming the activities I have in mind.

Author's Note

Longhorn concludes the *Texas Empires* series that began with *Crown of Glory*, a July 1998 release, and continued with *Lone Star*, June 1999.

Through fiction, set against a historical background as accurate as research could make it, the series has described the establishment of early cattle ranches in Texas in different landscapes and different times, from the Republic of Texas to Reconstruction.

For more than a hundred years, cattle and cowboys in the American West have retained a romantic image around the world. Their reality was far grittier, more dangerous, and filled with the risk of failure. It took real-life heroes and heroines to settle the wild country. The

Texas Empires characters have been created to represent these prototypes.

In *Longhorn*, Illusion is a fictional town. Dimmitt County and the Nueces Strip are real; so is the underground water Isaiah Jones found for Maddie. This part of South Texas, once called El Desierto Muerto, is now known as the Winter Garden Region, one of the most prolific vegetable-growing areas in the country. Still, successful cattle ranches abound.

I welcome your reaction to the series. Write me at the address below, including an SASE for a reply, and please check out my website.

Evelyn Rogers
8039 Callaghan Road
PMB #102
San Antonio, TX 78230
http://www.evelynrogers.com

WICKED
Evelyn Rogers

Gunned down after a bank robbery, Cad Rankin meets a heavenly being who makes him an offer he can't refuse. To save his soul, he has to bring peace to the most lawless town in the West. With a mission like that, the outlaw almost resigns himself to spending eternity in a place much hotter than Texas—until he comes across a feisty beauty who rouses his goodness and a whole lot more. Amy Lattimer is determined to do anything to locate her missing father, including pose as a fancy lady. Then she finds an ally in virile Cad Rankin, who isn't about to let her become a fallen angel. But even as Amy longs to surrender to paradise in Cad's arms, she begins to suspect that he has a secret that stands between them and unending bliss.

___52359-0 $5.50 US/$6.50 CAN

Dorchester Publishing Co., Inc.
P.O. Box 6640
Wayne, PA 19087-8640

Texas Empires: Lone Star
Evelyn Rogers

The Lone Star State is as forthright and independent as the women who brave the rugged land, and sunset-haired Kate Calloway is as feisty an example as Cord has ever seen. A Texas woman. He has not dealt with one in a long time, but he recognizes the gumption in her blue eyes. He would be a fool to question the threat behind the shotgun leveled at his chest. He would be still more a fool to give in to the urge to take her right there on the hard, dusty ground. For though he senses they are two halves of one whole, Kate belongs to the man he's come to destroy. That they will meet again is certain; the only question is: how long can he wait before making her his?

___4533-8 $5.99 US/$6.99 CAN

Dorchester Publishing Co., Inc.
P.O. Box 6640
Wayne, PA 19087-8640

Please add $1.75 for shipping and handling for the first book and $.50 for each book thereafter. NY, NYC, and PA residents, please add appropriate sales tax. No cash, stamps, or C.O.D.s. All orders shipped within 6 weeks via postal service book rate. Canadian orders require $2.00 extra postage and must be paid in U.S. dollars through a U.S. banking facility.

Name_____
Address_____
City_____ State_____ Zip_____
I have enclosed $_____ in payment for the checked book(s).
Payment <u>must</u> accompany all orders. ☐ Please send a free catalog.
      CHECK OUT OUR WEBSITE! www.dorchesterpub.com

BETRAYAL Evelyn Rogers

By the Bestselling Author of
The Forever Bride

If there is anything that gets Conn O'Brien's Irish up, it is a lady in trouble–especially one he has fallen in love with at first sight. So after the Texas horseman saves Crystal Braden from an overly amorous lout, he doesn't waste a second declaring his intentions to make an honest woman of her. But they have barely been declared man and wife before Conn learns that his new bride is hiding a devastating secret that can destroy him.

The plan is simple: To ensure the safety of her mother and young brother, Crystal agrees to play the damsel in distress. The innocent beauty has no idea how dangerously charming the virile stranger can be–nor how much she longs to surrender to the tender passion in his kiss. And when Conn discovers her ruse, she vows to blaze a trail of desire that will convince him that her deception has been an error of the heart and not a ruthless betrayal.

___4262-2 $5.99 US/$6.99 CAN

Archer's Crossing — Jean Barrett

Crossing Archer Owen seems like the last thing anybody would want to do, or so Margaret Sheridan thinks. Bringing dinner to the convicted murderer is terrifying—for though he is nothing like her affluent fiancé, he stirs a hunger in her she has never known. Then the condemned prisoner uses her to make his getaway. In the clutches of the handsome felon, Margaret races into the untamed West—chasing a man Owen claims could clear his name. Margaret wonders if there is anything Archer won't do. And then he kisses her, and she prays there isn't. For if this bitter steamboat captain is half the man she suspects, she'd ride to Hell itself to clear his name and win his captive heart.

___4502-8 $5.99 US/$6.99 CAN

Cinnamon and Roses

Heidi Betts

A hardworking seamstress, Rebecca has no business being attracted to a man like wealthy, arrogant Caleb Adams. Born fatherless in a brothel, Rebecca knows what males are made of. And Caleb is clearly as faithless as they come, scandalizing their Kansas cowtown with the fancy city women he casually uses and casts aside. Though he tempts innocent Rebecca beyond reason, she can't afford to love a man like Caleb, for the price might be another fatherless babe. What the devil is wrong with him, Caleb muses, that he's drawn to a calico-clad dressmaker when sirens in silk are his for the asking? Still, Rebecca unaccountably stirs him. Caleb vows no woman can be trusted with his heart. But he must sample sweet Rebecca.

Lair of the Wolf

Also includes the second installment of *Lair of the Wolf*, a serialized romance set in medieval Wales. Be sure to look for future chapters of this exciting story featured in Leisure books and written by the industry's top authors.

___4668-7 $4.99 US/$5.99 CAN